INDIGO

Richard Wiley

INDIGO

A DUTTON BOOK

DUTTON
Published by the Penguin Group
Penguin Books USA Inc., 375 Hudson Street,
New York, New York 10014, U.S.A.
Penguin Books Ltd, 27 Wrights Lane,
London W8 5TZ, England
Penguin Books Australia Ltd, Ringwood,
Victoria, Australia
Penguin Books Canada Ltd, 10 Alcorn Avenue,
Toronto, Ontario, Canada M4V 3B2
Penguin Books (N.Z.) Ltd, 182–190 Wairau Road,
Auckland 10, New Zealand

Penguin Books Ltd, Registered Offices:
Harmondsworth, Middlesex, England

First published by Dutton, an imprint of New American Library,
a division of Penguin Books USA Inc.
Distributed in Canada by McClelland & Stewart Inc.

First Printing, September, 1992
10 9 8 7 6 5 4 3 2 1

 REGISTERED TRADEMARK—MARCA REGISTRADA

LIBRARY OF CONGRESS CATALOGING-IN-PUBLICATION DATA
Wiley, Richard.
    Indigo / Richard Wiley.
        p.   cm.
    ISBN 0-525-93547-9
    I. Title.
PS3573.I43315   1992
813'.54—dc20
                                                    92-183
                                                    CIP

Printed in the United States of America
Set in Goudy Old Style
Designed by Eve L. Kirch

PUBLISHER'S NOTE
This is a work of fiction. Names, characters, places, and incidents either are the
products of the author's imagination or are used fictitiously, and any resemblance to
actual persons, living or dead, events, or locales is entirely coincidental.

For my daughter, Pilar,
and for Morgan, my son

The author wishes to thank the University of Nevada, Las Vegas Foundation, and the University of Nevada, Las Vegas Research Council for generous financial support during the writing of this book. In addition the author wishes to thank Stan & Ebba Jacobson and the faculty and staff of the American International School of Lagos, Nigeria, for their kindness and hospitality, and Mr. Patrick Okoh and his associates, for advice and help concerning the Nigerian legal system.

NIGERIAN DISCIPLINE CAMPAIGN:
NO SPARING THE ROD

The New York Times
August 10, 1984

LAGOS, Nigeria, Aug. 3. The television advertisement can be seen many times each evening throughout Nigeria. In the first scene an office worker is shown sprawled across his desk, fast asleep. In the second, a secretary paints her fingernails, oblivious to the telephone ringing at her desk. A voice asks, "How do you spend your day?"

To drive the point home, the camera shifts to a Nigerian air-traffic controller efficiently coordinating arrivals and departures, and then to a baggage handler energetically loading a Nigerian Airways jetliner.

The commercial is one of several promoting the "War Against Indiscipline," declared in March by Tunde Idiagbon, one of the two top men in the military government that overthrew Nigeria's civilian administration in a coup last December 31st.

Prologue

February 10, 1984

The students were assembled in the courtyard and the principal was waiting for the artist to arrive so that he could begin his speech. The music teacher was playing a medley of Gershwin tunes on the piano, but the students, though previously quieting to the gentle nature of the music, had discovered that the program was delayed and were soon chatting again. Nigerian and American, Israeli and Indian, they were nevertheless all speaking good English, as easy on the ears as the music that they heard. Their teachers, who were nearly all American, were standing behind them and chatting too.

The principal was uncomfortable with the idea of the installation of the three panels of art, though not with the art itself. He was uncomfortable because the school board had purchased the art as some kind of tribute to him, an act insisted upon by the school board president, though the principal had several times discouraged it, saying that he simply wanted to continue on with his life, letting the events depicted in the art affect him, if they would, in a strictly private way.

The principal was sitting with the school board president and other board members on a makeshift stage at the center of the courtyard, but he felt completely alone in his loose-fitting suit, and he looked into the audience to see if he could find a

1

friendly face among the adult Nigerian guests. Even a bit of indigo would have buttressed him, or the sight of someone wearing heavy glasses on a string.

From where he sat he had a good view of the school gate, which was open and through which he could see the continuing turmoil of ordinary Nigerian life, people walking past with bundles on their heads, uniformed students on their way to the local schools, which they could attend at a hundredth of the cost of attending his. It was clear that the artist would not arrive on time, and it was equally clear that the others on the stage were losing patience. They all had places to go, and the principal could see that even the board president, though he'd been the one to insist on this ceremony, thought it would be better if they just got on with the school day.

Though the morning had not yet given way to the oppressive Lagos heat, the principal had removed his jacket, and when he stood to approach the microphone he had trouble getting the jacket off the back of his chair. A part of it had worked its way under the left back leg of the chair, the only leg not covered by a rubber bumper, so he had to lift the chair to free the jacket and when he did so he saw that the jacket had been torn by the jagged edges of the chair's leg. This struck him as a kind of sign. Not only did his clothes still fit him poorly, but perhaps he should not have gone back to wearing them at all. He remembered the loose-fitting Nigerian clothing that he'd worn, the way the breeze had come through it even during the hottest times of the day, drying the sweat under his arms.

The principal leaned into the microphone and said, "Good morning." He adjusted the microphone and smiled out at the students, who quieted so quickly that he was caught looking down at his jacket again.

"Recent events have been turned into art by one of Nigeria's great artists and today we were supposed to be able to meet the artist and receive the first installment of his work."

The idea of paying attention to the art really was a good one, but buying it the way the school board had still troubled the principal, seeming, somehow, like clear evidence of a continued misunderstanding.

"Though life sometimes seems endless and routine, it is not," he told the students. "It comes and goes according to a set of rules that we cannot understand. But a school is a place for learning, and our school years, though we rarely know it while we are living them, should be the most wonderful years of our lives, with nothing to do with our time but learn, nothing to carry back home with us but books. It is a time when ideas win out over pragmatic concerns, a time when our hearts understand more purely, and a time when each piece of information, each new idea, seems invented especially for us, at the very moment of our learning it."

The good quality of his opening remarks had put the principal into a certain rhythm, and once speaking he might have continued for a very long time, suddenly sure that he could tell his story as well as the art could. But when he looked up at his audience he saw some of the teachers pointing to the courtyard's side, where the artist, stepping into the school's isolated world, cheerfully stood. And the artist was smiling so benevolently that the principal let himself go. He remembered that the artist had spent weeks on the work, and by doing so surely did understand what had happened better than anyone else, better, even, than he did himself.

The principal held his hand out toward the artist. "Hello, LeRoY," he said. He then sat back down with the others, waiting while the artist came forward, his assistant trailing behind him with the piece of art.

"Hello, good day, everybody," the artist said. He spoke too loudly, so the A.V. man turned the microphone down. "What happen over dese las' weeks belong to us all, every one in some small way, dat is why I wan' make it into art."

The students applauded and the artist bowed. "It took me too long to made dese panels and I apologize for bringin' 'em 'round so late. I don' want to take all de time I took, but I can only hope, now, dat my panels will satisfy, speakin' to dose who look at 'em well. Of course, I tried to pound dese my panels wit' de truth, but when you look at 'em de truth will move aroun' a bit, depending on who is looking. Get it? Dat is de way wit' art."

The students applauded again so the artist told his assistant to unwrap the first panel. "Les do it like dis," he said. "Today let us enjoy panel number one. Den les wait a short while. Panel number two is already done, but les put it up nex' week. Dat way you can all grow 'ccustom to de beginning before proceeding to de middle. An since de school board wan' me to pound my third panel right here on de school groun' on de auction night, later on you can all see de end unfoldin' before your eyes. Dat's de way I like things to happen anyway, firs' de beginnin', den de middle, den de end."

Without further comment the artist and his assistant put panel number one up on the nearest wall of the school, between the nurse's room and the main office door at a spot that had been prepared beforehand. He hung two small talismans from it, two leather pouches that swung down the panel's sides, sending out an aura of safety and good luck. The students were dismissed, and though they filed past the panel, pressing against one another in order to see it well, the bell soon rang and the courtyard was quickly deserted. Later they'd come down to look at it one class at a time.

The school board members hurried out to their cars, but the principal and the school board president stayed by the panel, both of them trying to make sense of it. Though neither man had seen the panel before, as they looked at it now they would not have been able to come to any agreement on what they saw. The principal ignored the whole, staring instead at the far left side, where the nearest talisman hung. He touched the talisman lightly and then tried reading the panel as if it were a book. In this way he was drawn into something that surprised him, once again, by its complexity and magic and depth.

The school board president, on the other hand, saw the same jumble he always saw when he looked at African art. The panel told the story, he supposed, but it was a story that he already knew too well. And in the art the story was longer than he thought it should be, and considerably more complicated, not simple, like stories about real life should be.

Looking at the panel made both men late for work.

PANEL NUMBER ONE

One

November 28, 1983

Before leaving his flat to walk down the stairs and across the athletic field to his office in the school, Dr. Jerry Neal looked through the peephole in his door. Though there was rarely anyone else on the stairs at that hour, the action was habitual. He liked to take his morning walk alone, without the obligation to chat. He also liked to be the first one at school, to walk through the hazy air without the sounds of other people's voices buzzing in his ears.

The school's chief custodian, a Nigerian man with his shirt off and his trousers unbuttoned, was washing himself at the side of the courtyard and called out brightly when the principal came into view. "Good morning, sir!"

Jerry Neal nodded to the man but he did not speak. The chief custodian always arrived before him. He was the one exception.

The principal put his lunch in the teachers' room refrigerator and, once inside his office, hung his jacket from a wire hanger that swung from a hook on the back of his door. He loved the silence of this early morning time, when no one came to speak to him and when the noisy air conditioner, his constant companion once the day got hot, had not yet become a necessity.

Since it was Monday the principal took out his calendar for

the week and shook his head, overcome by the work load, but pleased with it as well. There would be a school board meeting and several subcommittee meetings. There was the problem of salary increases for the locally hired teachers and the mystery of the missing cans of toner for the school's copy machine. Someone had been stealing the toner, but though the chief custodian had twice set traps, the thief had not only proved difficult to catch but irritating as well, leaving such things as dead birds and bats' wings around to try to frighten the Nigerian maintenance crew. Jerry Neal kept an empty toner can on his desk as a reminder to keep the problem firmly in mind. He suspected that once the toner was safely off the campus it came back by way of the copy-machine-supplies salesman, who bought it from the thief and then re-sold it to the school. He hated seeing the toner can on his desk each day, but since the problem was infuriating, he wanted to infuriate himself further with the unsightly pres-ence of the can. Christmas vacation was less than a month away and he would have the problem solved before dismissal.

The principal had worked on his school board reports for about an hour when, at slightly before seven-thirty, someone knocked on his door. The knock came twice, but he finished the sentence he was writing before sighing and calling out, "Come in!" He didn't like these interruptions at all.

Since it was still early he had expected an adult but when the door swung open a student stood there, a Nigerian boy with his head down, hands at his sides. This boy's name was Nurudeen, and Jerry remembered that there had been some trouble the previous week.

"Ah, Nurudeen," he said.

"Good morning, sir," said the boy.

"Well, come in. Are there others, or are we going to get to the bottom of this alone?"

Nurudeen didn't reply so the principal told him to close the office door. "All right, son," he said. "Did you speak with your parents?"

The boy shook his head. "My father has traveled," he said.

"What about your mother? You were told to bring one of them with you today. Wasn't that our understanding?"

"My mother lives elsewhere," Nurudeen said.

The principal sat back and looked at the boy. This boy had been stealing lunches from the teachers' room refrigerator. He had been caught but had denied the thefts. One of the lunches he had stolen had been Jerry's own, but since Jerry at first thought hunger had played a part—even rich Nigerians sometimes left such things to chance—he had been slow to react. Now, though, he believed that the thefts were malicious, an act of boredom perhaps, or something done on a dare.

"So what is it going to be?" he asked. "Have you decided to tell the truth?"

Nurudeen nodded gravely. "In a way I took your lunch," he said.

The principal leaned forward but Nurudeen had closed his eyes and continued to speak. "The real truth is too strange to tell," he added.

Jerry Neal laughed sharply, but at that instant there was another knock on the door, which combined with his laugh to make it sound harsher and more cynical than he'd intended. He had only wanted to exhibit his disbelief, but the knock made it seem as though he had barked at the boy, and it startled them both.

Without waiting, Sunday Aremu, his administrative assistant, came into the office, forcing the principal to get up and walk him back toward the door. "What is it?" he asked. "What's up?"

"We are due at the ministry at ten," said Sunday. "I am collecting the particulars now." Sunday was a big man with a wide-open face and a pair of black glasses forever hanging from his neck on a string.

The principal nodded and when Sunday left the office he went with him, back into the teachers' room for coffee. He believed that Nurudeen's days in the school were numbered anyway, so missing the beginning of his first-period class wouldn't make much difference. And being in the office alone would give the boy a chance to think.

The relationship between Jerry Neal and the faculty of his school was complicated. Most of the teachers had been hired by him, either out of the United States or away from other international schools, but the remainder were hired locally and were paid considerably less. The difference in pay was a volatile issue at the school and the warmth of the principal's reception, upon entering the teachers' room, was greatly dependent upon who was sitting there. This morning there were mostly locally hired people about, so rather than stay a while he got his coffee and wandered back through the hallway to his office. Nurudeen, to his surprise, was pressed against the nearest wall when he opened the door. The boy's eyes were rolled tightly up into his head and his hands were pulled against his chest.

"Nurudeen! My God!" the principal shouted. He was about to run for the nurse, but at the sound of his name the boy deflated, immediately coming back to himself and walking over to a chair. "What?" he asked.

Jerry Neal sighed. "Look, son," he said. "You don't need such histrionics and you don't need to steal my lunch. If you want to go to another school just say so. Do you want the British system again, is that it?"

"All of my thefts were involuntary," said the boy.

"The devil made you do it, right?" said Jerry, and Nurudeen looked at him.

"It was my stepmother," he said.

The principal glanced at his watch. Soon he would be in the office of the minister of internal affairs, and he wanted to finish his paperwork before he left. Since the first-period bell had rung, a quiet had taken over the outer hallway and everything seemed peaceful again. Jerry looked at this boy and decided to give him another chance.

"What does your stepmother want with my lunch?" he asked. "Has she been coming around to eat with you?"

"You think everything is funny," said Nurudeen. "Americans try to make too many jokes."

In truth Jerry Neal did not try to make too many jokes, but he said, "OK, I don't think it's funny and you've got my full attention. Convince me that I should send you back to class."

Nurudeen looked quietly down at his shoes and the principal, despite his intention to keep staring at the boy, began rereading a letter that was lying on the top of his desk. The letter was from his sister-in-law in Tillamook, Oregon. Though she was well into middle age, she had recently become a chiropractor and had written insisting that a spinal adjustment would help Jerry end the grief he still felt concerning the death of her sister, his wife. Jerry's wife had been dead for five years, but whatever grief he still felt was certainly not centered in his spine, and he grimaced at the letter. He took some pleasure in hearing from his sister-in-law but she was a foolish woman sometimes. She and his wife had been twins but they had not been alike. Once, however, during his courting years, the sister-in-law had fooled him into believing that she was her sister. That had been three weeks before his wedding. He had taken her for coffee and they had held hands. When he called for the check his sister-in-law had suddenly grown serious, saying that she was Marge, not Charlotte. She had made Jerry furious by telling him, "It's the lack of focus for your love that is making you mad."

"My stepmother is my father's wife," said Nurudeen. "My mother is not. My stepmother has a son and that son is older than I." Nurudeen stopped speaking, as if that pretty much explained everything, but when the principal asked for more he said, "My stepmother does not care for me because I am to be the recipient of my father's wealth. My father has decided so, even though it was her son who was first born. She wants such things for her own son, but my father has decided in favor of me because I am clever and my older half-brother is not."

Nurudeen was looking at the principal carefully, but Jerry had been in Nigeria long enough by then to know how to hide his intentions well. If Nurudeen understood that he was not about to be expelled, there would be nothing more that Jerry could learn.

"All right," he said, "now let's get to the part about my lunch."

Nurudeen sighed. "It is my stepmother's will that I steal, for by stealing I will disgrace myself and jeopardize my place as rightful heir." Nurudeen touched his forehead with both his hands. "She casts spells," he whispered, "she uses witchcraft. That is the part I know you will not believe."

Jerry sighed; the boy was certainly right about that. If the Nigerians wanted to believe in all this voodoo—juju, they called it—that was up to them, but he had little patience for it, little desire to let this boy explain to him how it worked. His paperwork came to mind again and he had that meeting, but since he had decided not to suspend Nurudeen he had to take another moment to extract a promise that Nurudeen would not allow his stepmother's mischief to take hold again. Otherwise how could he justify leniency?

"If I send you back to class what will happen next?" he asked the boy.

"Who can say?" said Nurudeen. "When I defy her she causes me pain." He pointed to his previously puffed-up chest, and Jerry realized that Nurudeen was telling him that the stepmother had been at work while he'd been out of the room getting coffee.

"But if you steal again she will have won," he said. "If you steal again I will dismiss you from school."

"Maybe now that I have spoken her power will be less," said the boy. "I have been told that mentioning such things has had that effect before."

The principal wrote out a tardy slip and stood, walking Nurudeen to the door. "If you feel the pain returning ask your teacher to send you to the nurse. The nurse will then call me and we will deal with the pain together."

Nurudeen's eyes were bright as they walked together toward the bottom of the stairs leading to the junior high section of the school. And when Nurudeen was out of sight he stepped into the nurse's office to tell the nurse what arrangements had been made.

The Ministry of Internal Affairs was at the Federal Secretariat, and it was always difficult to predict how long it would take to get there. Since the school had recently hired a driver, parking, at least, would not be a problem, but when Jerry and his administrative assistant left the campus it was nine-fifteen, not nine o'clock as they had planned. Though they would surely have to wait once they arrived, it would not be good to be late.

"I've been thinking," Jerry said. "Maybe, at this level, we could end it all. Today, right now."

Sunday shook his head. "Our chance was with one of the lower boys. Now things have gone too far. Even if we could dash this man, it would cost too much."

This was the problem: Jerry Neal had hired eight new teachers on his recruiting trip to the United States the year before. Since the recruiting fair had been on the West Coast he had made visa applications, on behalf of the new teachers, at the Nigerian consulate in San Francisco. He had been told at the consulate that a new government policy mandated that the teachers arrive in Nigeria with tourist visas which would then be changed to working status by the Ministry of Internal Affairs. Jerry had argued the matter for three days, staying in San Francisco and taking the consul general twice to lunch, but in the end he had been convinced that the new policy was real. There were too many foreigners in Nigeria, the consul general had said, too much hard currency was leaving the country and the government had decided to take a firmer stand. Once he was back in Lagos, however, Jerry quickly discovered that the Ministry of Internal Affairs knew nothing of the new policy. What's more, the ministry had told him that all eight new teachers would have to return to San Francisco so that their documents could be vetted and the proper visas issued.

When the school van entered Alagbon Close, the traffic snarled and then stopped. Hawkers came onto the road, dozens of young boys but some women and older men too. They were walking past the vehicles, holding up items for sale, food and pieces of clothing, alarm clocks and replacement parts for automobiles. Sunday looked at his watch. "If we walk we will arrive on time," he said. Jerry knew that was true, but if they walked he would arrive in the minister's office sweating, and he wanted to appear cool.

A boy at the van window had a selection of videotapes in his hand and smiled when Jerry opened the door. "Oh, look," said the boy. "*Dallas! Wheel O Fortune!* Yes, America. Twenty naira, cheap!"

Jerry didn't speak to this boy, but a taller boy, standing just behind the first one, drew his attention. This boy was selling ironing boards and Jerry remembered that his steward, Jules, had been complaining that their ironing board was no good. The boy with the ironing board saw a look of interest in Jerry's eyes and pushed the other boy away. "Fifty naira," he said. The ironing board was wrapped in butcher paper and tied with string.

"I don't have time," said Jerry Neal.

"OK, las' price forty-two. Very fine board dis one. English ironing board, jus' like de one use by de queen."

Sunday looked at his watch again so Jerry closed the van door and told the driver to make his way to the front of the Federal Secretariat and wait.

"Let me show you," said the boy. He began tearing the butcher paper away from the ironing board, but the two men weren't waiting, so he tucked the torn paper under the string and tried to keep up. Sunday was carrying the teachers' files in his briefcase, which he clutched to his belly with both hands.

They cut through a pathway that led past various stalls. Here there was clothing for sale, the stall owners sitting on low stools or lying down on cardboard under hanging trousers and shirts. When they slowed once to decide which way to turn, the ironing-board boy banged his board into the back of Jerry Neal's neck.

"Ouch!" said Jerry.

"Do you want that thing?" Sunday asked.

"Jules tells me we need a new one," Jerry said, so Sunday spoke to the boy and then said, "The real last price is thirty naira."

"OK," said Jerry, "tell him I'll take it for twenty-five if he's around when we come back. If I pay him now he won't take the ironing board back to the van."

"Oh yes," said the boy, and Sunday, embarrassed by the principal's lack of trust, said, "I think this one always works here." They settled on twenty-seven naira and when Jerry paid the boy he restrained himself from giving another warning. He watched the boy walk back toward the van with the ironing board and the cash.

The Ministry of Internal Affairs was on the sixth floor of a government office building and since the power was down they had to walk up the stairs. Still, by ten o'clock they had opened the door and stepped into the minister's outer office, right on time.

The secretary was asleep on her typewriter, but she stirred when she heard them come in. "We have an appointment with the minister," Sunday said. "We are from the International School."

The secretary pulled her head up and pushed some papers about until an appointment book came into her hand.

"No," she said. "Here I see no man's name."

"I spoke with the minister myself," Jerry said. "Maybe it's written in his own appointment book."

The secretary looked at him and yawned. She was wearing

traditional Yoruba clothing, a yellow cloth wrapped around her and tucked in here and there, but to Jerry she was the picture of incompetence, a good example of why Nigeria never made any progress with the outside world. "No man's name," she said again.

"Is the minister on seat?" Sunday asked. Though the principal had been ready to yell, Sunday's voice had grown softer.

"He is on seat," said the secretary.

"Is he alone?"

"He is working."

"It is now ten o'clock," said Sunday. "Though I can see we are not written in his appointment book, maybe we can go in small? Just for a minute or two."

The secretary stared at them but then pushed herself away from her desk, tucked at her clothing, and ambled across to the inner-office door. When she left the room both men sat down and Sunday placed a thick hand on Jerry's arm. "Too much palaver," he said. "But it is importan' to go through each step slowly. Then we will be fine."

Sunday smiled, but after that the two men were quiet, content to sit down low on the broken couch. Aside from this couch and the secretary's desk, the room was empty, but it was still a little cooler than the street outside, making them both realize that the power had not been down too long.

When the secretary returned she walked heavily over to her desk but managed to say "He will see you" under her breath.

The minister's inner office was thickly carpeted and heavily draped and chaired. There were official-looking photographs on the walls, and the minister's desk alone was nearly the size of his entire outer office.

The minister was staring at a ledger of some kind and made them stand before him for a full minute before waving a hand and telling them to sit down.

"How can I help you?" he finally asked.

"Alhaji, you might remember that last week we spoke by phone," Jerry Neal began.

"Of course," said the minister.

"Concerning visas for teachers at my school . . ."

The minister closed his ledger and sat back. His chair was big enough to be a small country's throne. "If I broke the law in America would I be allowed an audience with the secretary of state?" he asked.

"I'm sure not," said Jerry Neal.

"Would I be allowed, even, to enter your country if my intention was to work and I arrived with documents stating that I was a tourist?"

"Probably not."

"Are the tourists in question teaching now?" asked the minister.

"They are not tourists," Jerry said. "We were only obeying instructions from your consulate in San Francisco."

"Then if it is the consulate's mistake it is up to the consulate to rectify it. Send the tourists back and let them do things properly this time."

"In that case we must close the school," said Jerry.

The minister shrugged. "There are many good Nigerian teachers who would love to teach in such a school. I myself could provide you with a list. Hire Nigerian teachers. Surely you are not unaware of our indigenization program?"

"Of course not," said Jerry Neal, "but our charter states that our teachers must be U.S.-trained."

"Why?" the minister asked.

"So that the children of U.S. citizens will not have the nature of their education interrupted when their parents work abroad. It is not intended as a comment on the quality of Nigerian teachers."

The minister laughed, smiling for the first time. "Of course it is," he said. "Why not tell the truth?"

"I am telling the truth," Jerry Neal said mildly.

"Do you have Nigerian students in your school?"

"We do."

"How many?"

"Very many. Perhaps twenty-five percent."

"Are they the children of ordinary citizens, ordinary men and women?"

"Of people who can pay the fees," Jerry said.

"Which are how much?"

"Five thousand per annum. In the end a little more."

"That is steep," said the minister of internal affairs.

Now Jerry Neal shrugged. "It is the same everywhere," he said. "Among international schools."

"I have children," said the minister. "Could my children go to your school?"

"It would depend upon their ages. Some of our classes are full, some are not. Also they must take a test, to discover at what level they can read."

"And if they read poorly you would turn them away?"

"We would do our best to find them tutors who would help them read better," the principal said.

Jerry was beginning to feel uneasy. He had supposed that the minister might seek admission for his children as payment for allowing the visas to be changed, and he knew his school board would say no. But he could not think of a way of changing the direction of the conversation.

"I would be glad to show you the school sometime," he said.

For the last minute Sunday had been pushing his foot against Jerry's, trying to tell him that things weren't going well. They had powerful weapons they could use and he was telling Jerry that now was the time to use them. And the minister, finally, asked a question that opened things up a bit more.

"Do the children of my colleagues go to your school? Are the children of other ministers enrolled?"

The principal leaned forward, touching the edge of the desk and lowering his voice. "Not of ministers, perhaps, but of the president. The president's youngest child is there."

There it was, their best card played. Now the minister

knew that he could not decide to close the school. Jerry had been careful to present this information only as a statement of fact, not as a threat. Nevertheless, the pause grew long while the minister studied him. Finally Jerry spoke again.

"We are very sorry to have broken any laws. We would never have done so knowingly."

"Ignorance of the law is no excuse," said the minister. "Haven't you heard that somewhere before?"

"Yes," said Jerry. "It is an expression of our own."

Things had been so tense, to this point, that Jerry and Sunday both were startled when the minister slapped his desk and laughed loudly, nearly losing his balance in his chair.

"Yes, yes," he said. "I first heard it when I was driving badly in Washington D.C. I was a student at Georgetown and thought it rather fine. I have used it often since!"

Jerry took a chance. "Georgetown is a good school. I myself applied there once but was turned down."

The minister was pleased by this pronouncement and leaned forward. "And I'll tell you what," he said, "though ignorance of the law was not an excuse, that cop let me off. I told him I was Nigerian and he seemed to think my citizenship, rather than my ignorance, was excuse enough."

The minister looked at Jerry Neal and then at Sunday. The story was funny but Jerry didn't know whether or not to laugh. He had hoped that the minister would carry it through, telling him that he was going to repay the kindness of the Washington D.C. cop by allowing the teachers to remain. It was Sunday, however, who spoke next.

"Oh, yes," he said, "we are all brothers under the skin."

To Jerry the statement seemed trite and completely beside the point but it struck a chord with the minister, and Sunday, once again exhibiting his masterful sense of timing, opened his briefcase and placed the teachers' files in the center of the desk. "Alhaji, this is a serious matter," he said. "Maybe we could show that it was an honest mistake in some way that would do no harm to the children."

"Yes," said the minister. "I suppose it would be the school-
children who would suffer most were I to make their teachers
leave."

He seemed truly saddened by that thought, but before anything more could be said the secretary slouched back into the
room, mumbling something about an appointment elsewhere.
When she departed it was clear that their meeting was over.

"I will take it under advisement," said the minister. "I understand now that you are men of good faith, a point on
which I had serious doubts before."

The minister stood then and went out the door ahead of
them. The outer office was now full of petitioners, all of
whom leapt to their feet when he suddenly appeared.

"When may I call again?" Jerry asked, but Sunday put a
hand on his shoulder. The minister was collecting papers
from the men surrounding him and speaking hurriedly before
rushing out the door. Soon the office was as empty as it had
been when they'd arrived. The secretary, sitting down low
behind her desk again, had pulled one bare foot up and was
picking at her toes.

"Come," said Sunday. "I think it will be fine now."

But nothing was settled and Jerry said, "We don't know
what the man is going to do."

Sunday put a finger in front of his nose. "I will come back
in a day or two," he said.

The principal wasn't satisfied, but he opened the door and
had gone out into the hallway before he realized that Sunday
had not come along. Sunday was still inside the room, sitting
on the edge of the secretary's desk, quietly laughing with the
woman and stroking his chin.

The principal was hungry, but when he looked inside the teachers' room refrigerator, his lunch was gone. His paper sack was there, but his plastic sandwich box and his thermos were missing. It was two o'clock and he had just returned from taking his new ironing board back to his flat so that it would be waiting when his steward returned from his afternoon break. Jerry had made a mistake with Nurudeen. He should have expelled the boy. This time he'd not only lost his food but his sandwich box and thermos as well.

At four p.m. Jerry left his office for the day. He had to drive to the home of the school board president by seven that evening, and he wanted some time to rest. But when he saw the chief custodian he remembered that he hadn't done anything more about the missing copy-machine toner, so while the two of them pretended to engage in small talk, they made plans for the chief custodian to sleep in the copy room once again that night. He had done so previously, without results, but though he pretended not to be, he was nervous about doing so again. The thefts were too mysterious to be easily explained and the chief custodian, like Nurudeen earlier in the day, was beginning to have the spirit world in mind. The thief's malicious plantings had had an effect even on this good man.

Nevertheless, the chief custodian said that he would leave the campus at five-thirty and asked that Jerry drive out shortly after that to pick him up on the main road. That way, should the thief be watching, it would appear that the chief custodian had gone home for the night. Once safely back on campus, sneaking him into the copy room would be easy. They said good night loudly, and Jerry walked back to his flat alone. When he opened his door he found Jules there ironing, but on the old ironing board, not the new one.

"Didn't you see the board I bought today?" he asked.

Jules, who was Togolese, put on a French West African pout and cast his head toward the back of the living room. "There it is, the terrible thing," he said. "It is too tall and its cover is torn. Also it is warped. How much did you pay for that thing? Why didn't you look at it first?"

Jerry went past Jules and found the new ironing board leaning against the living room wall. He set it up and put his hands on it. It was too tall. And looking across the board was like looking out over the surface of a rumpled bed.

"What a waste," mumbled Jules, but Jerry was not in the mood to be scolded by his steward, and he cast the man a look that made him stop. Tomorrow he would take the ironing board over to the school carpenter and get the legs shortened and a new top cut, but now he wanted a drink and some time alone in his chair, sitting under his assortment of masks and thorn carvings and other pieces of Nigerian art. He had collected these pieces carefully over the last three years, and he was proud of the quality of what he'd bought. He was most drawn to his masks, but he liked the juju pieces as well. Though there was too much nonsense concerning magic around the school these days, he really did think that the art was fine.

Jerry's dinner would be ready whenever he wanted it— Jules was great that way—so he would sit for an hour and then shower and eat before going out again to the meeting. Ah, but he had forgotten already about the chief custodian. And since it was four-thirty he had only an hour before he had to pick the man up. What a life he led. Before Charlotte's death he could not have imagined a life that encompassed worries such as what to do about a faulty ironing board or how to catch a toner thief. Jerry often wondered what Charlotte would have done had he died first. Would she have run from his death by leaving the country as he had? A frequent daydream of his was to imagine her living on without him, and in the daydream she always did it so very well.

Jerry went into the kitchen to get some ice and pour himself a drink. There was another letter from his sister-in-law on the counter so he opened it before handing Jules the lunch sack and telling him about the loss of the sandwich box and thermos. This new letter contained five name cards, with only a brief note scribbled on the back of one. The name cards were in the shape of the human spinal column and were stiff little plastic things, made to look like bone. The note said, "Hi Jerry, I met a female chiropractor from Nigeria and I told her to look you up. I've forgotten her name. Do you like my new name cards? I can see you now, looking down your nose." Jerry held the name cards out, arrayed like a poker hand in his palm. Spinal-column name cards, the letters of Marge's name spaced evenly along the vertebrae and made to look like the ligaments and muscles that supported them. His sister-in-law was fifty-two years old, the same age, of course, as Charlotte would have been. Their birthday was January 1, a date that had let them easily calculate their ages throughout their lives. When Charlotte's cancer finally killed her she'd been forty-seven years, one hundred and forty-seven days old—that had been on May 27, 1978. Now, more than five years after her death, Jerry was ten years older, he was fifty-seven, and would not marry again. He had occasionally imagined that he might marry Marge, but that had only been a game. His love for Charlotte had been too complete for him to see her face again, hellishly housing the countenance of Marge.

Jerry took a second scotch with him to the shower and when he came out a plate of West African curry and a bottle of Star beer were set out nicely on the dining-room table. Jules had finished ironing and had put on a white shirt, something he always did for dinner. It was nearly five-thirty and Jerry imagined the chief custodian over at the school, letting people see him preparing to leave. He sighed and said, "I would love to be able to stay in tonight, but I have a meeting." His comment was not so much intended for Jules, but was a testament to the vocal habits of those who live alone, and Jules did not reply.

Jerry finished his dinner and got up from the table at five thirty-five. He put his jacket back on and picked up his folder of meeting materials. There would be time to spare, but he did not want to come back into his flat after getting the chief custodian into the copy room. Jules would clean up and leave the flat by seven, locking it and making his way to Moroko where he lived. Jerry had been to Jules's house once or twice and knew it was a terrible, dark place, two small rooms housing Jules and his wife and children. Jerry paid Jules well—at three hundred naira a month he was the highest paid of all the stewards in the building—and since he worked for a single man he had the easiest job. Whenever Jerry had a dinner party he paid Jules overtime.

Since he was going out on school business, Jerry took the van, starting the engine and waving to the security guards as he drove out through the gate. It would take the chief custodian ten minutes to walk to his bus stop, so Jerry drove slowly, circling out past the Eko Hotel and then back to where the chief custodian stood.

"Good evening, sir," he said, climbing quickly into the van. "Tonight we will find our thief."

Jerry turned the van around and drove, this time all the way out to Bar Beach, while the chief custodian snuggled down onto the van's floor, pulling a blanket from the seat and covering himself.

"I don't want to go back too soon," said Jerry.

"No, sir," came a muffled reply.

The Bar Beach road wasn't crowded so Jerry pulled onto the shoulder, looking out over the sand dunes and trying to see what progress the sea had made in taking back the reclaimed land. All of Victoria Island, the land where the

school and the flats stood, had once been underwater, yet
now it held some of the most expensive homes in Lagos,
with rents and purchase prices doubling and tripling every
year. Jerry looked out at the water and the ships as they
moved into Apapa, the Lagos port. Nigeria was such a difficult, troublesome country that even after three years he marveled that he was living in such a place. Before Charlotte's
death he had been content with his school administrator's
job in Oregon. Ironically it had been Charlotte who had
sometimes said that their lives might benefit from a change.
And after her death, it was for Charlotte that he had taken
the job in Abidjan, in the Ivory Coast, for Charlotte that he
had moved to Lagos when the opportunity arose.

"Sir?" said the chief custodian, and Jerry put the van in
gear, driving back toward the school. When he got there he
waved to the night guard, then pulled the van up close to
the school's back entrance. When no one was looking he slid
the van door open and pulled the blankets off the chief custodian's back. They got into the air-conditioned room easily
and unnoticed.

"What about your dinner?" Jerry asked.

The chief custodian laughed, rubbing the sweat from his
arms and face, so Jerry went back to his flat after all, to see
what he could do about getting some food. On his way he
met one of the teachers, who told him that there had been
a call. "The Ministry of Internal Affairs," the teacher said.
"Someone wants to see you again tomorrow."

Back in his flat the after-dinner cleanup was finished and,
though it was barely six, Jules was already gone. Jerry took a
plate from the cupboard, then found the leftover curry and
rice and put it in the oven to heat. If the ministry had called,
then he was sure that he was expected at some specific time
but the teacher had not told him one, and for some reason
that made him imagine the minister's secretary, her slow
walk, her half-shut eyes, all her weight down low. Surely it
was she who had called.

When the food was ready Jerry walked back over to the

copy room, but when he opened the door he thought for a moment that the chief custodian was gone.

"Joseph?" he said.

"Yessir," came a voice, this time not muffled by wool but echoed in tin, and when the lower door of the copy machine swung open the chief custodian smiled up. He had the blanket over him and had placed an empty toner can under his head.

Jerry left the food on the floor and thanked the chief custodian for giving up another night at home. And by the time he went outside again the lights from the surrounding buildings, huge blocks of flats housing government officials, had come on.

The school board president's house was at the edge of Victoria Island, about fifteen minutes away. Perhaps the one predictable moment of the day would be what happened at this meeting. Still, as the principal drove there he reminded himself that his job meant everything to him, that he was dedicated to doing it right. He continued to miss Charlotte, his sister-in-law was right about that, but he was most sorry for what Charlotte was missing by not being here with him now, to see Africa, to have such an adventure as this. These were the thoughts he had every night. The joy in Jerry Neal's life came twofold, from work and from imagining Charlotte. He knew what would be said at this meeting and he knew what his responses would be and how he would feel about it in the morning. When Christmas vacation came perhaps he would go home for a while, or, more likely, he would visit Europe by himself, but imagining Charlotte seeing all those sights too. And when he returned he would be ready, once again, to continue it all. He remembered a time not so long ago when to continue anything, without Charlotte by his side, took all the strength he had.

The school board meeting was scheduled for seven the following morning, so though Jerry had not returned to his flat until midnight he was back in his office by six, going over his papers and wondering how best to discuss the issues at hand. On his way to the office he had stopped at the copy room but the chief custodian was gone, and when he found him in the courtyard he was told that the night had been uneventful, the thief had not come. The chief custodian vowed to stay again, but the principal really thought that the thefts were taking place during the day.

"Listen," he said. "Let's just lock the rest of the toner up, bring it out when we need it and have you there to put it in the machine. That way at least we'll keep what we have."

"Yessir," said the chief, but he disapproved of the plan. Catching a thief was preferable to stopping thievery, and locking up the toner would only add to the atmosphere of suspicion and guilt.

The major focus of the school board meeting would be the same thing that had dominated the committee meeting the night before: what to do about the eight new teachers and their improper visas. As he had with the committee, Jerry would tell the school board what had taken place at the ministry, and he would have his secretary telephone the ministry as soon as it opened so that he could clarify the previous afternoon's call. As he wrote, preparing each aspect of the issue carefully, Jerry felt the pure pleasure he got from running such a school. The issue was a thorny one but he would conquer it in the end. It was, after all, the unpredictability of his work that drew him, the improbability of a thing occurring only a moment before it did.

Members of the school board filed in slowly, but by seven-fifteen the president had called the meeting to order, and the first monotonous items on the agenda were introduced. Jerry paid little attention during this part of things. He knew the minutes of the previous meeting would be accurate, that the charts and tables he had prepared were ready for those who wanted them. For Jerry this was a time to relax, to prepare himself for the meatier issues that were at hand.

Just as Jerry began to settle into the rhythm of the meeting, however, someone moved to suspend the normal agenda and get right to the matter of the visas. Then the school board president addressed Jerry directly. "You've been around too long to make a mistake like this," he said. When he spoke, the other board members turned in their chairs.

Jerry waited a moment, looking at the man. He respected the school board president as a man who handled his job at the American Embassy in much the same way that Jerry ran the school. He was a no-nonsense kind of man, and Jerry was momentarily embarrassed to understand that the president saw his handling of the visa problem as a mistake. He nevertheless looked at the man evenly. "When I was in San Francisco I was convinced by the Nigerian consul general that the law had changed," he said. He was angry to have been taken by surprise by the suspended agenda and by the president's comments, and he would have continued strongly, but just then his secretary came into the room, telling him that he was wanted in the outer office. Jerry didn't suffer interruptions gladly, but he remembered that he had asked the secretary to get the ministry on the phone, so he stood and followed her out of the room, contenting himself only by staring calmly into the president's face and by saying that perhaps he could come back with a firmer statement on how to clear the matter up.

But when Jerry got to the main office and picked up the phone, all he heard was a dial tone, and when he looked at the secretary she shook her head. "No," she said. "In your private office." Had someone from the ministry actually come out to the school to see him then? he wondered. Surely it wasn't the minister.

Jerry went quickly down to his private office door, pausing only to straighten his tie. He had an automatic smile on his face but when he opened the door and saw who was waiting for him his smile collapsed. Nurudeen was there with a man who was probably his father, a well-dressed man standing with one hand on top of that empty toner can.

"I'm sorry," the principal said, "but I'm in the middle of something; all this will have to wait."

Nurudeen had Jerry's thermos in his lap and on his face was a look of pure pain, as if his stepmother were even then twisting away at him.

"We are here on a matter of great urgency," said the man. "We would not have asked your secretary to call you from your meeting for anything less."

Jerry knew that his secretary would not have dared call him from the meeting for anything less, so he stood there quietly a moment, calming himself so that he would not speak rudely. Finally he said, "If you would like I can see you just as soon as this meeting is over."

Nurudeen's father was wearing tribal clothes, white robes and a beautifully embroidered cap. He was short, but quite handsome. He wore thick glasses and he seemed about ten years younger than Jerry Neal. His demeanor was formal. "My son is under a great deal of strain," he said.

Jerry was about to repeat his suggestion that they talk when the meeting ended, but Nurudeen's father raised his hand. "I am, however, not here exclusively about my son. I am here also on behalf of my brother, who is the minister of internal affairs. It was he who put Nurudeen up to the tricks that have occurred."

Jerry paused, a little vertigo settling in. "The minister told your son to steal my lunch?" he asked slowly. Then he added, "Nurudeen said it was your wife."

Nurudeen tensed in his chair but his father remained calm above him, placing one smooth hand on his shoulder. "A boy in trouble will grasp at improbable straws," he said. "Could I trouble you for a moment alone?"

Jerry knew that several of the school board members would be irritated by his absence, but how could he dismiss such a claim? He looked at Nurudeen and then spoke softly, saying, "Son, you go on up to class. If you ever steal anything again you are expelled from this school, is that clear?"

Nurudeen nodded, so Jerry opened the door for him. And once the door was closed again he sat down, offering Nurudeen's father the chair his son had warmed.

"Now," he said. "How could this be possible? What would make you say such a thing?"

Though Nurudeen's father had taken the offered seat, he held both hands in front of him, shaking his head. "Please," he said, "it will all be clear to you soon. Isn't it about time that we get started for the ministry?"

The principal sat forward. "He's expecting me now?"

"Of course," said Nurudeen's dad. "You didn't get his call?"

Nurudeen's father stood, and Jerry went back into the staff room.

"Our little drama is coming to a head," he said, standing in the doorway and pretending to be amused. "It seems the ministry has sent a car. I've been asked to go back down there now."

Some of the board members wanted details, but the president waved Jerry away. "Good," he said. "We'll be pleased if you can get this thing straightened out today."

Jerry Neal smiled, but when he turned back toward his office he saw Nurudeen's father going out the other door, past the secretary and out to the school's front gate. He didn't like the man and he tried to remind himself, one more time, that he was in this business for the fun of it, for the surprises of each new day.

Still, though he tried not to hurry, when he got outside the confounded man was already in his car and was pretending impatience, about to have his driver pull away.

Though Nurudeen's father had been slightly cordial in Jerry's office, once inside his automobile he seemed to concentrate on the outside world. Jerry carried the teacher files with him, and since it was clear that Nurudeen's father preferred not to speak, he opened the files and went over everything once more, making sure that there was no detail about which he was unsure. The traffic was light so the trip went quickly, but when they got close to the Federal Secretariat everything stopped again. Jerry looked out the window and could see that there were police cars around. He could feel a certain lively excitement in the morning air.

"It is better for us to walk," said Nurudeen's dad, so Jerry gathered his files and slid across the seat, getting out after the man and straightening his jacket as he stood.

"Ah, masta," said a voice, and Jerry looked to see the ironing-board boy. It was he who had opened the car door.

"You sold me a piece of junk," Jerry said. He felt real anger and he glared at the boy. "The legs are too long and the top is warped."

"Oh no," said the ironing-board boy, but Nurudeen's father had not waited, so Jerry didn't speak again. He followed the man toward the ministry, and it really did appear as though something strange was going on. The path ahead of them was crowded, a murmur floating above it like a chant.

Nurudeen's father slowed and turned. "Something is truly wrong," he said. "Everyone is going where we are." He found a traffic policeman and asked him what had happened.

"Nigeria's disgrace," said the cop. "Another someone has started a fire."

They edged their way into the crowd, respect for Nurudeen's father making people lenient and allowing them to get up to where the police had cordoned off the area immediately in front of the Ministry of Internal Affairs. Jerry was surprised to understand that everyone seemed to know Nurudeen's dad. When he looked behind him he could see that the crowd stretched all the way back to the road. He saw the ironing-board boy in a nearby group, following along.

They were pressing up against the cordon when Nurudeen's father found another policeman and told him they had business with the minister. They could see the building plainly now, flames coming from a set of windows up high. Workers were milling about, craning their necks upward on the other side of the cordon.

When the policeman went off to find his commanding officer, Nurudeen's father turned to Jerry and said something Jerry couldn't understand. The mood of the crowd was bad and Jerry really did hope that they would soon be able to get past the cordon, where, if nothing else, there was a little more room to stand. Only a few months before someone had set fire to another big building, and ordinary citizens were beginning to lose patience.

When the commanding policeman came over he greeted Nurudeen's father formally, lifting the cordon and allowing them inside.

"Where did the fire start?" Nurudeen's father asked. "I hope this time it was an accident."

"The fire is contained, sir," said the policeman, "but it was not accidental. We already have our evidence."

The man said that the floor on which the fire had started housed the Ministry of Internal Affairs, and Jerry began to feel a little strange. "Were there injuries?" he asked the police captain. "Was anyone hurt?"

The policeman looked at him, but directed his answer to

Nurudeen's dad. "One hurt badly, two more suffering from the smoke," he said.

"I trust the minister is safe?" Nurudeen's father said, and when the policeman pointed to a group of automobiles parked at the side of the building they walked that way.

From where they had been standing the area that they now approached appeared to be crowded with police and fire vehicles, but as they got closer they saw that there was an ambulance as well. Nurudeen's father asked for the minister again and was directed toward a black Mercedes-Benz, its doors opened, a small crowd forming a crescent around its near side.

"Excuse please," he said, edging in among the people. Jerry was right behind him but he was not at all prepared for what he saw. The minister of internal affairs was sitting in the back of the Mercedes-Benz, turned sideways with his feet down on the ground. He cradled his head in his hands and his robes were filthy, covered with soot and pulled around so roughly that he looked like he had just been in a battle for his life.

"Alhaji," said Nurudeen's dad. "Minister, are you not fine?"

The minister looked slowly up, but when he saw Jerry standing there he reacted violently, jerking to his feet and staggering forward.

"Why are you all so evil!" he screamed. "Whenever there is tragedy, whenever a truly loathsome act occurs, there is always a white man involved!"

It was clear that the minister was in shock but Jerry, nevertheless, had no idea what to do. The minister nearly lost his balance, and then to everyone's surprise he came at Jerry wildly, actually scratching his face with one of his out-of-control hands.

"Hey!" Jerry yelled. "Ouch! Stop it!" The minister's blind thrust had hit him just above his left eye, tearing the flesh somewhere around his eyebrow. Jerry dropped the teachers' files, both hands shooting up to his face. He arched forward so that wayward drops of blood would not come down on his clothing, and at the same time he tried to find the teachers' files, kneeling and feeling around for them on the ground. Though he couldn't see, he could sense that everyone had been stunned by what had happened, and once he had the files again he stood up.

"Surely there must be medical help nearby," he said. He meant for the minister but Nurudeen's father thought he meant for himself, and when he went off to bring a medic back, the minister struck again, grabbing Jerry's arm and shaking him. "Here he is!" he screamed. "This is the man who started the fire!"

The minister spun Jerry around so hard that Jerry nearly dropped the files again. "Why do you despise us so?" he shouted.

Jerry's eye was burning but he could see out of it again, and he tried to stop himself from going in the direction that the minister wanted him to go.

"Come!" screamed the minister. "Cast your eyes on what your evil has wrought!"

The minister pushed Jerry back toward the side of the building and pointed at a spot on the shady ground. Mindless of the blood now, Jerry jerked his arm free and wiped a sleeve across his eye. He then looked down at the spot where the minister's finger led.

"My God," he said.

The minister's secretary was there, the lazy one from the outer office. A piece of torn cardboard partially covered her oddly angled body, but she was wearing the same yellow dress she'd worn the day before, and her face held that same bored look.

Jerry wanted to ask if she was alive, but by then Nurudeen's father was back, not with a doctor but with the same police captain who had opened the cordon to let them in. The minister seemed to have calmed by then but the policeman poked a stiff finger up against Jerry's shirt. "Do not speak," he commanded. He then pulled Jerry hard, jerking

him away from the secretary and back along the shady side
of the building to where another group stood.

"Look," said the policeman, "and explain, please, what it
is that you see."

Jerry's eye still throbbed, and when he looked at the
ground he expected to see someone else hideously hurt. This
time, however, there was nobody. Rather, on another piece of
cardboard stood five one-gallon cans of copy-machine toner.
And on top of one of the cans was Jerry's plastic sandwich
box, his name written on a piece of masking tape and stuck
across its lid.

For a moment Jerry was unable to take in the meaning of
what he saw. He remembered turning in the direction of the
captain of police once more, but then someone struck him
and he was on the ground.

"Keep back!" he heard the captain yell. "I want a car here
now. Keep those people back, do you hear what I say?"

Though someone was kicking at him, hard unopposed
kicks to his arms and side, someone else, perhaps two or
three someone elses, was soon pulling him from the ground
and shoving him into the backseat of a just-arrived automobile. He tried to speak but his mouth contained blood and
there was a piece of something that might have been a tooth,
which fell into the hand that he used to support his chin.

There was a roaring in Jerry's ears, but he wasn't clear
about its source. He wasn't alone in the back of the car, but
he had been pressed against the far door, and it occurred to
him that he might simply open it and run. When he looked
up, however, he saw a thousand angry faces just on the other
side of that fragile thickness of glass. The young ironing-
board boy was there again, his eyes oddly hurt-looking, his
mouth shouting with the voice of the crowd, his head bent
toward the sky.

As soon as the car began to move Jerry Neal spoke. And
he surprised himself by hearing that his voice was normal
and clear. "I'm not guilty of anything," he said, and though
the policemen around him had been as focused on the crowd

as he was, they were shaken by the sound of his voice, by the breach of prisoner etiquette that it entailed. Had a Nigerian spoken thusly, during the dangerous ride from arrest to jail, he might have been beaten beyond words.

Once Jerry spoke, though, some of his confusion left him and the pain began to set in. His mouth hurt more than his ribs or his arm, but he could not remember having been struck in the mouth. And now that his head was clear, he began to understand that someone had actually taken the toner with the idea of using it to start the fire. Miraculously, he still had the teachers' files, and when he thought of the teachers he thought of the minister, and when he thought of the minister he thought of Nurudeen's dad, and then he thought of Nurudeen and of his own little sandwich box, sitting up on top of the toner cans, complete with an imprint of his name. Good Christ, Nurudeen had taken the toner. Nurudeen, an eighth-grade boy, was involved in some kind of plot to bring him down.

Jerry looked at the policemen sitting around him. These guys weren't speaking, but he knew that Nigerians responded far more quickly to friendship than to threats, so when he spoke again his words were calculated and his face was calm. "This will all be cleared up shortly," he said. "After that we can all go out for a beer."

He smiled and turned in the seat when he spoke, but the man next to him stared straight ahead. It was the officer in the front seat, the one next to the far door, who would tell the others what they should think, and this man did turn slowly around. He was not the police captain who had treated Jerry badly before, but was an older man with a kinder face.

"Indeed," the man finally said.

"I am a guest here," said Jerry. "But I understand how mistakes like this can happen, believe me."

The police officer gave him another look, seemed about to respond, but then turned silently forward again. Jerry had not been paying attention to what part of town they were in, but just as he was beginning to believe they had been on the road too long, the car pulled in somewhere and stopped.

"Where are we?" he asked. "What police station is this?"

Again there was no response, but when the ranking officer came around and opened his door there was also no sign that he would again be treated roughly. The man held his arm, but gently, telling him with a slight pressure that he was to walk inside.

"If I could just call the school. We have our own solicitor who could begin to set things straight." It was unlike Jerry to be so free with words and he was slightly ashamed of it. He knew that sooner or later he'd get home, and once this was over he understood that he would know how best to take advantage of the horrible mistake.

The policemen surrounded him and marched him down a narrow hallway to a dismal room. There was a table in the room, and there was a chair.

"Empty pocket, take off shoe and belt," said one of the younger men. His entry into the station had caused a stir and he could not now be sure whether this young man had been in the car with him or not. But he did as he was told, moving slowly and trying to remember how much money he had. He usually carried one hundred naira or so but he didn't think he had that much today. He remembered, however, that there was a one-hundred-dollar bill tucked inside the photo section of his wallet, behind a favorite photograph of Charlotte. He kept it for emergencies, though it alone was illegal enough to keep him here. He took his wallet out and counted the money before placing it on the table.

"Watch," said the young policeman.

Jerry unstrapped his wristwatch and buckled it around his wallet, which was inside the circle made by his belt. The young policeman held out a detergent box, and when Jerry moved his belongings from the table to the box, the policeman told him to hold out his hands.

"Ah," he said. "Ring also."

Jerry's only ring was his wedding ring, which he never removed. "My wife gave it to me," he said, but the young policeman shook the box, so he took the ring off, then reached back into the box and picked out his wallet once again, unstrapping the watch and placing his wedding ring down into the wallet's pocket, among the worthless coins.

"I want these things back," he said, but the young man left the room without speaking, closing the heavy door and locking it from the outside.

Once Jerry was alone fatigue hit him and he sat down hard. He was injured and filthy and no one knew where he was. And the reality of what had happened, that someone had actually gone to the trouble of setting him up, still seemed dreamlike and completely impossible. He was beaten and broken-toothed and waiting in the dismal back room of a police station. It was too much to believe and he wanted to get to a phone.

Jerry went to the door and spoke. "I want my phone call," he said, but the sound of his voice made him feel pitiful so he sat back down. Now was not the time to show fear. He concentrated on his belief that he would be home before nightfall, and that thought calmed him.

An hour passed and Jerry used it to assess the physical damage done to him and then to stretch out on the table and try to nap. The table wasn't long enough to hold him, but with his knees up he could just catch his heels on the edge of it. He was surprised to find that whatever he had spit from his mouth had apparently not been a piece of tooth, and when he pressed his palms against the places on his body that ached he thought he was discovering that there was no serious damage done, nothing broken anyway, and probably no blood seeping quietly into him and sapping his strength.

Though Jerry did not actually sleep, he was able to breath evenly and keep his eyes closed, and by the time he heard the key in the door he had regained some of the buoyancy of his spirit, his naturally optimistic mood.

When the door opened the captain of police came into

the room. He was carrying a clipboard, and Jerry thought of
Nurudeen again.

"Mr. Jerry Neal?" asked the captain of police.

"Yes," Jerry said.

"It is my duty to inform you that you are being held pend-
ing charges by the Republic of Nigeria for the crime of arson
in the first degree." The captain paused, watching for the
power of his words to register on Jerry's face, but Jerry had
prepared himself, and all he did was nod.

"Have you anything to say? I have always found that a
confession makes things easier. After that the days go by."

"I am not guilty," Jerry said. "Surely you know that."

The captain looked at his clipboard, then began searching
his pockets for a pen.

"I had a biro when I came in here," he said. He looked at
the floor. "I never start interrogation without my biro."

The word *interrogation* didn't do much to help Jerry's calm,
but the captain hadn't noticed. He was down on the floor
now, looking behind the table legs and making Jerry move
his feet. When he stood back up he checked his pockets
again and then felt behind his ear. "Be right back," he said.

When the captain left, Jerry thought he would close and
lock the door again, but this time he left it ajar. Jerry could
hear his footsteps leaving. What the hell, he thought; does
he want me to try to escape? He knew of cases where foreigners had been left to rot in Nigerian jails for weeks, even
months at a time, so was this captain telling him that he'd
better take his chance now, that he'd better leave while the
leaving was good? Jerry walked over to the door and looked
out. There were several similar doors along the corridor, but
all of them were closed and silent. Across from him, along
the opposite wall, the hallway was composed entirely of windows, with a view out to a parking lot two stories below.
Jerry had no memory of climbing stairs when they'd come in
so perhaps the building was constructed on a hill, the other
side butted up against a street. Beyond the parking lot there
was nothing he recognized. He saw the low houses of a res-

idential area and he could see children playing in the dirt, but he didn't know where he was.

Though the captain took his time, Jerry didn't step outside the room. And when he heard the footsteps again he did not go back to the table. Rather he remained where he was, leaning against the jamb, watching the captain come.

"Now," said the captain. "Have you had time to reconsider? I believe you saw our evidence at the Federal Secretariat."

"I saw it," said Jerry Neal. "Why would anyone go to such trouble to involve me? I don't have enemies here; I am not political."

The captain took the cap off his pen and started writing. Jerry saw the paper in the clipboard, but he could not read what the man wrote.

"I want to know what you intend to do," said Jerry, "and I want access to a phone." He spoke quietly and the man continued writing, as if he were taking down requests.

Finally, after Jerry had been quiet for a while, the captain looked up. "This is not America," he said. "If you confess you may use the phone; if not you will be placed in a holding cell."

Jerry believed that if he were really being charged with such a huge crime there would be more people asking him questions now, an attempt to publicly announce the name of the villain, just as there had been with previous fires. Surely there would be men of higher rank. "I didn't do it," he said.

The captain capped his pen and stepped back toward the door. "Very well," he said. "Please, come this way."

Jerry wasn't handcuffed or restrained in any other way, but the captain went first. Then about halfway up the hall he thought better of it and pressed himself against the windows, letting Jerry pass him by.

When they got to the door at the end of the hall the captain reached around and opened it, giving Jerry a gratuitous shove, making him stumble, barefooted, into the next room. Here were the dozens of people he had expected, but they were not high-ranking officers. Rather the room contained prisoners, perhaps thirty of them, all jammed into three small cells.

"These are our holding facilities," said the captain, opening one of the doors. "Since you are not guilty I know you will want to be with others who are not guilty, too." He didn't shove Jerry this time, so Jerry held back. "What about my call?" he asked. "What about some kind of bail?"

But the captain made Jerry step far enough into the cell so that he could close the door. And then everything remained quiet until he went back out of the room again.

These cells were freestanding, unattached, like cages. Jerry had been placed in the smallest one, but one that contained seven or eight others, all of whom looked at him as if his presence among them were some kind of trick.

Jerry turned around and put his hands up on the bars, but with his back to the other men he began to feel a little cold. This wasn't funny. So far as he knew everyone at the school still thought he was at the ministry, negotiating proper visas for the teachers. He turned back around quickly, startling some of his cell mates. This room was darker than the one he'd been in earlier, but now that his eyes were adjusting he could see that the floor ran wet with urine and that in one corner there were even piles of feces, like ant hills. He turned around to face the bars, then back to face the men, then back to face the bars. He had no idea what to do.

By the time he had been in the holding cell for about five minutes his cell mates began to move. Jerry slid down the bars into a sitting position but as soon as he was seated a hand came to him, touching the edge of his leg.

"Oga," said the man connected to the hand. "What you bring us dis day?"

Jerry jerked away, frightened, but trying desperately not to show it. He pulled the pockets of his pants out and let them hang, like deflated balloons. "Nothing," he said. "I have nothing to give."

As time went by he understood that each man in the small cell was trying to claim as much space as he could, though nearly all the space had been soiled. There was no camaraderie among these men, and little conversation. An hour passed but Jerry seemed unable to concentrate or think about anything but staying where he was. When six o'clock came the outside door opened and several policemen came in carrying water. Jerry was thirsty, but when a bucket was placed in the center of his cell he stayed away from it, not claiming any of it as his own. He was hungry too but no food came and when the sun went down and the cell grew dark he pulled his legs up under his chin, holding them tight and forcing himself to be still. After more time passed he put his hands against the bars and pushed his crumpled legs out and tried to lie flat, hoping he knew where the dry places were, his feet stretching among the others until they moved, giving him room. He put his hands behind his head and stared up into the darkness.

Jerry Neal had been in World War II. As an eighteen-year-old he had been on Guam, sleeping with his buddies in the tall grass, terribly worried about the Japanese. There really had been snipers then and he had heard gunfire, so he listened to see what he could hear now. There were thirty men in these three cells and he could hear them breathing and alive. He was too exhausted to worry anymore or to think about what tomorrow might bring and in a while he felt as though he were floating, and he would have slept, as deeply, at least, as he had in the deep grass on Guam, but he was awakened by the sound of movement near him and then by the feeling of that hand again, pushed out and touching him from another world.

"Oga, do not fret," said the hand. "I myself sleep small and will stay nearby. I can warn you should trouble be coming your way."

But however long the night, Lawrence Biko, the school's attorney, was in court the next morning at ten, and by dinnertime Jerry Neal was out of jail and on his way back home. He had been charged with arson in the first degree, but he was free on his own recognizance, a move that got the presiding judge criticized in the press and on the evening television news. Never before had a foreigner been charged with such a public and politically important crime, and to let him back out onto the streets seemed absurd, neocolonialist at best, and at worst a clear violation of the law.

Lawrence Biko did not speak to Jerry at the police station, but once in the parking lot, he smiled. "Well, well," he said. "We have much to discuss. The court has ordered me to tell you that you cannot leave Lagos state without permission, do you understand?"

Lawrence was a big man. He had always reminded Jerry of a well-dressed and better-educated version of his administrative assistant, Sunday Aremu. He wasn't approachable like Sunday, but he was as expansive and humorous. Jerry occasionally had the feeling that Lawrence had too many irons in the fire, but he had always done a masterful job for the school. He had been the school's attorney since long before Jerry's time, and Jerry had never found cause to complain. He was not at all sure, however, that he wanted this man as his personal representative. Criminal law, so far as Jerry knew, wasn't Lawrence's cup of tea. Besides, if Jerry had any say in the matter, he wanted an American.

Lawrence edged his car into traffic. Now that he was out-side, it was possible for Jerry to tell what part of the city the police station was in. It was in a part he didn't know well, a part where expatriates rarely came, but once the car was on the Marina, heading home, he looked at his solicitor and sighed. "Tell me what you think is really going on," he said.

Lawrence Biko laughed. "Ah, Jerry, it is easy, don't you know? You are not important here. This is not about you at all. You were a mere convenience, a window of opportunity. The school's small visa problem gave them their chance, don't you know; it is nothing more than that."

"Their chance for what?"

"To blame someone, of course, to find a dupe."

Since Jerry didn't speak again, Lawrence continued. "Well, think about it, man. The government is cracking down on corruption, isn't that right? Auditors are going to all the ministries. The Ministry of Internal Affairs will surely have its audit soon. Put it together and what do you get?"

"So they burned the place down and blamed me?"

Lawrence laughed again and raised his hands off the steer-ing wheel. "The fire started in the filing cabinets, with the school's toner fluid poured all over the place. It's a joke, but a typically Nigerian one. Clumsy perhaps, but effective in the end."

"Then who really started the fire?" Jerry wanted to know. "Surely not the minister? And who is Nurudeen's father? He told me he was the minister's brother."

"The minister, one of the vice-ministers, who knows?" Lawrence shrugged. "Whoever was skimming the money set the fire. You should know by now that if you're looking for corruption it isn't hard to find. And Nurudeen's father and the minister are from the same part of the country. That's what we call brotherhood in Africa, don't you know?"

"So they recognized our visa problem as a motive and framed us? Nurudeen's father came to get me so that I'd be on hand?"

"Maybe so," Lawrence Biko said.

This was a lot to take in. The toner had been disappearing from the school for a month. And what a strange thing to use. Jerry wasn't even sure that it was flammable. He thought of Nurudeen and wondered if the boy had any idea to what use his handiwork had been put.

"You don't suppose it goes as far back as San Francisco, do you?" Jerry asked. "The consul general, all that talk about the laws having been changed."

"Well, well," said Lawrence. "I hadn't thought of that one. Won't it be fun unraveling all this!"

When they arrived at the school it was dark, but though Jerry was desperate for a shower and for his bed he wanted to get the board president on the phone, wanted, if possible, to see the man that night. As they passed through the gate he took Lawrence Biko's hand and shook it. "Whatever happens, I am sure the worst is over," he said.

But Lawrence lost the lightness of his look when Jerry said that. "Oh no, my friend, the worst is yet to come. I'm afraid I can guarantee you that one."

Was he joking? Jerry wondered. What could be worse than the last day and a half had been? "I mean for me personally," Jerry said. "I never want to go through yesterday again."

"But you surely have not forgotten the secretary, have you?" Lawrence whispered. "If she dies you will be charged with murder, which is another kettle of fish."

Though he had seen her damaged body, Jerry indeed *had* forgotten the secretary. He hadn't thought of her once since his arrest. "How is she?" he feebly asked.

Lawrence put a calming hand on Jerry's arm. "No change," he said, "no one knows what her chances might be."

Until that moment Jerry had not allowed the prospect of going back to jail to enter his mind. He could handle the pressure of this situation, but he did not want to think any-more about that cell.

"Really, Lawrence, don't say such things," he said, and for some reason that brought the robust Lawrence back. "Ah,

but never mind!" said the lawyer. "Chin up! We don't cross
our bridges until we come to them, don't you know?"

When Jerry got out of the car some of the teachers were
waiting, ready to welcome him home. He smiled at them and
was about to close the car door when another question occurred to him. He leaned in and asked Lawrence, "How did
you know where I was? How did you find me and get me out
so quickly?"

"Ah," said Lawrence, "did I not say? I was awakened yesterday evening quite late. Indeed, it must have been past
midnight when I got a phone call from a lady representing
Nurudeen's dad."

After Lawrence Biko drove away Jerry spoke to the teachers for a while, but though they had prepared food for him, he was too tired to eat and asked to be excused. He was surprised at the degree to which the experience had shaken him, and he wanted to be alone.

Inside his flat he was pleased to find that Jules was gone, with only a note reminding him to leave money for shopping before he left for work in the morning. Jerry ran water for his shower and while he undressed he tried to get the school board president on the phone. But just as he heard the man's voice he put the receiver down. What if the president took him to task for letting such a thing take place, or worse, what if the phone was bugged? Such an idea would not have occurred to him before, but if what Lawrence said was true, perhaps he'd better not take chances of any kind.

When he got into the shower he shut his eyes and let the water wash away the dirt of the prison floor, the stink of the urine and the memory of all those men. At the spot where that unattached hand had touched him he washed himself especially hard, and only when the water began to turn cold did he get out and wrap himself in a towel. He then found a pair of starched pajamas in his bottom drawer. The pajamas were lovely to step into, the legs opening crisply as he put them on.

Jerry walked through his flat, turning off lights and bolting the door. He then got Charlotte's photograph from his desk,

brought it to the bed and crawled in, holding it for a while
before placing it on the table by his side.

When he turned off his lamp the quality of the light in
the room changed, and he pulled his legs back quickly on the
chance that another prisoner's foot might be lingering at the
bottom of his bed. God, what a plot these strangers had
hatched. Not since he was a child had he felt so vulnerable,
and it made him consider what life would be like without orderly laws. How could men live under the old sets of rules,
survival of the fittest, an eye for an eye? Not since he was a
child had he thought of himself in terms of whether or not
he was physically brave. Not since he was a child had such
thoughts had any place in his life.

As he lay there, exhausted but completely awake, Jerry
imagined himself relating the experiences of the last day and
a half. When he told this story would he embellish, would
he, perhaps, make it humorous, or would he recount accu-
rately the depth and the surprising quality of his fear? Jerry
Neal turned in his bed and decided that this was a story that
he would not tell. And as sleep came down to take him he
understood that not since Charlotte's death had an event
outside himself made him feel so exposed and alone. He was
not an introspective man but he did feel uneasy with the
idea that should he choose to mine the depths of his heart
he was not sure what he would find there, or whether he
would like what he found at all.

Though Jerry had set his alarm for six, a group of teachers found Jules and told him to turn the alarm off, to let the man sleep until he woke. Jules took pleasure in stealing into the darkened bedroom and pushing the alarm's button down. The slack flesh of his employer's face drew him, and for a moment he looked at Jerry Neal and felt sorry. He could see the old man who would come in the next few years, the dormant evidence that death waited for us all.

Jerry's bedroom had thick curtains, and when he finally awoke he assumed that, as sometimes happened, he would have another moment or two before his alarm sounded. On these occasions he thought of the extra time as a gift from Charlotte, and he used it to remember a pleasant moment that they had shared or merely to picture Charlotte in some contemplative or restful mood. It was Jerry's practice, during these times, to try to remember an aspect of Charlotte as yet unremembered since its occurrence during her lifetime, and on this morning he remembered Charlotte's outrage with the city of Tillamook over the upkeep of a memorial for those who died in the famous Tillamook fire. Charlotte's grandfather had died in the fire and she was furious that the memorial was unkempt. Jerry envied Charlotte's capacity for outrage and wished he'd found more in himself at yesterday's fire.

Long moments passed and when Jerry heard a pounding on his outside door and looked at his clock, he discovered that it was nearly ten. He jumped from his bed and stormed into

the living room, ready to scream at Jules, but the board president was there, and Jules was giving him coffee.

"Jerry," said Leonard Holtz, "do you need to see a doctor?
God, what an experience that must have been."

"I overslept," the principal said.

Leonard Holtz threw his briefcase onto a chair. "I've spoken with Biko and I've informed the ambassador. This kind
of thing is uncalled for, man. Let them frame another Niger-
rian if they're going to frame somebody."

"I would have called you last night," said Jerry, "but I
didn't trust the phones."

Leonard said that he'd scheduled a special school board
meeting for ten. "Whatever happens," he said, "I know this
time we will be united."

Jules brought out orange juice and crepes and put two
warmed plates on the dining-room table. Jerry wondered if
his steward knew the details of what had happened, but
when he looked at Jules he couldn't tell, and when Jules was
gone again Leonard Holtz lowered his voice. "When the ambassador first heard about this he told me to get you out of
the country today," he said. "He's changed his tune about
that but he's calling the president's office this morning.
When this ambassador gets worked up there's always hell to
pay."

Jerry guessed he should be grateful for the official American support, but all that had really happened was that he'd
been pushed around a little and spent a night in jail. It had
not, after all, been so much, and he was embarrassed by his
imbalance, by the unreasonable fear he had felt.

"It wasn't really that bad," he told Leonard. "Once everything's straightened out I'll have another good story to tell."

The school board president smiled and stood up. "Good,"
he said. "I'm glad to hear your spirits are up. Let's get on
over to the school and meet the others."

But Jerry excused himself, saying he'd be right along, and
when Leonard left he dressed and then went into the
kitchen to pick up his lunch. When he looked inside his sack

he could see his thermos, but his sandwich was wrapped in waxed paper, across the top of which Jules had written his name. When Jerry saw it he experienced a little dip in his mood and reached down to tear the name away, leaving a portion of the sandwich exposed. It was a silly thing to have done, perhaps, but it made him feel better. Now whatever happened there would be no evidence that this sandwich, or anything else in the sack, was his.

As Jerry hurried over to the school the chief custodian found him and reported that he'd just spent his third consecutive night sleeping inside the copy machine. "It is strange," he said. "Like some man know I am there."

"It's over, Joseph," Jerry said. "I'm sorry you weren't told, but I know who took the toner."

"Yessir," Joseph said, "the culprit is who?"

Jerry found Nurudeen's name on the tip of his tongue, but he held it there, deciding that it might be better to retain some secrecy for a while.

"It was not one of your men, Joseph," he said.

"Yessir, not one of my men."

Jerry could see that Joseph wanted to be told, but he suddenly needed to know immediately whether or not Nurudeen was in school, so he left Joseph standing there, saying he'd tell him everything later on. It was good luck that he hadn't expelled the boy. With Nurudeen around, perhaps the key to the truth was at hand.

Inside the main office the school secretary said she was sorry and then handed him a stack of pink message slips, as well as copies of the morning newspapers. The story of his ordeal was everywhere, but there were no photographs. Somehow, during all the time he'd been held, no one had taken his picture, and that suddenly seemed very strange to him, giving him, however briefly, the idea that maybe someone was working on his behalf on the inside.

Leonard Holtz came in and took his arm. "Everyone's waiting," he said. "Some of them can only stay a minute."

Jerry was rested and his head was clear but he wanted to use his time finding Nurudeen, reading the stories in the newspapers, and deciding what he should do. A school board had its place, but at the moment it was far less important to him than it wanted to be. Still, Holtz was pulling on him so he tucked the papers under his arm and followed Leonard down the hall, glancing first at the messages that he held. The top one said, "Pamela called." His secretary had written the additional word "twice" on the memo, but there was no phone number, and no other clue as to what her business might have been.

The school board meeting was short and its tone was supportive. Jerry was told that the school's attorney could be used and that school time could be spent getting to the bottom of it all, but when the meeting ended and he went into his office again, his mood had darkened, and his anger rose, focusing, oddly enough, on the people around him, on the board members and on his steward, on the worthless phone messages that his secretary took. And as he sat there he realized that somewhere along the line he had lost the teacher files. Now what would he do about the damned visas?

There was a knock on his door but Jerry didn't move, and in a moment another message appeared on his floor. "Nurudeen is ill today." He had asked his secretary to check on the boy, hoping that if Nurudeen were in school he could perhaps push him up against the wall and scare the truth out of him.

Jerry read each of the newspaper articles carefully, but they didn't say much. Each one gave his name, relating the fact that he had been arrested and then released. The papers assumed his guilt and had reserved much of their wrath for the judge who had let him go. "If a Nigerian had committed such a crime what would 'his own recognizance' mean?" one of the papers asked, and in another, though there was no photograph of Jerry, there was one of the judge who had freed him and a caption which read "Justice thinks American too slow to run."

Jerry pushed himself away from his desk and smiled into the empty room. He picked up his phone and dialed Lawrence Biko's number and was told that Lawrence was gone. Good, maybe that meant he was on his way to school. Jerry stood and went out into the hall. The best thing now would be to attend to business. There was a school to run and the best thing that he could do was to run it.

In the outer office Jerry told his secretary that if Lawrence came he could be found in the English room where he would be observing class. The school's English teacher was a favorite of his, a woman named Hortense Blyth whom he'd recruited the year before. He loved the woman's name, and since literature had been his own subject, when he'd taught so many years before, he really did enjoy it when he and Mrs. Blyth were occasionally seated together at dinner parties.

As soon as he entered the room, however, Jerry realized that the class being taught was the one that would have contained Nurudeen had Nurudeen been in school. The class quieted, and he feared for a moment that Mrs. Blyth might actually speak to him. But she only smiled, and then continued her lesson, knowing quickly that he was there in an attempt to structure his time.

Jerry felt the tension leave him as he listened to the class. Perhaps he should have remained a teacher when he'd had the chance, all those years ago. He remembered a discussion he and Charlotte had had on the eve of his first administrative job, a sudden appointment that took him from his classroom in the middle of the term. He and Charlotte had talked about what it would mean to lose contact with the students he loved, but his administrative star had risen, and in the end he hadn't missed teaching very much. Now, though, he saw the wonder of the classroom freshly and the thought struck him that, in the end, he might go back. Some administrators did that, he was sure that they did. Some went back and taught again.

He had not been aware of the time and was surprised when the period ended only a few minutes after he entered the room. He would have stayed for another one, but as the students filed out his secretary appeared at the door and waved until he looked at her.

"Someone is here now," she said, so Jerry went back to the office slowly, to the rhythm of the passing students and the sudden belief that someday he would teach again.

But when he entered the office it wasn't Lawrence Biko who was there. Instead an attractive woman sat in the reception area, and Jerry thought he knew immediately that this was Nurudeen's stepmother. She was a poised and calm-looking woman, and Jerry was suddenly certain that she was fed up with the turncoat nature of Nurudeen's dad. She would tell him now what was really going on.

"Pamela," said his secretary, reading from a slip of paper in her hand.

"Good morning," the principal said.

The woman was young, perhaps not yet thirty-five, and she was quite tall. She had an open and beautiful face and eyes that seemed to scan Jerry quickly, ignoring his principal's facade and looking directly at the man underneath. She was delightful. "Good of you to see me," she said.

Jerry opened the door to the inner office and waited while the woman walked through. She moved like an American and he quickly thought of the comatose minister's secretary again. Once inside the room he turned and shook the woman's hand. "How do you do?" he said.

He felt foolish, a little nervous to have such a beautiful woman so close, but he nevertheless sat down on the same side of his desk as she did. It then occurred to him that perhaps he'd picked up a virus in that cell; he was flushed and suddenly so nervous he thought he might be ill.

"Would you like some coffee?" he asked. "Perhaps a cup of tea?"

"No," the woman said. "I have only come to pay my respects. I promised I would do so, so here I am."

Jerry didn't understand but he pressed forward, asking, "How is your family? I trust everyone is well." Now, if she chose to, she could tell him the truth. Though she had said barely a word Jerry was hopeful that he'd found someone he could trust. Perhaps this woman would be his friend, someone familiar with the enemy camp.

But the woman seemed surprised and said only, "Actually they are in the east and I have not yet had time to look in on them."

Good, thought Jerry. Nurudeen was not in school because he was in the east. Already this conversation was proving to be beneficial.

"I am very glad that you have come," he said. "Now, at least, we will be able to clear up some of the confusion."

The woman smiled. "I am very happy to be here," she said, "but I am beginning to think we are talking at cross-purposes. I am Pamela ... ? I left a message before. I was under the impression that you were expecting me."

Jerry tried to remember Nurudeen's family name. He wanted to address the woman formally, to tell her that he admired her courage, he wanted to take her hand. "You aren't Nurudeen's stepmother, are you?" he asked.

"Goodness, no," said Pamela. "I am Marge's friend, the chiropractor. Didn't she write you that I would come?"

Jerry was stunned and then he actually did, for an instant, touch the woman's hand. He remembered Marge's letter and reached into his pocket, fishing around until he found one of her spinal-column name cards.

"Yes, yes," he said, "forgive me. I've been under such strain. I'm afraid I've been acting like a fool."

But Pamela put her hand up. "I know," she said, "I've been reading the papers. I didn't want to bother you, but I did want to fulfill my promise to Marge."

Jerry had no clear idea why, but he felt downright light-hearted, glad to have Nurudeen out of the picture, happy to have someone new around. He smiled and smiled. "It's good

to meet you," he said. "How is Marge? Please, tell me everything that's new."

But Pamela didn't want to talk about Marge. She saw that
Jerry was on the verge of some kind of breakdown and she
gave him a careful look. "You really are a wreck," she said.
"And what an awful situation."

Jerry was hunched up in his chair, looking at her out of a
crooked head. "It's a terrible situation," he said. "I still have
no idea what I will do."

Pamela nodded and then stood up and began clearing the
papers and other items from the broad expanse of Jerry's
desk. "This is not proper," she said, "but it will have to do."
She then slipped out of her shoes and ordered him up onto
his desk, telling him to lie down along the desk's near edge.
The expression on her face was one of serious calm; it was a
professional face, but Jerry was incredulous.

"Not really," he said, but without answering him Pamela
went over and turned the lock on the door.

Jerry Neal was a dignified man, the principal of the school,
and if anyone had suggested that he would allow a strange
woman to lock his door and order him up on top of his desk,
he'd have been shocked. It was during school hours. "On my
stomach or on my back?" he wanted to know.

Pamela said that for the moment she wanted him on his
side, and as close to the desk's edge as he could get. She then
pulled his top leg, the left one, out toward her, making it
bend at the knee. "Relax now," she said. She touched his
back and when the muscles there began to loosen she actually fell on top of him, pushing his entire torso toward his
chair, away from the natural bend of his upper knee. Jerry
heard a line of bones crack, like the tumblers in the school
safe. "Hey," he said.

Pamela had him roll over to the desk's other side, and
when he was situated properly again she repeated the proce-
dure. After that she popped his neck, cradling his head
against her bosom, the softness there nearly making him

swoon. Then she pulled on all his fingers and toes. "Easy," she kept saying. "This won't do you any harm."

And Jerry did feel easy. He paid attention to what she was doing, and it felt good and he told himself such a thing was not at all untoward in a widowed man's life.

"That's enough for now," Pamela said.

Jerry looked up at her. It wasn't enough, he wanted to say, how could anyone think that it was? But when she said, "Well, stand up, walk around," he propped himself onto one elbow and tried to give her a smile.

Pamela helped him off the desk and watched him as he walked toward the door. He felt marvelous—better anyway than he had before—and when he said so Pamela laughed. "You see," she said. "Marge was right and you were wrong." And then she said, "You really should be seeing someone regularly. At least until these trying times are over."

"Yes," said Jerry, "I will. What about lunch?"

It was a ridiculous thing to admit, but Jerry had not been smitten since the day he'd met Charlotte, thirty-five years before. Pamela, however, was businesslike. "I don't eat lunch," she said, "and I really do need to get on with my day." There was a knock on the door that prevented him from saying more, and when he opened it his secretary was there with news that Lawrence Biko would be out of town through the weekend.

When the secretary left again, Pamela slipped back into her shoes. "It's been lovely," she said. "Would you like me to call again?"

"Of course," Jerry said. "I mean, yes, I would."

They shook hands, and Jerry said that he hoped she'd be back soon.

"I am quite busy," said Pamela. "But yes, sometime soon. We can catch up on everything that's happened. I mean, of course, everything that's happened to Marge."

Pamela left quickly then, and soon after that Jerry did too. He went home and took another shower and sat alone at the end of his dining table and slowly ate the food that Jules had prepared, washing it all down with wine. Now he was back on track. It had taken time, but he was over the fear he'd felt and ready to face whatever he had to face, ready to clear his name and to get on with the running of his school.

When he finished his meal Jerry took the wine bottle over to his reading chair and went to the bedroom for his dictionary and his copy of *Madame Bovary*, in the original French. Reading this book was a project he'd started in Abidjan but had discontinued nearly a year before. Perhaps meeting Pamela had brought it back to mind, perhaps it had been the English class.

Nothing could have been further from the truth of his own life than the sexual longings of a nineteenth-century French woman, but to read about her made Jerry realize that he might be capable of leading a different sort of life someday. He could decide, for example, to teach again, or he could decide to be less private. He could even decide that his loyalty to Charlotte could continue should he discontinue his marathon homage to celibacy and living alone.

Jerry Neal marveled at himself. He had learned a great lesson from the experiences of the last days and he decided that it had pretty much all been for the good. Unlike Madame Bovary, for him the world was wide. As he read he realized that he was not tied to anything from which deceit was the only escape. That, in fact, was what made him free. Jerry poured himself another glass of wine and felt a sense of wellbeing and warmth. Christmas vacation was coming and if he was no longer under house arrest by then he would use the time to travel and think. Or perhaps he would stay in Lagos after all, where he could pay close attention to the school, where he could solve the visa problems and look after the continued well-being of his spine.

Two

On Saturday morning at eight o'clock the police came knocking on Jerry Neal's door. Jerry had read until nearly two, struggling through the language of Madame Bovary's life, so though the knocking awakened him, he took his time getting dressed before going out to see who insisted on doing business so early in the day.

The same police captain who'd interrogated Jerry had pushed Jules back into the flat and was glaring at him. Jules had a frying pan in his hand, but when Jerry spoke, suggesting that Jules bring coffee, everything calmed down quickly.

Jerry felt refreshed and in charge, and though he did not take the policeman's visit as good news, he was determined not to be afraid. He waited until Jules had brought the coffee, and while the captain and his assistant took their own sugar and cream he spoke firmly. "Tell me why you are here," he said. "How can I help you today?"

"There has been a development," said the captain. He had lowered his voice too far. He did not like being in this man's flat, and he worked his fingers around the edges of his coffee cup before saying, "The minister's secretary has expired."

Jerry stared at the man, but then he made a small mistake. "I am so sorry," he said, and when the policeman looked at him sharply he added, "for the woman, I mean, for whatever family she has that remains."

60

"Then you are confessing?" asked the incredulous cop. "Right here in my presence?"

"Of course I'm not confessing," Jerry said. "You know I had nothing to do with that fire."

Jerry wished the authorities had seen fit to send news of the secretary's death through Lawrence Biko, and he asked why the captain thought it necessary to come himself. "It was kind of you," he said, "but you needn't have bothered."

"I am not a messenger," the offended captain said. "You were released on your own recognizance concerning the crime of arson, one count. Now that you may be charged again you must surrender yourself again. If the chief criminal investigator decides to go forward with this case you will remain in detention until your day in the dock."

The captain's face had grown sterner as he spoke, and when Jules came back to offer more coffee, he and his assistant both declined, putting their cups back onto Jules's tray. Jerry was looking away from the man, trying to think fast. They were telling him that he had to go with them now. They would put him back in that holding cell with those awful other men. The smell of urine came into his living room but before he could speak again the police captain held up a hand. "If you want to collect a change of clothing, that would be permissible," he said.

Jerry felt the urge to panic, but he held it at bay. "May I use the phone?" he asked. Then he added, "Surely this can wait until Monday, when my solicitor is free."

The policeman sighed. "If it could wait until Monday I would have come on Monday," he said, so without pausing further Jerry stood and went over to the phone. He quickly dialed Leonard Holtz's home.

"Come," said the policeman. "You can telephone from Ikoyi jail."

The phone had rung five or six times when the police captain took the receiver from Jerry's hand, hanging it up.

Jerry found a loose twenty-naira bill in his pocket and placed it next to the telephone. "One more call," he said.

He wanted to call the ambassador's house. Even if the ambassador wasn't in, the ambassador's wife was a friend. She would know what needed to be done. But Jerry could not remember the ambassador's home telephone number. He had it on the Rolodex in his office, but he'd called it many times before and should have been able to find it in his head. Finally he dialed the U.S. Embassy's main switchboard, letting the phone ring nine times before a marine guard picked it up. It was one of the guards he knew.

"Eric, this is Jerry Neal," he said. "You know, from the school."

"Oh, hi," said the marine.

"Listen, have you heard about the trouble I'm in? The arson charge and all that?"

"What a joke," said the guard. "When is this country going to get serious, that's what I . . ."

"Listen, Eric," said Jerry. "The police are here at my house now and they are taking me back to jail. Is the ambassador there? Is Mr. Holtz there or anyone with power?"

"No, sir," Eric said.

"Well, I won't be able to call anyone after this and I need to be able to rely on you. I want you to get in touch with the ambassador and with Holtz, with anyone you can. They are taking me to Ikoyi jail and . . ."

Though the twenty naira was gone from the table, the police captain had put his finger down on the button, disconnecting the call.

"These things are classified," he said.

Jerry had somehow regained a portion of his previous composure and instead of protesting, only nodded briefly. He then went into his bedroom to collect his things. He quickly scribbled a note to the teachers, leaving it on his bed for Jules to find. He emptied his wallet of its cash and took his hidden one-hundred-dollar bill out from behind Charlotte's photograph. He found a few one-naira notes on his bureau, so he stuffed those into his pocket toward whatever favors they could buy in jail. What else would he need? Now was the time for careful thought. He packed his razor and his toothpaste and brush. Finally he took Charlotte's photograph from its frame and slid it into his jacket pocket too, where it got hung up on his toothbrush and would not go all the way down.

When Jerry came back out he spoke to Jules in halting French, telling him to deliver the note and to tell everyone where he had gone. Then he told the police captain he was ready. He tried to keep an active mind, searching for something that would help, but all he could come up with was this: In a moment I will be in the police car and a moment after that I will be clear of the school compound and at the mercy of this man. Jerry wondered, absurdly, what Madame Bovary would do in a situation such as this, and when he did so he realized that his fate, too, from that moment on might not be subject to any action of his own.

When they left the flat the policeman made Jerry walk in front of him. Twenty naira for one phone call. He really did despise the rich. If the man had only asked contritely he would have let him make the call for free.

"When it be night no man can see me in de shadow of de bush or tree. No man can see me in de shadow of de house."

"When it be night no man can see anodder man in dem place, not only you. Properly it mus' be in de day no man can see you in dose very place. Properly in de night you mus' exis' wit' quietude, like only de night go by. In de day you mus' blen' in, become de man anodder man don' see, like de invisible man. Dat is how to get by during de day."

The man who had spoken last laughed and turned to Jerry. "Of course, we are all of us caught and put in here, Oga. When dat happen talk is cheap."

These two men were Jerry's only cell mates this time, though the nearby cells held as many as seven. Jerry's cell mates assured him that they were only three because he was Oyibo, a white man. They also said they were glad of it. Across the hall there was another non-Nigerian, an Indian merchant whose sad eyes sought Jerry's every time he looked that way, but this merchant, somehow, was in the most crowded cell of all. He spent his time huddled near the door, like Jerry had during his first, and much worse, incarceration.

This was Ikoyi jail, and several days had passed. But though Jerry had not spoken to Lawrence Biko or to anyone from the embassy, and though Christmas vacation would begin in less than two weeks' time, he had remained calm and was even beginning to consider himself lucky. Now there was a mattress for him to sleep on, and there was a pail in the room that was emptied each day. Also, this time they had selected his cell mates carefully. They were informants, perhaps, but he was nevertheless now confident that he would not be physically harmed. The Indian across from him, by contrast, seemed to be paying for protection. He was a pitiful man, and though Jerry had at first felt a foreigner's kinship with the man, he had recently begun to despise him, thankful that they were separated by the bars.

The Indian prisoner did, however, have one ritual that Jerry watched and longed for. At noon each day another man came into the cell block and brought this man his food, large supplies of curry with chapati and rice. The man ate all the food while the other man was there, chatting urgently with him through the bars. The two men spoke Sindhi, but though the man was presumably Muslim, he pushed thick hunks of things into his mouth and let it bulge there, flowing down his chin and falling onto the floor.

In Jerry's own cell, small plates of yams and eba were pushed through a wide section in the bars. On the Saturday of his arrival he wouldn't eat anything, but by Sunday evening he began to take a little of the food, and now he was eating whatever he could, though he did so slowly, examining each bite and tearing parts of the food away.

Of his two cell mates, the most articulate was Parker Akintola, a confidence man who had been jailed for selling tickets to a fictitious reggae concert presumably to be given by the Caribbean star Bob Marley. He would have gotten away with it but in May, 1981, Bob Marley died and Parker was caught. Since then, Parker said, he had been in and out of one jail or another, awaiting trial.

When a guard came into the cell block on the morning of Jerry's fifth day, he brought news that Lawrence Biko would arrive that afternoon. Jerry had maintained himself well over the days; he had not panicked and though he'd eaten the jail food he had not been ill. But now that word of Lawrence had come, he began to worry again. Why had it taken five days? It all seemed so absurd, such trumped-up charges and such a lot of time gone by.

Jerry spent that afternoon waiting at the cell door, but he was not called out until after the evening meal, and by then his mood had turned bad. He had just sat down on his mattress and was gazing at one of Parker's magazines, at a selection of African women's hairstyles, when keys began to rattle in the outer door and a guard came in. "Someone come to call," he said.

Jerry would be seeing Lawrence in a private room, and when he got up to go his other cell mate, a young thief, told him to take his personal things along. "You may see we two nevermore," he said, and Jerry took hope from that.

The guard walked ahead of him down the corridor, ushering him into an unbarred room at the end of the hall. It was not, however, Lawrence Biko who sat at the table waiting for him.

"Please," said a thin man in a good-looking suit, "have a seat."

"Who are you?" asked Jerry. "Where's Biko?"

"My name is Tunde Phelps-Neuman," the man said. "I came in the hope that we could clear things up. Far too much of your time has already been taken by these events."

"I was expecting my barrister," Jerry said. "I was told that it was he I would see."

"Alas," said Phelps-Neuman, "it is only me. But shall I inquire on your behalf? It's Lawrence, didn't you say? I'll give him a call."

"Lawrence Biko," Jerry said. "Will I be allowed to go home tonight?"

The man did not reply, but Jerry understood that it wasn't because he was considering the question. He had a pad before him, three sharp pencils stationed at its side.

"I apologize for the delay," the man said, "but let me explain that I have come for two reasons. First to bring news

that will cheer you, and second to get your statement, a sum-
mation of things as you understand them."

"What news?" Jerry asked. "It's been nearly a week and no
one has come for me. What's happened to the U.S. Embassy
in this matter? And what of Lawrence? What of the school
board, for crying out loud?"

Phelps-Neuman held his palms up in a gesture that said
though the questions were good ones, he didn't know the answers. He then said, "Let me be clear, Mr. Neal. I am the
senior police investigator assigned to this case, and I am here
to make a determination. It might be best, in fact, if you
considered me your adversary."

Jerry lowered his eyes and then closed them. This was all
a bad dream and he was stupid to have maintained his opti-
mism. Five good days had gone by! These things happened in
movies, perhaps, but all he'd wanted was proper visas for the
teachers in the goddamn school.

Jerry looked at the man quickly, asking, "Do you know
where my teachers' files are? They were taken from me on
the day of my first arrest. If I had them now I could show you
why I went to the ministry that day. And the minister's files,
too, should say that our teachers were in need of working
visas, nothing more than that."

"The ministry's records were burned, of course," Phelps-
Neuman said. "There is now nothing to show anything of
the kind. That's what makes you a suspect, don't you see? We
call it a motive."

"But they have tourist visas in their passports!" Jerry
shouted. "That means that without a change they'd have to
leave the country after ninety days!"

Jerry paused, trying to control his voice. "You mentioned
something about good news," he said. "What the hell could
that be?"

Phelps-Neuman waited a moment but then smiled. "I
want to tell you that we are considering a reduction in
charge, a move that will renew the possibility of bail." He
looked at Jerry carefully again. "If you will write your state-

ment I will recommend bail in the morning. And then Mr.
Lawrence Biko will have no trouble getting you out."

"My statement?" Jerry asked. "Do you mean you want me
to write down my movements of that day, that sort of thing?"

Phelps-Neuman pushed the legal pad across the table.
"Yes, certainly," he said. "And something about the copy-
machine fluid. If you weren't involved what's your theory
about how it got off the school grounds in the first place?
Write down anything that will help us clear it all up."

Jerry pulled the pad toward him and looked at it. "Who
are you really after?" he asked, but all Phelps-Neuman would
add was, "Why not spend your time at home?"

Jerry Neal had no idea what was going on, but whatever it
was he felt sure, once again, that the ultimate target could
not be him. Nevertheless he said, "I would like to write my
statement in the presence of my lawyer. You know, an advocate, someone who's on my side."

Phelps-Neuman pushed himself out of his chair then, but
reached back down to touch the legal pad. "At any rate
think about it," he said. "I will come back again tomorrow."

After that Phelps-Neuman left the room, but though Jerry
was sure he'd stop at the door, when the door did open again
it was not Phelps-Neuman but the guard, telling Jerry to
come along back to his cell. Phelps-Neuman was nowhere in
sight, nor was there any other sound.

As they were walking past the row of offices, however,
Jerry saw an open door. Inside the room there was a desk
with a phone sitting on it. This door had not been opened
earlier and he looked at the guard. "Wait," he said. "That
man told me I could make a call. He said I could use this
phone."

The guard looked at him but didn't speak, so Jerry went
into the room and picked up the receiver, sure that if he
showed any hesitancy he would be stopped. He looked at the
dial, wondering whether or not he had an outside line. The
dial tone seemed normal so he called Lawrence Biko's office,

hoping, though the hour was late, that he might be in. Lawrence answered at the first ring. "Biko," he said.

"Lawrence, this is Jerry Neal. Do you know what's going on? Do you even know where they're keeping me?"

"Not too clearly," his advocate said.

"I am in Ikoyi jail. I have just been interrogated by someone named Phelps-Neuman. Do you know him?"

"As a matter of fact, yes," said Lawrence. "He is very high up, very tough. How did you get to a phone?"

"Never mind that," said Jerry. "Tell me what I need to know."

"I have been waiting for word that I could see you. Even the American ambassador has not been able to discover as much as what you told me just now. It is all very unusual, Jerry. I have never had trouble seeing a client before."

Jerry looked at the guard. "I'm not alone," he said, "so listen carefully. I want you to get to Nurudeen. He's the boy who took the toner. Get him and hold him. Make him tell you the truth about what's going on."

Lawrence laughed. "That's kidnapping," he said. "And of course I have already spoken with the boy, and with his mother too. I already know what's going on. The difficulty now is getting you out. Once you are free we'll put our plan into action. But, of course, we can't discuss that on the telephone."

Jerry had felt cool when telling Lawrence Biko to grab Nurudeen. Now though, with his attorney dismissing the idea out of hand, he began to lose his resolve.

"I can't stay here much longer, Lawrence," he said.

"But didn't they tell you? You are set for arraignment next week. That much I've been able to settle without seeing you. And you are a newspaper headliner now. It's really quite astounding. Because of all the publicity your trial will be quick, no adjournments, I'm quite sure of that much at least."

When Jerry looked at the guard again the man pointed to his wrist, where, on a richer man, there would have been a watch.

"Phelps-Neuman said they might reduce the charge in exchange for a statement. He said he could arrange bail."

This time it was Lawrence who answered quickly. "That might be a trick," he said. "Did you write anything down?"

"No, but he left me the paper."

"Don't use it. Bail before arraignment is impossible."

The guard had walked down the corridor but was back.

"I can't talk anymore," Jerry said, "but surely I have the right to see you before I'm arraigned. Don't I have that right?"

"You have it under the law," Lawrence said.

Jerry had pushed the use of the telephone too far but there was one more question he had to ask. "You said you spoke with Nurudeen and his stepmother. Tell me, what was the woman's name?"

Lawrence laughed again. "Well, yes," he said, "let's see. I believe she told me her given name was Pamela."

Over the remaining days before his arraignment, Jerry learned the name of his other cell mate and came to the decision that it was just possible that two Pamelas had entered his life at the same time. The other man was Louis Smith-Jones, whose high-sounding name did little to improve his impoverished face.

And however adversarial Tunde Phelps-Neuman had been or intended to be, he did one thing for which Jerry would forever be thankful. He arranged for Jerry's food to be brought in by Jules, every morning, from the outside.

Jules's first visit was on Saturday, and though Jules was by nature a taciturn man, something in the current situation brought him out. He smiled when he entered the cell block, greeting Jerry with a spirited description of what his bundle contained. "I have strawberry crepes with sugar-o, home-made bread, and coffee fresh-ground!"

Jules stayed, each time, only long enough for Jerry to receive his food, but the visits ordered Jerry's day. And the food, very quickly, meant everything. Jerry loved the wonderful variety of it, adored the sanitary way it was prepared. And after that first day he asked that enough be brought for all three of them. He had learned that lesson from the Indian man across the hall.

Of his cell mates, Louis Smith-Jones liked to sample bits of Jerry's food but Parker Akintola was as transformed by it as was Jerry. They still had their jail meals, of course, but all of them now looked forward to Jules. They took his arrival as a celebration and it allowed them to become chums.

"We go release someday, have reunion chop same," Louis said one morning when Jules brought in meatloaf for them to try. He picked up a slice of meatloaf and smelled it.

"Dis be pork?" he asked.

"No, only mince," Jerry said. "And onions and raisins and bread."

"I go smell pork," Louis said, so Parker took the meatloaf from him and ate it, running his tongue around his mouth.

"Oh, you are right, Louis," he said. "Is pork, no question. I be careful for you every time from now on."

Despite the anger that stayed with him, this kind of banter made the time go by. Louis Smith-Jones was a sweet-natured young man, and Parker kept proclaiming his own innocence by saying that for an ordinary Nigerian just holding a Bob Marley concert ticket was such a satisfying thing that actually going to the concert was beside the point. He had given everyone pleasure and was only in jail because the authorities had failed to understand.

Jerry didn't see Tunde Phelps-Neuman again until the morning of his arraignment on Tuesday of that second week, December 13, three days before Christmas vacation was to begin. On that morning Jules arrived early, carrying food but also bringing a clean suit of clothes. The guards let Jerry wash himself privately and change in one of the interrogation rooms. He shaved and dressed, and when Phelps-Neuman came in Jerry could immediately see that he was surprised.

"Your arraignment is before Justice Felix Ogunde," Phelps-Neuman said. "The charge will be arson plus murder, but the state will not oppose bail. We will then recommend deportation within forty-eight hours of the plea."

He had spoken as if he were reciting something memorized, but Jerry got stuck on the word "deportation." It hadn't occurred to him that they would make him leave the country, but why should it have? Why would any prosecutor settle for deportation when the charges were so serious? This was arson and murder and none of what was going on made any sense. "Aren't you interested in finding the ones who really set the fire?" Jerry asked. Phelps-Neuman, however, only stared at him, then turned and went back out of the room.

Jerry didn't know what to think or do. He had expected Lawrence, and he was irritated with the way Phelps-Neuman had treated him, irritated with himself for not knowing more. He knew he had to start doing better, to make some kind of plan, but in the end all he did was wait in the room until nine o'clock, when three guards came in, placing him in actual shackles and escorting him down the hall.

Jerry's big surprise was that Justice Felix Ogunde was a man he had met before. Though the judge was wearing robes and a white wig, Jerry was sure that he had spoken with him, at a party, perhaps, or even on the school grounds.

The judge had Jerry stand in the dock and wrote in his ledger while Lawrence presented himself for the defense and an oddly thin woman introduced herself as representing the prosecution. The courtroom was a shabby, poorly painted affair, and though it was not large, the loudness of the air conditioners made hearing difficult, and since Justice Ogunde did not seem inclined to shout he had to repeat himself many times.

"Madame for the prosecution, what case do you have? What strength is there in it? Tell me truly now."

"We have a strong case, sir," said the thin woman. "We have evidence and we have cause."

"Mr. Biko," said the judge, "your client is free of a criminal record, is he not? I mean in his own country as well as in Nigeria."

"Yes," said Lawrence, "as he will be throughout his life."

Jerry thought he saw the judge frown, but he merely looked back at the prosecutor and asked, "Is it the prosecutor's intention to carry this thing to trial?"

"It is," said the woman. "I am sure the court is aware that there was loss of life. The penalties here are statutory."

The judge looked back at Lawrence. "Mr. Biko, what is your plea?" he asked.

"We are innocent," said Lawrence. "And we plead so using the acceptable terminology of the court, that is, not guilty. Also, the defense would like to state for the record that to accept deportation would mean that our innocence could not be proved and we therefore decline, in advance, any such offer."

What the hell? Lawrence had not discussed any of this with him and Jerry was glaring at his attorney when the judge glanced over at him and smiled. "Mr. Neal, can you understand all of this? I know it's noisy in here; can you hear what is being said?"

Jerry felt the shackles dig into his ankles as he stood in the dock and the judge leaned forward in his chair. "My Lord, Mr. Neal, are you bound?" he asked. He looked at the prosecutor and then at the nearest guard. "Who ordered this man shackled and who's got the key? Could anyone possibly have thought that this man would run away?"

The judge was staring at the guards, so everyone was surprised when Phelps-Neuman spoke from the side of the room. "We did not order him bound because of the nature of the man, but because of the nature of the crime," he said.

But the judge ignored Phelps-Neuman and slumped back in his chair. "You there," he said to the nearby guard, "unbind this man. Go find the key and unbind him now."

The guard left quickly and while everyone waited Justice Ogunde looked at Jerry and spoke in a kindly way. "I hope that you will accept my apologies on behalf of the court," he said. "We have procedures, but we sometimes do not have the common sense to make judicious decisions as to when

not to follow them." He had started out speaking softly but
had ended on a sharp note, and Jerry, though still angry with
Lawrence over the deportation thing, knew enough to keep
a serious face. "I'm fine, sir," he said. "The guards were only
doing their jobs."

As a matter of fact, Jerry thought it was great. The judge
was mad and when the guard came back and unlocked the
shackles Jerry sighed and rubbed his wrists, happy to have
the shackles gone but wonderfully glad, now, that they'd
been put on him in the first place.

"All right," said the justice, "Mr. Biko, you are entering a
plea of not guilty, isn't that what you said?"

"Yes, sir," said Lawrence.

"Very well. For the record of the court, Mr. Jerry Neal, res-
ident of Lagos state, citizen of the U.S. of A., you are
charged with the crime of arson in the first degree and with
the wrongful death of a certain Mrs. Purity Ono and you
have entered a plea of not guilty on both counts."

The judge looked away from Jerry and spoke out into the
room. "The defendant has entered a plea of not guilty to the
charge of arson in the first degree and wrongful death under
the heading of murder. Under the guarantees of a speedy
trial, and due to the unusual publicity in this case, I hereby
set the trial date for January, 1984, the first working day after
the New Year. Madam Prosecutor, Mr. Biko, are your calen-
dars clear on that day?"

Lawrence and the thin woman nodded, and then Lawrence spoke again. "Your honor, the defense requests that the
defendant be granted freedom, within the confines of Lagos
state, on his own recognizance, up to and including the final
day of his trial." He had spoken softly but Jerry stiffened.
This was the point about which he was desperate.

Justice Ogunde looked at the prosecutor and then at the
guard who still stood nearby with the shackles, and then,
briefly, at Tunde Phelps-Neuman over on the other side.
"Does the prosecution object?" asked the judge.

"We do," said the thin woman. "What purpose, other

than that of personal comfort, would be served by granting such a request?"

"Why, the easy preparation of our defense," said Lawrence. "And we will, of course, relinquish the defendant's passport as a guarantee."

The justice then spoke to the prosecutor. "The court is aware of the bailability of the charge, and I know that the prosecution is aware of the discretion of the court." He then allowed bail, on Jerry's own recognizance again, and pounded his gavel recessing the court for the day.

Jerry watched as Lawrence and the prosecutor shook hands, talking with each other as they walked out the door. He knew, now that he'd had time to think about it, what Lawrence would say about refusing deportation. He would say that the charges were too easy to beat, that they had logic and the evidence of the school's records on their side, a paper trail concerning the visas that went all the way back to San Francisco. He would say that it was impossible to lose. But Jerry had wanted the confounded man to consult him *before* making such fateful decisions, and the confounded man hadn't.

Still, now that he was free it was hard to maintain his anger, so while the two lawyers talked Jerry looked around the courtroom for friendly faces, someone with whom he could share the moment. It was late in the day and no one appeared to have come. As he walked toward the back of the room, however, he met a group of teachers coming through the outside door. Jerry smiled at them all, but as he walked toward them Lawrence quickly joined him again, pulling him off to the side of the room, under the noisiest air conditioner.

Jerry was about to thank Lawrence, to say, at least, that he was terribly glad not to be going back to jail, but Lawrence shushed him. "There is something rotten in Denmark," Lawrence said.

Jerry knew that well enough. What was rotten in Denmark was the trumped-up charge and the prolonged inability of Lawrence to get him out of jail. But now that he *was* out he was of a mind to forget all that, to get back to his office and see what was going on with the school. He was sure there was a great deal of work to be done and there was nothing he looked forward to more than doing it.

"I don't know," said Jerry, "the judge certainly seems to be on our side."

"That's what I don't understand," said Lawrence. "You have just been freed on your own recognizance for the second time. I am proud to have pulled that off, but now that I've done it, I don't trust it at all."

"What do you think?" said Jerry. "Now that I'm free should I fool them all and get the hell out of town?"

He had meant his comment to sound light and he was ready to laugh when Lawrence did, but Lawrence's demeanor was serious and no laugh came. "This is not the place to talk about it," he said.

Jerry Neal was not guilty of any crime but now that it appeared that he would not be deported for what he had not done, was his attorney telling him that something else was up and that he ought to run away? Jerry wanted to say something further, but the teachers were standing nearby and Lawrence, when he saw them, stepped away a little.

Jerry looked at his watch, which had just been returned to him along with his other belongings from the jail. It was December 13, 1983. If he stayed in Nigeria, he would be standing trial for murder in just about four weeks' time. What he wanted to do now was get together with Lawrence, to talk about the difference between deportation and flight, to discover what it was that Lawrence seemed to think had gone so terribly wrong.

Jerry slept fitfully that night but spent the next day back in his office, trying to catch up on his work and meeting with various groups of teachers, most of whom would be leaving town for the three-week period of Christmas break. Since he was under house arrest he could not, of course, leave himself, but it didn't matter. The idea of being alone on the campus appealed to him, giving him the feeling that he was breaking back into ordinary life in stages. That evening, however, he did attend a party, given in his honor at the home of Leonard Holtz, the school board president. He had become a kind of celebrity in the international community, and it was only by the strictest enforcement of his will that he avoided agreeing to a reception line.

All of the school board members were at the party, as were many of the teachers and most of the people from the embassy who had children in the school. Leonard Holtz lived in an elegant house, one that overlooked the harbor. As he stood at one of the picture windows, Jerry could see ships leaving, and he imagined himself on one of them, creeping away.

Jules's food notwithstanding, Jerry had lost weight during his eleven days in jail. Now his best suit fit loosely, allowing him to twist his trousers half a turn around. He had his hands in his pockets and was thus experimenting when Leonard came over to him, accompanied by Lee Logar, a black American diplomat, new to town. Jerry had met Lee once before, but Leonard introduced them anyway. "Lee has been working on your case from the embassy side," he said. "He had someone at the jail every day but nothing went according to plan. We did try, I hope you realize that, Jerry. If we weren't in bloody Nigeria we'd have had you out on that first day."

Though Jerry was irritated with Leonard's tone he and Lee shook hands, and then Jerry suggested that they step outside. The moon was over the water and he wanted to be under it when he talked about how he was going to get away.

The three men walked across the lawn and sat at a picnic table on the edge of a bluff, far away from the house. Lawrence Biko was at the party but Jerry wanted to leave Lawrence out of this. Though he'd thought constantly about Lawrence during his time in jail, and though the idea of leaving had come from Lawrence too, Lawrence's version of things was too cryptic. And with the hard involvement of the U.S. Embassy, whatever was going on in his attorney's mind seemed beside the point. It was as if he were being asked to choose between the two countries, and the choice was instantly in favor of the United States. Jerry had, however, seen Sunday walking around, and he knew that if he was going to trust any Nigerian to help with his plan, his administrative assistant would be the one. When a steward came by he asked him to call Sunday over, and to bring fresh drinks as well. After that he simply said, "I've decided to think, again, about finding a way to get out. I mean now, of course, before my trial. Let Lawrence Biko prove my innocence after I'm gone."

Leonard Holtz said, "All this is completely off the record," but Lee Logar nodded, saying, "We think so too. It would be easiest to go by way of Accra. Overland through Benin and Togo and then by air back to the States."

Leonard Holtz stood, saying he didn't want to hear any discussion that would leave the school without a head, so Jerry asked him to keep Sunday away for another five minutes. And when Leonard left Lee spoke up. "This really is the strangest damned thing," he said. "It's much more complicated than it seems. You've probably guessed that the whole visa thing was a setup, but I've got to tell you, we haven't got a clear idea as to why."

"No shit," said Jerry Neal.

Jerry Neal rarely spoke like that, but he was suddenly too impatient for other words. Why was he sitting here with this young man? He should be talking to the ambassador or to the D.C.M. He had expected that his government would know by now whatever they needed to know to extract him from this mess. Who had done the setting up, for example, and why? And was Lawrence really right in believing that it was only the coincidence of the visa problem that made him the hapless dupe that they'd used? Jerry wanted answers and he wanted a plan, a way to get out of the country without mistakes.

Lee Logar stared out across the lawn. He could feel Jerry's disregard for him but he nevertheless continued. "All right, listen," he said. "The majority opinion is that this has nothing to do with the ministry's books. If you were to stay, and if your attorney went into court ready to take that line, arguing that it was all a cover-up for a financial scam, it might be a big mistake. The prosecution would likely pull out sets of unscorched records and the ministry would be cleared. You might then find out that what was really burned were records having to do with the permanent residencies of foreign nationals, in other words nothing more than the files containing visa information about the school, and that would put a strain on Nigerian–American relations. We think, as a matter of fact, that that's the point of this whole thing. They want you to think exactly what you are thinking, don't you see? If you believe the case is ridiculous you won't be afraid to stay and stand trial. So far, except for the secretary's death, everything seems to have gone just as they've planned."

Leonard and Sunday were standing off to the side but Jerry said, "What are you talking about? Who are the *they* you're referring to? Everyone knows Nigerian officials are corrupt. And what possible purpose could there be in all of this if not to cover up the theft of huge amounts of cash? Who wants Nigerian–American relations to be bad?"

Jerry saw the moon and the water and the ships sailing by. Lee Logar's face was darkly serious, but since he remained quiet Jerry sighed and spoke again. "All right, then," he asked, "if they're so eager to make a fool out of me at the trial, why did they talk about deportation? And won't they get the same results if I leave? Won't I be seen as guilty for having run?"

Lee shrugged. "I think the deportation offer was made to see how you would react. I think they wanted to see what kind of man you are. Some of this, after all, is still dependent on you."

But Jerry had had enough and he waved his hand. "So what is it?" he asked. "What is my government's position on me getting the hell out of here?"

"With you gone there won't be a trial and without a trial everything will stay confused, which, right now, your government considers to be to its advantage," Lee said. "Also, in light of what went on at your arraignment yesterday morning it should be easy getting you out. After all, they have your passport and that judge believes he is dealing with a man of principle here."

Jerry looked hard at the man. What the hell kind of thing was that to say? He was a man of principle! Lee Logar, however, heard the insult in his words and spoke again. "I only meant to say that they are now sure you have understood the elements of the trial the way they want you to and will stay because you think you can easily win." He then added, "Anyway, I've almost completed the arrangements for your departure. All you have to do is wait to hear from me. And be ready to go, of course."

When Leonard came back with Sunday, Lee left, going off toward the house. But when Jerry looked at Sunday sitting there, a large beer in his hand, he suddenly thought of the school again. Who would take care of the school once he was gone? He had missed too much work already, and he realized that what he had really been looking forward to was using the three weeks of Christmas vacation to catch up. Besides, if he left, where would he go and what would he do with the rest of his life? He had not yet begun to think of that.

Jerry suddenly decided that whatever Lee Logar thought, whatever plans his embassy had made, he would, after all, put off his decision about leaving until he had the school in order once again. And with that his mood suddenly lifted. Sunday called to one of the waiters, asking for more beer, and when Jerry looked at the man he said, "Let me tell you about my time in jail—have I got a story for you."

Jerry pulled his chair around and put an arm across Sunday's broad back, and Sunday smiled, looking at Leonard Holtz so that Leonard would feel included in whatever it was that Jerry was about to say.

"Is good," said Sunday. "Nothing so fine as a good story when the beer is coming and it is warm."

The next days went by without incident. Jerry worked furiously to catch up on all that he'd missed, but he didn't speak to Lee Logar again, and though he saw Lawrence Biko daily, he let Lawrence continue working on the case as they had originally understood it, telling him only that for the moment he would not be running away. He lived his life, as a matter of fact, as if he were going to stay in Lagos running the school for years to come.

It wasn't until the students and teachers left on Friday, heading out to various holiday destinations, that Jerry began to feel at sea again. It was Christmas vacation and though the teachers gave him sympathetic looks, he could see their vacation smiles hidden beneath those looks. He roamed the campus alone over the weekend, and though he worked as hard on the following Monday as he would have had his teaching staff been around, by Tuesday he was beginning to lose his concentration. Joseph and his crew were still there, washing and painting the walls, but what did he really know of these men? He certainly couldn't talk to them about the decision he had to make, asking their opinion of what he should do. There was Jules, of course, but when he went home for lunch Jules seemed upset that he still had to work, while all the other stewards got three weeks off.

Late on Tuesday afternoon, Jerry found himself alone in his office, staring out the window at two large lizards on the wall and wondering what it meant to be ready to go at any time. Could he pack a suitcase, could he say his good-byes, a parting word to Joseph or Sunday, a farewell note to the teachers who were now gone, would he be allowed that much?

Without really thinking about it, Jerry realized that he had decided to run again. He couldn't face jail, nor could he think, for very long, about that fiasco of a trial. He really didn't think that this was an anti-American thing, he didn't believe Lee Logar, but he also could not grasp Lawrence's apprehensions, that "something is rotten in Denmark" sensibility, his attorney's poorly articulated fear. Jerry only knew that the truth of the moment, the one that he came to in the lonely clarity of his air-conditioned room, was that there was no one for him to go to, no one with whom he could discuss these things. Of course he knew that even if the teachers were on hand he would not confide in any of them—when Charlotte had died Jerry's interest in the act of personal confidences had pretty much died with her. But though he had always viewed that fact with a good deal of pride, by the time he left his office that night he had nevertheless decided that he'd kept his own counsel long enough. Five years was long enough.

Jerry locked the office door and had walked halfway across the empty school playground before turning back, unlocking the door again, and copying Nurudeen's address from the student files. He then walked off the campus and down to one of the federal housing units across the street, the one in which Nurudeen lived. These buildings were all around the school, and though they were huge, sprawling things, he had no trouble finding the right one. He took a stairway to the second floor and walked along the outside passageway until he found the right flat. He quickly walked to the end of the corridor, but when he came back he stopped in front of the door, trying to listen. What if Nurudeen's father was inside? What if Nurudeen's stepmother was someone other than the Pamela he knew?

Since he was leaving the country all of this was foolishness anyway, and he had just about decided to let it go when the door opened and Pamela came out.

"Something's come up," said Jerry Neal. "I think we will have to put off meeting again for a while."

Good God, he thought, what an idiotic thing to say. As he stood there staring at her, he felt as though he might step back and fall over the railing, down to his death below. "I don't understand anything," he said.

"It isn't what you imagine," Pamela told him.

But how could it not be what he imagined? "Goddamn it," he said, "how did you know about my sister-in-law?"

"Come inside," Pamela said.

"I don't want to come inside! Who's in there? Is Nurudeen there? Is that father of his around?"

Jerry was quickly furious again. He'd been nothing but a stupid victim, a pawn.

But Pamela held the door calmly open, so he finally did step inside. "I am alone," she said. "I guess it never occurred to them that you might actually come over here."

"So you live here with Nurudeen's dad. You're the one who put the spell on Nurudeen and made him steal my lunch!"

It was such a silly-sounding statement that Pamela laughed. "Nurudeen's an imaginative boy, but no, that wasn't me, that was his grandmother." She paused, suddenly serious again. "I should say that when his grandmother does something it should not be treated as a joke. I, by the way, am not his stepmother. I'm not a chiropractor either, I guess you know."

"What are you then?" asked Jerry. "And what did you hope to gain by visiting me like that?"

Jerry had shouted, but the door was closed and his voice didn't carry far.

"Sit down," said Pamela. "What can I get you?"

"I want the truth," said Jerry, but he did sit down. There were only two chairs in the room. Now that he took a moment to look, in fact, he saw that the place was more like an office than anyone's home. He was flustered and stood up again. "I think I'd better go," he said. "There's no point in this. I won't believe anything you say now anyway."

"Suit yourself, I suppose," Pamela said, "but I only lied a little, and I meant you no harm."

"OK," said Jerry. "How did you know about Marge? Let's start with that."

"Easy," she said. "Nurudeen's father's been screening your mail."

Jerry hadn't expected such an answer and he paused, finally asking the real question. "Is this about stealing money or is there something else at hand?"

Pamela looked at him. "Your lawyer will handle all of that," she said.

"Who is Nurudeen's dad?" Jerry asked. "And where is Nurudeen?"

"His father has been a great many things," she said. "Once he was minister of health, another time he was Nigeria's ambassador to Mexico. He is now between posts and working very much on his own. Nurudeen is in Anthony Village, just off the airport road, living with his mom."

"Who are you?"

"My name is Pamela, just like I said."

"And what are you to Nurudeen's dad?"

Pamela paused then before shaking her head. "Look," she said, "none of this is over yet. I've already told you most of what I know."

"Your job was to keep an eye on me? Find out what I was thinking, what I might do, right?"

"That's right," she said.

"How could you do such a thing?"

Pamela sighed, then smiled. "I was asked to take one small part, to get to know you and see what you were up to. When Nurudeen's father intercepted Marge's note he saw to it that I got a lesson on what it is that chiropractors do. He knew I could convince you because I have lived in the United States. I have only recently returned, as a matter of fact."

"Then you don't live here?"

"Certainly not," said Pamela. "Nurudeen lived here when he was attending your school, and his father did too, on and off. Now that Nurudeen is gone this place more or less sits empty, but to give it up would be foolish. These places are hard to come by in the best of times."

"Where do you live?"

"I live out in Anthony Village, too. I live with my son who is twelve."

Jerry wanted more, but he couldn't think what to ask, and since he had a certain sense that she was now telling him the truth, he didn't want to press it.

"OK," he said, sitting down again and finally speaking normally, "if what you have said is true then why are you here now? Why are you hanging around this flat alone?"

Pamela shook her head. "Look at the view this flat has of the school," she said. "I was to stay here and be ready. If I received a call I was to go over and try to see you again. Make myself useful by staying in touch, making it harder for you to run, making it harder for those embassy friends of yours to take you away. I was to make myself interesting to you. Do you know what I mean by that?"

Jerry's heart swelled a little; he knew exactly what she meant by that—even now he was drawn to her but he had also heard that embassy comment of hers. Surely they had no idea that he'd been talking to Lee. He wanted to ask about that, but what he asked instead was, "What do they care if I run? They can find me guilty in absentia, without even taking the time for a trial. And who are 'they'? Who in the hell are we talking about?"

Jerry closed his eyes. This was all too complicated. He tried to go over everything but he couldn't think.

Finally Pamela said, "Look, your trial date will soon be at hand, and I'm quite sure I'm not the only one watching the school. We will be lucky, as a matter of fact, if no one saw you coming over here today."

Jerry heard the "we" she'd used and it pleased him. Still,

if she had agreed so readily to spy on him in the first place, why was she turning around now and telling him what it was that she'd agreed to do?

"Tell me why you're speaking so frankly," he said. "You wouldn't have if I hadn't caught you here."

"I might have," she said. "Such intrigue really doesn't suit my natural frame of mind. And though you may not think so, I'm taking a chance by talking to you now. This is not a game, Mr. Neal. This conversation, as a matter of fact, could get me into very hot water indeed."

There seemed to be nothing more to say, nothing for him to do other than leave. She wouldn't tell him who "they" were, but though he told himself he was foolish, he believed everything she *had* told him. He was not, however, going to mention the escape. He only hoped that when she found out about it, she'd be happy for him and relieved.

"I think I'd better go," he said. "If you like you may come to the school later, playing your part out, if you know what I mean."

"Yes," she said. "I think I would like that."

Jerry knew he was stupid. He knew that when she showed up again he'd be gone. But he had wanted to find out that she wanted to come. He would carry that idea with him, thinking about it in Ghana and perhaps again in the U.S.A.

Early on Friday morning, December 23, Jerry got a note on embassy stationery telling him that he was to pretend that the school's copy machine had broken down and call the repairman to come and get it with his truck. Jerry did so immediately, and when he put the receiver down he sat for a long time, marveling at the plan. The empty space in the bottom of the copy machine, the space that had previously contained Joseph, would soon contain him.

Jerry spent the day writing memos. He had no idea who would take his place, but he had run the school for three years and its orderly continuance was important to him. There was still the problem of the visas to attend to, still the inequitable salaries of the locally hired staff, and any number of students with whom he had special contracts concerning behavior and academic improvement. Had someone asked him earlier he would have guaranteed that, though some of those contracts might surely be broken, they would not be broken by him.

At four o'clock Joseph sent his crew to work on another part of the school and stood guard outside the copy-room door. Inside the room Jerry was nervously pacing around. Sunday was there and had stacked the reams of paper off to the side. Jerry had told Joseph and Sunday of the plan out of a sense of camaraderie and trust, because they had worked together for years, but he had not told Lawrence. He had relied on his attorney, it was true, but he wanted Lawrence's denials of involvement to be authentic. Also, he wasn't sure how Lawrence would react if he absolutely knew that Jerry was going to run.

The copy-machine doors were open, its internal compartment gleaming. Jerry had practiced getting in and out of the machine a couple of times, and when word came that the repairman's truck was there, he ducked down quickly, taking only his thermos and a sack lunch, and not, in the end, saying good-bye to anyone. It was a tight fit—though the copy machine could hold fifty reams of paper, it was only five feet long—but he pulled his knees up and twisted his shoulders around, and when the doors were closed he felt the machine move off the ground. Joseph had called his crew back, and when they put him down he could hear them getting the replacement machine off the open back end of the truck. When they lifted him once more he felt the truck's bed under him and he heard the tailgate slam.

Jerry was afraid that the copy-machine doors might swing open again but he couldn't get his hand around to hold them. He heard Joseph ask the driver when the machine would be returned and he heard the man say, "Don' know, but les tie 'er down good."

There was silence then. The driver had a rope in his hands and wanted to string it around the machine, through the hooks at the side of the truck's bed. Jerry felt his stomach fall. Why hadn't they anticipated this? Had Lee Logar believed Jerry would simply be able to slide out of the machine freely, crawling over and jumping off the side of the moving truck? Good God, here he was, already locked inside the copy machine before realizing how stupid the whole plan was.

Jerry could hear Sunday stalling for time, telling the man that his ropes were old, that it was better to go without them than to risk having the police see the condition they were in, but the driver immediately believed that Sunday was trying to steal his ropes, so there was nothing left for them to do but allow the man to tie the machine down tight.

"OK," said the man, "have 'er back before too long." He

checked around, satisfying himself with the way the copy machine sat in the back of his truck and trying to speak to them, now, in a friendly way.

Not only was Jerry tied down, but all this was taking a great deal of time. He could see from the luminous dial on his watch that it was after five. And though he had been in-side the machine for less than fifteen minutes, his legs ached from the position they were in, and he was having trouble taking a full breath.

Joseph's crew had moved across the school grounds again and Sunday had taken the truck driver inside to get him a drink of water when Jerry heard another voice nearby. Pamela was there, standing at the side of the truck and ask-ing Joseph where Jerry lived. Jerry was sure she had contin-ued to watch the school, but since she couldn't see inside the rooms, how could she possibly know about the copy ma-chine? Jerry imagined that it was all a coincidence because of his asking her to visit him once again, and in his mind's eye he saw her pointing off toward the flats. He saw Joseph shift-ing his weight, searching for a good reply.

"His flat is that very one, madam," Joseph finally said. "Firs' floor, lef' side." Joseph paused then, and Jerry could feel him holding on, trying to decide whether to let the woman walk toward the flat or to tell her that he was away. Jerry, however, had suddenly had enough. He'd need spinal adjustments for the rest of his life after this and it was, fi-nally, all too odd, and too much against his view of himself, for him to let it go on. Let Lee Logar find another way of spiriting him away.

"Joseph," he said, and there was another long pause.

"Yessir," Joseph finally said.

"Tell the lady to wait a minute and then get a knife—get me out of here."

But immediately Pamela spoke again. "Never mind, Jo-seph," she said, "I think I understand."

"But I'm tied in here," Jerry said. "I can't get out and I'm so late that I might even get left in here overnight."

That possibility hadn't occurred to him until he'd said it, but Pamela said, "Shh, here comes the driver again." What, had she now completely come over to his side? Was she now going to help him find Lee Logar in the downtown Lagos streets?

Jerry knew that Joseph would not ignore his request to be freed, but as soon as Sunday and the driver got back Pamela asked the driver for a lift into town, asking him where his shop was and saying it was near where she wanted to go. Jerry imagined her with her hand on Joseph's arm, keeping him quiet with her eyes and tone.

So in a minute Pamela and the driver got into the cab of the truck and Joseph and Sunday stood around the tailgate at the back.

"Sir?" Joseph said quietly, once the driver had turned the engine over and put the truck into gear.

"Never mind, Joseph," Jerry heard himself say, "let's give it a try." And then, as the truck lurched forward, he said, "Thank you and good-bye."

That was all. He was away from the school, away from his pleasant and orderly life with no more fanfare than that given a broken copy machine. The ride into town was long, and though Jerry had never been more uncomfortable, he remained still and tried to think of other things. He thought of the memos he had placed inside some of the files, the lists of things to do that sat on his desk, the little insights he'd tried to relay to whoever would next occupy his chair. He thought of the pride he'd taken in being appointed principal of such a school, the unblemished quality of his long and good career. And of course he also marveled at Pamela, helping him out of it, riding along as his aide.

The truck had been moving well, zooming into town, but Jerry was suddenly jarred by a quick stop. Horns blared, and after that the truck crept forward, stopping for long periods before rolling slightly forward again. They were in a go-slow, a Lagos traffic jam, and he pushed at the copy-machine doors, so that he might see out a little.

Boys surrounded the truck, hawkers from the side of the road, and Jerry thought of the ironing board he'd bought. He could hear the truck driver buying something through his window and he could tell from the sound of things that both the driver and Pamela had their windows down, were exchanging comments with the hawkers who walked by. The truck was not moving and he could hear, now that the traffic noise had dimmed, a certain give-and-take, a friendly sort of chatter. Pamela had bought something to eat, and when a beggar approached he could hear her telling him to wait while she searched around for a coin. Jerry had never done that. When beggars approached him he always stared straight ahead until they went away. He ignored them all, even the legless ones who scooted through the traffic on those horrible skateboards of theirs.

By the time the go-slow broke up the sun was down, and when the truck stopped again they had reached their destination, were inside some kind of garage. Pamela got out of the cab and the driver ran off somewhere to report his arrival.

"Cut me loose," said Jerry.

"Shh. Give us a moment," Pamela said.

She untied the ropes from the side of the truck and had pulled them from the main body of the copy machine when the driver came back with a friend.

"I only thought I'd give a hand," she said, but the driver and the other man laughed, telling her that it was late, that they could take the machine off the truck in the morning when they had a full crew.

"Come, madam, let us lock our door," said the new man, and Jerry heard the three of them walk away. He heard the big double doors close and he saw the light leaving and he heard the quiet coming in. When he moved against the copy-machine doors they opened a foot before becoming entangled in the ropes. Still, he was able to get an arm out, and then a shoulder, and soon he was on his knees in the bed of the truck, born of the copy machine but looking pretty much like himself. He lay down and pointed his toes and stretched his body out.

Jerry was in a new and different world, but in a moment he remembered that businesses in Lagos often had night guards and he froze, listening. Maybe the guard was not on duty yet or maybe he was still outside, standing in the road with the guards of other businesses nearby. Surely, if he were in the shop he'd have heard the noise Jerry made and come to investigate by now.

The copy-machine repair shop wasn't large. The truck, in fact, occupied most of it, and around the truck copy machines were stacked, their doors and lids fallen open like unhinged mouths.

Jerry let his eyes adjust and then grabbed his lunch and stepped over the side of the truck, landing lightly and turreting around like a military man, his thermos held above him like a club. He had been athletic as a youth and continued to be proud of the fitness he had maintained.

The smell of copy-machine toner was everywhere but Jerry could see, from the mix of broken parts, that he should never have sent the school's machine here. Though they might fix whatever was wrong with the machine, they would steal from it as well, switching newer parts for poor ones like an organ bank in America might do.

Just as Jerry stepped around the back of the truck, the front door opened and the guard came in. Jerry had seen the man's face in an outside slice of light and he stepped up to the man quickly, before he could secure the door.

"Good," he said loudly. "I was afraid I was going to have to call for help."

"Allah!" said the security guard.

But when the guard saw Jerry's white face he calmed and Jerry said, "I fell asleep in the truck. I guess they forgot to wake me, must have forgotten I was there."

Jerry pointed back over his shoulder as he spoke, then asked the guard to open the door. The security man still had his hands on his chest, but in a moment he did what Jerry asked, letting the door slide open far enough for Jerry to walk through it into the unfamiliar night. "Is no good down here for de white man," the guard said, but Jerry didn't reply. He wanted to get far enough away so that if the guard decided to seek him out again he wouldn't be easy to find.

The area outside the shop was candle-powered, and there was a low burning fire with men standing around it. Jerry remembered Pamela and hoped she might be waiting nearby. Would it be better to let her find him or to slip away? Surely Lee was waiting as well and would be furious to find Pamela.

"Oh, dare you are," said a voice, and since it wasn't Pamela's or Lee's, Jerry tensed, ready to punch and run. "Who's there?" he said. "What do you want?"

"Oh, I am wounded now," said the voice. "You forget me quick like dat? Time get better a man don' remember 'is own pas' friend, dat's de trouble wid people dese days."

Jerry looked then and saw a face he knew. It was Parker Akintola, his old cell mate, the Bob Marley ticket man. "Parker," he said. "What are you doing here?"

"Same ting I was doin' in jail," said Parker, "workin' on takin' care o you. I work for Lee, de been-to from America. Louis Smith-Jones is my driver."

Jerry thought it was impossible that Parker worked for Lee. Surely Lee would have mentioned him. But before he could respond Pamela came out of the dark. "Is this man bothering you?" she asked.

A few of the nearby street people had begun to take an interest in what was going on, so Parker led them back past the repair shop and down an alley. Jerry had hoped to see the red diplomatic plates on Lee's embassy car but what he found instead was a Lagos taxi, the driver's door open and, sure enough, Louis Smith-Jones behind the wheel.

"Where's Lee?" asked Jerry. "What the hell's going on here?"

But Parker shook his head. "Lee can't be out here his own self. Dis is only stage one. Lee is our stage-two man. And so far everything has gone wrong. You was supposed to come

alone, widout a lady frien'. You was supposed to come early
and you come late. Lee will be upset. I don' even know if he
is still at our number-two rendezvous place."

Parker got in front, so Jerry and Pamela both slid into the
backseat of the cab. Louis jerked the car once and in a moment they were rolling out of the alley and onto a road that
seemed to lead farther into this unknown part of town. Jerry
had not been told anything about what would happen after
he left the school, but now that he thought about it, he realized how idiotic he was to have followed instructions that
Lee had sent him in a note. Anyone could have sent that
note. He looked at the others in the car, trying to gauge
something by the way they sat, but he couldn't tell a thing.
His heart fell a little, though, when he remembered that
when Pamela approached him on the street, Parker hadn't
been surprised.

After Louis drove past the same spot three times, after
he'd gone around the same roundabout and up the same
drive, Parker said, "Dis is what I was afraid of. . . . Lee has
not waited. I don' see any sign of de stage-two vehicle either."

There was still a chance, of course, that Parker was telling
the truth, that he really did work for Lee, so all Jerry said
was, "What do we do now?" It was Pamela, however, who responded. "We aren't far from my house," she said. "Let's all
go there."

Jerry waited for Parker to dismiss Pamela's offer out of
hand, but he turned and looked at her. "Do you have a
phone at where you live?" he asked.

"There is a phone and I am between house girls. No one
will be coming in."

When Parker heard that, he nodded, and Pamela told
Louis to head out Western Avenue until he got to the Anthony Village road. This was a part of Lagos that Jerry didn't
know, a Nigerian part of town.

What was he going to do? He did not feel in physical danger. Parker and Louis, though they'd been in jail with him,

didn't seem at all tough, and Jerry felt sure that he could get away if he had to, slipping out of the car and running into the night. But where would he go if he ran, what would he do? Since he didn't know anything about the inner workings of the C.I.A., it was still possible that all of this was legitimate, that Lee Logar had truly orchestrated such an unlikely series of events. Also, Jerry wanted to find out more about Pamela, and seeing her house would certainly allow him a chance to do that. So he just sat there, clutching his thermos and sandwich, as if it were they who would leap from the car if he released his grip, giving them half a chance to escape.

Pamela directed them through several more turns, having them stop on a quiet road where modest frame houses lined both sides of the street. "There," she said, "the white one behind that wall."

When the car was parked, Parker asked Jerry to stay where he was while he and Louis checked the place out. Was that something they would do? Jerry asked himself. If they were trying to interrupt his flight in some way would they now leave him alone? Jerry looked into the night and fingered the door handle, but in the end he didn't move until Parker came back. "Is fine," Parker said. "We got de servants' quarters with no one living in 'em. It will be good for one day. I already call Lee and he tol' me so."

Parker smiled well and when Jerry got out of the car he reached back in to get Jerry's thermos and his lunch. "You don' want to leave dese things lying about," Parker said. "Too many thieves in dis part of town."

Pamela's house was small, but Jerry decided that if Nigeria had a middle class this must be it. The living room had chairs and a couch and a floor of bare cement. But what made the room interesting was that Pamela stood in it, having changed into a loose white blouse with a few yards of colorful cloth tied around her middle. She looked so wonderful that Jerry thought surely such a vision must be on his side.

"I am making something for us to eat," she said. "It will be ready soon." Had she done something with her hair too? Jerry couldn't quite tell, for the light in the room was bad.

Parker went over and picked up the phone. He then asked Pamela if it was the only receiver in the house.

"There is one in my room, upstairs," she said, and when Parker went to see about it, Pamela asked Jerry to sit down. "There is another little thing we must clear up," she said. "My son is upstairs and he wants to see you."

Jerry had been preparing himself to hear something else about the current state of his affairs, so though she spoke seriously, to him her words sounded light. "Sure," he said, "I'd love to meet your son."

"Good," Pamela said, and when she called up the stairs and he heard the boy's slow walk Jerry grew calm. He was excellent with children, probably Pamela saw that in him, and he realized, as the boy approached, that for the past three days he had been playing the game of seeing himself helping her out, perhaps even putting her child through school. He smiled at that. He was an educator, and it was pleasing to remember that when all of this was finally done, that was what he would be again, maybe in America, or who knows, maybe even back here, in Lagos once again.

Jerry had his back to the stairs, so Pamela put her arm on his shoulder and turned him slowly around. Acceptance was in his heart, but when he saw Pamela's son on the stairs he quickly knew that he had been wrong. There was nothing he could do for this boy. The boy, of course, was Nurudeen, and when Pamela said his name he held out his hand and, like a little gentleman, stepped down into the room.

This time Jerry would not hear an explanation. He backed away from Nurudeen, then went to sit in the upstairs room where the other phone was, looking at the phone as if Lee were about to call with news of how to get him out of town. He had been too much of a fool, but he would stop that now. Nurudeen was her son, yet Jerry had believed her when she had said that he was not. Pamela tried several times to speak to him, telling him that she had said only that Nurudeen was not her *step*son, but he would not respond to her knocks on the door. He only sat there, staring at the phone, his old re-solve coming back again.

But after a while, when Jerry slumped back against the headboard of Pamela's bed, there came a knock to which he responded simply by standing and opening the door. It was Louis Smith-Jones. "Here I am, Oga," he said. "De man won' call tonight. Les have good sleep for travel on tomorrow."

Louis seemed so friendly standing there that Jerry asked, "Who hired you, Louis? Were you working for Lee when we met in jail?"

"Oh no, Oga," Louis replied. "Dat man fin' Parker, Parker fin' me."

With Louis in the room Jerry felt better. Surely it was the truth after all; this boy could steal, perhaps, but from what Jerry had learned about him in jail he couldn't lie very well. Surely in the morning he'd be on his way with Lee, off to Ghana and then home. And it was just then that Pamela reappeared. She came out of the darkness carrying soup on a tray.

"I hope you will eat a little," she said. "I hope you will listen a little as well."

Jerry didn't respond so Pamela set the bowl down and then told Louis to leave them alone. The mattress on her bed was soft and Jerry felt his end of it rise when she sat down. "Nurudeen is my son," she said, "but he and I were apart for several years. During that time Nurudeen stayed with his father in that flat near the school."

"Am I supposed to believe you now?" Jerry asked.

"I couldn't tell you before, don't you see? I had to distance myself from the situation until I understood it better. I haven't had much to say in Nurudeen's upbringing. His father paid for my studies abroad, and when he asked me to play the role of Marge's friend I had to go along. If for no other reason than the chance it gave me to spend time with my boy."

Jerry tried to make his voice incredulous, but curiosity was its strongest influence. "Everything you did you did with Nurudeen's best interest at heart," he said.

"As always," said Pamela, "I knew you'd understand."

Her voice was matter-of-fact and Jerry was dumbfounded. He did understand. And he believed her again. "But why didn't you tell me the truth when I caught you in that flat?" he asked. "And why spring Nurudeen on me in such a dramatic way?"

"I didn't trust you enough then," Pamela said. "And I still didn't have Nurudeen physically with me. He was staying with his grandmother. Having him here is my payoff, I suppose, though it's all considerably more complicated than that."

Jerry took up his spoon and stirred the soup, letting steam rise up between them. During the years since Charlotte's death he had not had many fantasies about women. He'd had so few, in fact, that he had occasionally been ashamed. Now, though, in spite of everything, he was still strongly drawn to

Pamela, though she had told him only lies since the day they'd met, and though she might even be lying now.

There was a quiet knock on the door and when Nurudeen came in Pamela touched Jerry's hand, making him look at the boy, asking him with her eyes to say something.

"I'm sorry about your withdrawal from school," Jerry told the boy. "Perhaps when this is over you'll come back."

"Are my teachers all fine?" Nurudeen asked. "When you see them give them my hello."

It was ten o'clock when Pamela took Jerry down to the tiny servants' rooms, each with a made-up cot. Most Lagos houses had such rooms, but these were smaller than Jerry had imagined they would be.

Parker and Louis were already in their rooms, and when Jerry thought of them he had difficulty remembering them as they had been in jail. Now Louis seemed sweet-tempered and much younger than he'd appeared to be in prison. Louis was a boy, no more than nineteen or twenty, and Jerry understood now that if he was a thief he was a careless one, a thief without malice or plan and one who would always be caught.

Parker, on the other hand, now seemed far more like someone capable of succeeding in a fantastic con. He was likeable and he had the charisma of a politician, calm and seemingly honest. Jerry found himself wondering how Lee Logar had found Parker, though he soon remembered that he wasn't sure of any such thing at all. Still, if he was really leaving Nigeria in the morning, it suddenly seemed ironic that on the eve of his departure he was finally coming to know the place, and that was a feeling that added to his growing desire not to leave at all.

Jerry slept until nine, when he was awakened by Nurudeen with the news that breakfast was ready and that there had been a phone call, which Parker had answered, up in the main part of the house. When Jerry entered the living room, Parker was just putting the phone down. "Lee has read dis morning's papers," he said. "Your photograph is everywhere, with captions saying you are at large."

Parker then said that in Lee's opinion the newspaper articles dictated a postponement of their departure for a day or two. He also said that Lee wanted to move Jerry to a safer place. Jerry was to wait at Pamela's until eleven and then find his way to Jankara market, where he would be met. Parker and Louis were to go along.

"Do you know de market?" Parker asked. "He says he want to meet us by de monkeys."

Jerry said he had seen the monkeys, but Jankara market was huge, and too central to the everyday commerce of Lagos. Jerry thought it was a bad place to meet, and he asked Parker to get Lee back on the phone so that he could tell him so. The others, however, all said they thought that Jankara was ideal, a place with such rutted roads that no one, least of all the police, could easily go rushing about. And Louis said that he knew the market well. "Don' worry 'bout nothin'," he said. "My own good brodder stay aroun' dem monkeys. He fin' us housing if de been-to fail."

Louis had returned the car he'd driven the night before, but Pamela had a Peugeot 504, the most common car in Lagos, and when Louis backed it out of her garage at eleven, Jerry got into the backseat, Pamela on one side of him, Nurudeen on the other. Parker rode shotgun and told Louis where it was that he should turn.

At a roundabout near her home, Pamela rolled down the window and bought three morning papers. Jerry's passport picture was on the front page of two of them and on the back page of the third. He looked fat and clean.

When they neared the market—actually from an overpass just above it—they could look down and see the market sprawl, an endless array of buildings, corrugated roofs and collapsed sides. To their right were mounds of smoking garbage, rag pickers on top of them searching for salvage among the ruined food.

The highway and its off-ramp and the Peugeot in which they sat were made of materials from the modern world, but Jerry could see that what lay before him was of a different composition altogether. During the rainy season the off-ramp would run directly into a lake of mud, but now, with harmattan dust still about, it was embedded in a pathway so cracked and deep that no automobile could pass. There were cars parked along the ramp, but Louis managed to drive a hundred meters more, stopping in front of a line of other Peugeots. "Les walk," Parker said.

They all slid out the driver's side, depositing themselves on the rumpled ground. Though the market was before them, its entrances were numerous and Jerry had no idea how far they were from the monkeys.

"My brodder in de business of finance," Louis said. "De finance business be near de monkey business."

Parker was the tacit leader of the group, but Louis was making everything light, and Jerry was thankful for that. As they walked away from the car the market stretched before them like the canopy of a rain forest. Jerry knew he could get lost in there but when he tried to suggest that they ask about the monkeys and then walk around the market's outskirts until they got close, Parker took the newspaper from him and pointed at his photograph. "On de outside people got papers to read," he said, "but de inside of Jankara is safer than Ghana, perhaps."

From where Jerry stood the market didn't look safer than Ghana. He had been to this market only once before; on the occasion of his arrival in Nigeria he had come on a U.S. Embassy wives' tour. He had visited the fabric sellers then, walking tall among a tight group of women, marveling at the disarray.

They entered the market down a thin road walled on both sides with stacks of automobile parts. Jerry was surprised at the parts. He had always worked on his own cars, yet all during his time in Lagos he hadn't been able to find the parts he'd needed. When they passed a shop selling brake pads he seriously thought of stopping. He'd been needing new brake pads for weeks.

Jerry thought they might be near the monkeys when they came to a section of the market where parrots were sold. Here were dozens of African Gray parrots in wire cages, heads hanging sadly down. But the parrots were apparently not near the monkeys and soon they had passed into the section where there was food for sale and through it to a landscape of cups and saucers stacked on cardboard like fake Spode skylines of futuristic towns. Louis Smith-Jones led them here and there. He led them with confidence, but he couldn't find the monkeys. And as the morning heat rose, Jerry's anxiety did too. When he looked at his watch he realized that if Lee was really involved in any of this, they might miss him again because they were late.

When he asked Louis, Louis insisted that his brother lived around the spot where the monkeys were, and he said he wanted to find his brother so that they could ask for help.

"Good idea," said Parker, but Louis immediately got confused and began scanning the decrepit landscape, trying to recognize a doorway or a path, something that would lead them to that brother of his.

"Louis, what is your brother's name?" Jerry asked. "Why not ask someone for him by using his name?"

"My brodder name be Smart," said Louis. "Everyone know him down here. De door to Smart's own place be green; I remember it well."

Pamela and Louis walked off, asking shopkeepers if they knew Smart, but Jerry soon became so agitated that he took Nurudeen and Parker and started down a nearby pathway of his own. This was not a commercial path, and it didn't look like it led to where the monkeys were, but here, after they'd gone some distance, doors did begin to appear, and some of them were green. These doors were lined up so close together, though, that it was difficult to imagine that they led anywhere. It was more like a door store than any kind of entrance.

"Let's go back," said Nurudeen.

Jerry didn't want to go any farther either, but the anxiety he felt at being late was terrible, and it propelled him up to a dozen shirtless men, a few heavy women listening to a radio.

"Do any of you know the monkeys?" Jerry asked. "They should be around here someplace."

The men stayed quiet, but one of the market women smiled at him. "Say again, please," she said.

"The monkeys," said Jerry, but Parker took over. "If it please, madam, where go dem monkey seller? We go fin' quick fo' meet wid one anodder masta."

"Oh," said the woman. "Down 'roun dat way, den straight on to de other side."

Jerry had no idea what the woman had said but Parker asked, "Maybe de man Smart be close at hand? He behin' one green door, call de finance man. We be travelin' wid his own good brodder, Louis."

When Parker mentioned Smart the others in the crowd watched him. "What you wan' wid Smart?" the woman asked.

"Wan' make de introduction," said Parker. "Wan' talk small wid 'im, das all."

Maybe nobody wanted to say so, but it was clear to Jerry

that they all knew Smart. And when the heavy woman took Parker's wrist and turned with him, everyone followed along. "Back here," she said, and in a minute they were standing in front of one of the doors they'd passed before. It was a tall, surreal door. It was green, but it made them hesitate.

"Who de brodder o Smart?" asked the woman, and when she said it Nurudeen ran off to bring the others quickly back.

"Here," said Jerry. "It's Louis. He's the one."

Louis smiled. "What?" he said. "Did I not say de door be green? Hello, madam, hello everybody. I am Louis. Smart young brodder by de same daddy. Only de mama not de same."

Louis was proud, but Jerry could not imagine that he had ever been to his brother's place before. The people greeted him, though, and soon the heavy woman was pounding on the door, producing a deep echo. While they waited Jerry held the newspapers tightly under his arm. He was beginning to believe that it might be days before such a current paper made its way down here. The market wasn't such a bad meeting place after all.

Pamela stood behind Nurudeen, resting her hands on his shoulders. "It's nearly twelve," she said. "I fear we're late again." But for the longest time the woman's pounding produced only the echo. Louis's pride in bringing the outside world to his brother was making him as impatient as Jerry. When the green door finally opened, however, they all stood still. The person opening it was a boy.

"Smart's asleep," he said.

Beyond him there was only darkness, as if the boy stood in no space at all. Louis, however, jumped forward. "Elwood, my frien'. How do you do?"

Jerry felt that all of this might go on forever, but apparently the noise had brought Smart too, for another man stepped out of nowhere, coming up behind Elwood and moving him aside.

"May I help you?" he asked.

Smart looked at Louis with slow recognition and Jerry thought that if he was Louis's brother it was certainly a loosely knit family. Smart was at least fifty, probably older, and he gave the impression of being a man of calm intelligence. Louis, on the other hand, bounced around in front of him like a marionette until the man held a hand up.

"Howdy, Louis," he said. "Long time no see."

"Yes, brodder!" Louis said. "How do you do?"

Though everything was fascinating, Jerry couldn't stand any more family reunion and he said, "Excuse me, but we need to know where the monkeys are, and we need to know now."

Without the proper background the question was absurd and Smart laughed. "A fine question," he said. "I believe the urban sprawl has wiped them out. Try looking a little more deeply into the bush."

With that he appeared to be about to turn back into the darkness but Pamela stopped him. "We mean the monkeys in the cages," she said. "We have an urgent meeting that was to take place there."

"Ah," said Smart. He looked at Pamela keenly and then he said, "Very well, step inside."

Once the green door was closed, the visitors could see a sheet-metal hallway veering sharply to the left and down. There was light, of a sort, coming up from the end of the hallway and Smart walked toward it without speaking, letting them follow along. Jerry was so amazed at the place that he momentarily forgot the urgency of his mission and the lateness of his arrival to fulfill it. He was behind the green door walking deeply into some kind of den. Surely those other doors could not all have been real.

When they got to the end of the hallway they entered a room where kerosene lamps made the metal sides of things look soft.

"We've built this place between two green doors," said Smart. "The monkeys are outside the other one."

The room where they stood was not the room in which Smart had been sleeping. In its far corner was another hallway, but along the nearest wall were several doors of ordinary size. Jerry rather hoped that Smart would say something about how he had managed to carve a metal house into the middle of the marketplace, but Smart led them across the oddly angled room and up the other hallway, a two-minute walk to the next outside door.

"The monkeys are just here," he said, "you can't miss them."

"Oh brodder, thank you," said Louis, and Jerry, too, shook the man's hand.

When they stepped through this green door, however, they weren't standing on another path but in the back of some kind of shop, in a room all a-clutter with machine parts. They had to walk through the shop in order to get outside, and when Jerry looked back he saw that the shop's front was made of canvas. A wooden sign sewn to it read, "SMART'S APPLIANCES. REFRIGERATORS AND WASHERS FOR SALE."

At the spot where they stood the market was quite different, extremely busy, but in a vague way familiar to Jerry. He was sure it was to this spot that he'd come on the U.S. Embassy tour. Here men were pedaling through the crowds with boxes of audiotapes on their bikes; here, too, directly across from Smart's was a tribal doctor, a medicine man, sunk down on his stool but surrounded by vials and smoke; and here, just to their left, were the monkeys, most of them looking at Jerry as if upset with him for being so late.

"I don't see Lee," Jerry said.

"I know the face of his contac' man," said Parker. "Lemme walk a bit. Maybe he will see me in de crowd."

Parker took off, so Jerry and Pamela and Louis and Nurudeen stood near the monkeys and waited. These monkeys were forlorn things, more pitiful than the parrots had been. In some cases their cages were so small that they looked wrapped in the wire. Some of them were bleeding and all of them had a dull cast about their eyes.

Nurudeen was upset by what he saw and Jerry wanted to ask whether the monkeys were sold as pets or as food, but when he looked at Pamela all she said was, "I haven't been down here since I was a girl."

Jerry could not believe that Lee wouldn't wait, however

late he might be. It was Lee's job to see him safely out of the country, not to ensure that he was always on time. But when Parker came back he was alone. "I don' know," he said, "but Lee's no fool. Maybe he's sittin' tight somehow."

The monkey section took up more space than Jerry thought it would, and when Parker spoke Jerry got the idea that he should walk around the monkeys too, letting himself be seen. Pamela went with him.

Opposite the monkeys there was seafood for sale; in the nearest stall the long thin body of a shark stretched out in the dirt. It was a seven-foot hammerhead and the cold dryness of it brought Jerry back to the absurdity and danger of the situation he was in.

They circled the monkeys twice, but they were approached by no one suggesting Lee. "Goddamn him," Jerry said. When he spoke it was a whisper, but it drew the attention of the nearest monkey, a frail little thing slumped at the bottom of his cage.

They waited longer, of course, hoping to meet someone who would tell them what they should do, but finally Louis said, "Only Smart can help us now." Jerry would have stayed until the sun went down, but Pamela coaxed him away, having him look past the hopeless monkeys, through the forest of wires to where the dead hammerhead shark still lay. "It's too late," she said. "We've arrived too late once again."

Jerry saw a piece of newspaper stuck between the monkey cages and he pulled it out. It said December 4. He looked at his watch to confirm that today was in fact the twenty-fourth, the day before Christmas. Maybe they would have to go to Smart for help but he believed that, for a time, at least, he could come back outside whenever he liked, walking around the monkeys with impunity, hoping to find someone who knew how to get to Ghana, someone, even, who represented Lee Logar and who was willing to take him there.

Smart wasn't a Smith-Jones, and Louis wasn't either. But Smart's Appliances had been around since before Nigerian independence, and Smart once believed that the ultra-British quality of such a name would endear him to the colonizers and make his business a success. During those years all he'd wanted was to sell refrigerators and washing machines, to make a living off the people who ran things.

But the appliance business had not succeeded, and by the mid-1960s Smart expanded, first into musical instruments, later into the publishing of small pamphlets and books, the poetry and essays of Nigerians whose work could not find favor elsewhere. Thus the walls of Smart's house were made of metal stripped from old appliances, the vents from the bodies of accordions and the reamed-out throats of clarinets, and the seams and scars covered with the pages of works he had published but not sold, Hausa poetry and ageless fables from Ibo land.

For a time Smart's publishing efforts had garnered him a quiet sort of fame; for a time this odd house had served as a meeting place for artists and intellectuals of all sorts. In recent years, however, that had all died down. The natural audience for his efforts had been the common man, and the common man, these days, not only had no money for such things, but seemed to have a shrinking inclination for them as well.

When Jerry and the others stepped back into the appliance shop and opened, once again, that second green door, Parker said, "If there is a phone we could ring up this Lee, tell 'im to come one more time."

But Jerry, when he saw that he was standing in a room carved from old refrigerator parts, had no more patience for any of that. The question of whether Parker was really working for Lee or not could be answered by whether or not Jerry would be allowed to walk back up the other hallway, back out to Pamela's car, and have Louis drive him to the U.S. Embassy where he would stay. He had decided he would do that, but when he mentioned it, Pamela said, "That only works for political crimes," and thus he had to stop and think again.

Pamela sat next to Jerry on an enamel bench, while Louis began opening the side doors, looking for Smart. "Hello, brodder," he called. "Oh Smart, come out now, we need you here."

There were three doors along the wall and Louis didn't find his brother until he'd opened the third. When Smart did come out, Elwood, his young steward, came with him.

"Bring morning chop," Smart told the boy, "don' waste time," and when Elwood left, Smart listened while Louis explained what was going on and why they were back in his living room in this uninvited way. When he had finished Smart looked at Jerry. "What do you want from me?" he asked. "Help leaving the country or help clearing your name while you stay?"

It was a pivotal question and one Jerry could have answered better if he knew where he stood with these folks, but in the end he decided to answer honestly. "Help leaving the country, I think," he said, "or getting in touch with my contact man again. I will try to clear my name from Ghana or the U.S.A."

Smart laughed and shook his head. "Name clearing can't often take place in absentia," he said.

Smart was a thick-shouldered man, physically a lot like Sunday and Lawrence Biko. His dark-framed glasses were like Sunday's too, and his laugh was as explosive. But Jerry didn't want the unsolicited opinion and he said, "If you were in my place you would stay, I suppose."

He hadn't wanted to sound confrontational, but he let it stand, and Smart, instead of replying in kind, spoke softly. "It is not your place to worry about Nigeria," he said, "of course I understand that."

Elwood came back with the food, white bread and sticks of suya meat, and while they were eating Smart spoke again. "I have been to America and I have been to England," he said. "I was a student in England, but in America I traveled about, seeing the places where Africans live. Would you like to hear about it?"

Jerry had been very hungry and his mouth was full, but when he said that he would, Smart continued. "I visited Harlem and Watts and Philadelphia, which were all fine, but an interesting thing happened when I was there. Though I was in America for six long months I did not have a single conversation with a white man. Not one conversation. Doesn't that seem strange?"

"Yes it does," said Jerry. He had swallowed hard and was looking around for something to drink. "Why didn't you want to speak with white men?" he asked.

"It was their decision, not mine," Smart said. "In the beginning I had no idea that I would not be speaking to white men, but after a time I realized that white men were not speaking to me. And when I began to pay attention to it I came to the decision that I would not speak first, that I would wait and see what happened. That was my American experiment, to see how long such a thing could go on."

"But if you were in Harlem and Watts maybe there weren't many white men around," Jerry said, and Pamela agreed. "When I was there I spoke to white people all the time," she said.

Smart looked at Pamela pleasantly. "I stayed in Harlem and Watts but I was not confined to those places. And when I say white people did not speak to me I am, of course, referring to conversation. White officials spoke to me at airports. I sometimes purchased tickets from white people at museums and such."

Louis had gone away with Elwood, but Parker had been listening to the conversation and he nodded, leaning in. "I just now realize dat dis man here is de firs' white man I spoke to in a conversational way." He was pointing at Jerry and he added, "We are not countin' hellos and de like, are we, Smart?"

Jerry looked at Parker, but then Pamela said, "I'm sure it's all a matter of circumstance, Smart—I don't think it means a thing."

"But of course it means something," said Smart. "It means that it is possible for men to avoid each other. If for six months, then surely for any amount of time. If in America, then why not here?"

Jerry wanted to get back to his own situation again, but instead he said, "Americans come in many colors. And they have conversations all the time."

He had tried to give his voice a tone of finality, but the others were engaged by then.

"Maybe so," said Parker, "but de Africans in America was slaves and de real Africans is free people over here. Maybe de used-to-be slaves don't know how to have conversations with a white man. Maybe dey only think dey are having conversations. And if dat's de case it don't comply with de rules of conversation. It is only answering questions, or something like that."

Elwood and Louis had come back and Jerry stood up, looking at Parker. "Do you think, then, that Lee Logar doesn't have conversations with me?" he asked. "Does your experience with Lee tell you that he doesn't converse with white men well, that he only answers questions and by doing so thinks he is conversing?" He was irritated but he was also trying to use the moment to find out how much Parker was willing to say about Lee. It was absurd, but he still had no idea at all whether or not Parker even knew the man.

But Parker was careful again and only said, "Maybe Lee de exception which proves de rule. And who knows, maybe Lee is fooling his own self. I know from my years in de confidence game that if a man don' fool his own self once in a while he can' be fool by another."

Parker's answer was cool and it made the others smile. After that Smart said, "I brought it up only to say that you are the first white American with whom I have spoken in such a conversational and personal way. I thought it was strange since I have been to America, that is all."

It was after one p.m. by the time the meal was done, and when Elwood cleared the plates away he and Louis and Parker took Nurudeen out into the market for a walk. It was at that moment that Jerry first felt startled in another way. A comment had returned to him, something Pamela had said during the meal, an echo that would not fade away. "I'm sure it's all a matter of circumstance, Smart. I don't think it means a thing."

If Pamela had not met the man before, then why had she spoken to him in that way? Why was she being so familiar?

Smart was watching Jerry carefully and had leaned forward in his chair. Jerry felt sure that Smart had guessed his thoughts and would speak of Pamela himself, but instead Smart asked, "Have you ever noticed how most of Nigeria is broken down? I mean systematically—the banking system, the power authority, the government ministries. Is the breakdown of this country something you have noticed during your time with us?"

"Of course it is," said Jerry. "My problems all started with the Ministry of Internal Affairs. . . ."

But Smart interrupted him, waving a hand. "For the moment let's not talk about your problems," he said. "I am trying to ask you something else. Have you ever noticed what great trouble Nigeria is in?"

Jerry was surprised by the shortness in Smart's tone and he said, "It might be better if I left now. I want to go to my embassy and try to find my way with them."

But Smart only laughed, saying, "It amazes me, my friend, to realize that you still do not understand that the activity you've blundered into isn't criminal, not some plot hatched by the powers that be. Open your eyes, take a look at the country in which you've chosen to live and make your fortune."

Jerry's lips were thick, his tongue too numb to answer. He could only manage to say, "I have no idea what you're talking about."

"Then I will spell it out for you," Smart said softly. "The current government is about to come down. Everyone knows it, and many people also know that there are at least two military factions planning coups. But for all its ineptitude and corruption, this current government is still a civilian one, which means it was elected, and since there is definitely going to be a change, the people you are with now hope that the change itself will be a civilian one. What I mean to say is this: if we get there first, and do it correctly, perhaps we will have a chance of holding the military at bay for a while, of trying civilian rule again."

While Smart had been speaking Pamela had moved away, taking up only a small space on the enamel bench, but when Jerry said, "What has any of this got to do with me?" Smart lost his patience, sighing deeply. "I'm sorry, Pam," he said, "but you tell him. I'm not having a lot of luck here."

For a moment Jerry was indignant. Did Smart think that Pamela understood things any better than he did? But when Pamela said, "You *are* a bastard, Smart," he stopped thinking that.

Pamela put a hand on his arm. "I'm sorry, Jerry, but I do know a little something more than I have said. If you'd care to listen there will be no more secrets after this."

Jerry wrapped his knuckles around the edge of the bench, bitterly upset, but very quickly it was Pamela's turn to put a little edge in her voice.

"Stop that now," she said. "We are fighting for our country here and in the end you'll be fine. Just listen for a while.

Don't make one of those famous decisions of yours without understanding all the facts."

"What about your son?" Jerry asked. "What about Parker and Louis? Is everybody in on this?"

Pamela held up a hand. "Nurudeen's role in this is finished," she said, "but though the part about his father and I being estranged is true, our estrangement has not hindered my dedication to this project of his, the one that you are now beginning to understand. Nurudeen's father, as a matter of fact, is at the heart of it."

Jerry was speechless yet at the same time he was telling himself that he had known it all along. He wanted to protest, he wanted to shout, but he simply sat there like a tongue-tied dummy, catatonic amid the swirl of images in his head. After a long moment had passed, Smart sighed and said that since Jerry wasn't speaking he'd try to help things along by taking Jerry's part. He then looked at Pamela and said, "But why are you doing this? Why are you going to all the trouble of involving me?" He tried using an American accent, but Pamela didn't welcome his humor so he dropped it.

"You can't seriously not know why," said Pamela, touching Jerry's sleeve as if it had been he who'd spoken. "The plot against you is so transparent that we were sure the truth would come out in court no matter what idiot you got for a judge. You would be easily acquitted but it would look like the government was behind it, don't you see? And as this government's credibility crumbled one last and very public time, the leaders of our group would stage their coup. You were chosen because you provided us with good timing and because we had access to the school. All we needed was a widely publicized last straw and you were it. Your Mr. Biko, by the way, was beginning to get wind of us. That's another reason we thought you might try to run away."

"But what about the military?" Smart asked. "How would you keep them at bay?" This time he had pulled a hand inside his sleeve and moved it in the air as if it were the mouth of a puppet.

"That is the beauty of it," Pamela said. "We have already extracted the promise of a year from the senior officers, some of whom believe in civilian rule too. If, after a year, Nigeria is not on the road to prosperity and unity, and if corruption isn't curbed, then the military can come in and we will step aside."

Though Jerry had been unresponsive, he had been listening and he suddenly sat up straight. "So when Lee and I decided that I should run away it messed everything up. For me to run meant my innocence couldn't be proved and you wouldn't have your last straw."

"Bravo!" said Smart, and Pamela said, "With you out of the country we could only be sure of adjournment after adjournment. All our planning would have gone for naught. Luckily enough we have the sympathy of Lee Logar's driver, so we knew what he was up to all along."

So this was it, the final truth. Pamela and Smart were in cahoots with Nurudeen's dad, and Lee Logar, who had no clear idea of any of it, had not been involved with his escape plan at all.

"But if the current government is so bad, then why not catch them up on something they have actually done?" Jerry said. "It seems to me that they aren't the guilty ones here, you are!"

"It is a bit ironic," said Smart, "I'll give you that. But the government's corruption is so deep that to catch them up on something they have not done adds a little poetic justice, and we want justice of all kinds."

"Who's in charge?" Jerry asked. "Who's the boss of all of this? Surely not Nurudeen's dad."

"It's a coalition," said Pamela, "but as I've said I'm afraid my ex-husband is at the head of it. If anyone in Nigeria can pull this off, he can."

Jerry thought of Nurudeen's dad standing so regally in his

office. He could not abide the man but he simply said, "I don't even know his name."

"It's a name that will launch a thousand ships," Smart said, but Pamela waved her hand. "His family name is Abubakar," she said. "His given name, however, is such a travesty that everyone calls him Beany."

Jerry said, "Beany Abubakar," then said, "It's a stupid-sounding name." He had meant to be insulting but he only succeeded in making Smart laugh. "I know what you mean," Smart said, "but I've always thought it sounded rather American."

By the time they finished talking it was late afternoon. The others had come back, passing in and out of the room in quiet embarrassment, knowing that Jerry now knew everything. Everyone ate again at six, and after that Smart told Jerry to rest, that they would be going out that night and that it would be necessary for him to go along. Parker and Louis were sent to sleep up at the tops of the two tunnels, like guards, and Smart retired to his private room. Since Parker and Louis had taken Nurudeen home, only Jerry and Pamela remained in the main room, and they stretched out on mattresses, a little distance from each other, on the hard tin floor.

Jerry really understood, then, that anything was possible in this world. It even occurred to him that he might be dying soon, joining Charlotte on her perch, sitting up there. And it was then that he did the strangest thing. At the moment that the image of Charlotte came to him, when her face was most clearly in mind, he reached across the short expanse between them and put his hand on Pamela's cheek. He did it without premeditation, yet the completed act of it froze him, distressing him more, even, than the events of the day had done. How could he still want her after all she had done?

Pamela turned her head toward him, and when she did so

he removed his hand. That was all. He wanted to speak then, but he hadn't the slightest idea what to say. He felt moved but he did not know why. Pamela's interest in him was purely a matter of her dedication to her ex-husband's plan, any fool could see that, yet Jerry understood that he wasn't any fool, but a very specific kind.

Miraculously, however, though it was far earlier than usual for him, Jerry slept. And while he slept he dreamed that Charlotte was there, sitting on that enamel washing-machine bench in Smart's main room.

"I didn't see you come in," Jerry said to her.

Charlotte was wearing shorts and the printed top of an old favorite dress, and that made Jerry pause. Either she had cut the dress off, or she had tucked it down into those shorts, a situation that would account for the unsightly bulkiness of her hips and thighs.

"I've been here all along," Charlotte said. "Things are certainly more interesting than they used to be."

Jerry felt a tightness in his chest. All these years his longing for Charlotte had been great, but however much he'd wished it, he had rarely dreamed of her. Now that she was here, however, the awful countenance of her dress made him keep his distance.

"Wait a second," he said. "Who are you really? Tell the truth now, I'm tired of lies."

But before Charlotte could speak, Jerry understood that once again it was Marge, and that realization plunged him into a deeper despair than any he felt from the complications of his real life. "Goddamn it, Marge," he said, and he was suddenly across the room, standing at the enamel bench. He took Marge by the neck and shook her until the violence of the shaking woke him up. It was sometime after midnight and Marge had turned into Louis, who was kneeling at his side.

"Come," said Louis. "We must be quiet and obey."

Louis had Parker with him but it was left to Jerry to wake Pamela, to pass the message on.

Elwood gave them coffee and the others trooped about, but it took Jerry a moment to shake that awful dream. And then, as was the case with every dream he'd ever had, it was so completely gone that he would never remember it at all.

They left Smart's hideout very shortly after that, and when they did so Smart put a hand on Jerry's shoulder. "You and Pamela ride with me," he said. "Louis and Parker have their own work to do."

They walked up the front tunnel and unlocked the back door of the appliance shop. When they reached the monkeys, there was an excited stirring, small faces pressed to wires, small eyes following their movement as they passed.

At the edge of the outside street they stepped into two waiting taxis, dark yellow Peugeots but with Smart's men behind the wheels, and when the doors were closed the taxis drove away, not turning on their lights until they hit a main road.

The taxis moved through the back Lagos streets, weaving their way past the ever-present police checks, young soldiers with machine guns sleeping at the side of the road, and finally onto Ikoyi Island, taking only twenty minutes to get to the parking lot of the Ikoyi Hotel. Smart told Jerry and Pamela to wait with the driver, then he got out and walked through the hotel lobby with Parker and Louis, who had emerged from the other cab. Was this, Jerry wondered, his best chance to escape? Could he not step out the door and simply run into the surrounding night? But the driver had his eyes on him in the rearview mirror, so he looked down and sat still. And though he sensed that Pamela would speak, in the end she, too, let the quiet surround them, taking up all the remaining space in the car.

They sat that way for half an hour until Louis finally came out. He wasn't hurrying, and he opened the front door of the cab, getting all the way in before turning to face them. "Everybody's waitin' in room 512," he said. "Les go see what they want."

Jerry got into the hotel elevator, and once the elevator's doors were closed and the noisy thing began its climb he turned to Louis and said, "What should I do, Louis? Should I meet with these people, should I follow you along, or should I take my chance now and get away?"

It would be easy to run. Louis Smith-Jones, though thirty years younger than Jerry, was a small man and Pamela would only try to stop him with words. He could simply get off on a lower floor, run down a stairway, then find his way out of the building and into the night. There would be a marine guard at the embassy and once inside he would stay there. He could act on his own behalf now, all he had to do was push the elevator button.

But Louis seemed to read it all and said, "Oga, please, give de evening its one chance," and that somehow stayed Jerry's hand, though the elevator moved past each floor in a slow and surreal way.

The elevator stopped on the fifth floor but the door opened only about halfway before sighing and stopping, making the three of them walk out single file. Louis tried to close the door, and then he tried to push it all the way open, but it stayed where it was, unmoving, oblivious to the call button, which they could all hear impatiently buzzing, five stories below.

Room 512 was down a long hallway and as they walked over the worn carpet Jerry took up the rear. He imagined dropping away, stepping into one of the other rooms and out of this thing, but when they got to room 512 Louis opened the door too quickly to satisfy Jerry's sense of the dramatic, and Pamela ushered him inside.

"Ah," said Smart. He then told Louis to stay outside, to knock if anyone came down the hall.

As Louis closed the door again Jerry looked around. The room was larger than he'd thought it would be, and it was cleaner. The wallpaper was faded, but its rose pattern was still visible, though the seams had parted here and there to let the bare wall through. There were two beds in the room and there was a round table with chairs. Smart was in one of the chairs and Parker was in the other, leaning against an ivory-handled walking stick. Pamela had gone over to stand against the bathroom door, and on the second bed sat a man whom Jerry didn't know. This man wore jeans and a T-shirt. He was athletic-looking though he wasn't young, and Jerry believed that he was somebody's bodyguard.

"What now?" Jerry asked.

With one exception these were all people he knew, and suddenly Jerry understood that nothing would come of their plans for a coup and that, very likely, the only victim would be him. No one had answered his question, but before he could speak again, noises came from the bathroom and Pamela was jolted from her place against its door.

"Ouch," she said, and as she stepped out of the way Nurudeen's father came into the room, glowering around and focusing on Jerry Neal. Parker stood out of the chair, quickly handing the man his cane. When he had it he leaned against it hard, as if it were truly necessary for walking.

"Nigeria is failing on all fronts," he said. "We have brought you here to try to convince you to stand trial with enthusiasm, to join us in what we are trying to accomplish for our land."

Jerry laughed, imagining himself smiling from the dock. He didn't like this man, but at least the conversation was direct. "Here I am," he said. "Looks like I'll stand trial whether I'm enthusiastic about it or not."

"Let me try again," said Nurudeen's dad. "We want you to take an active part in proving how absurd the charges are. We want you to put your best energy into it until it becomes transparent how corrupt a government must be if it has to stoop to such stupid tricks."

Jerry sat down on the edge of the nearest bed and spoke quietly. "I really think that there is every possibility I will be found guilty and sent to prison. I think, in fact, that the only outcome of all your efforts is likely to be that. Why would I not take an active part in trying to see that it doesn't happen?"

Nurudeen's father glanced at Smart and Pamela and then took his weight off the cane, folding it under his arm like a baton. "We want more than that," he said. "We want you to join us in condemning the current regime. Is that clear enough? We want your help. You were not chosen as randomly as you suspect. You have a reputation at your school for being hard but fair, a reputation for good discipline, and we want that reputation for ourselves. Our countrymen need pluralism, respect, and involvement from all sides, and we're going to give it to them."

Jerry had been prepared to speak sarcastically, but he did get some small satisfaction in listening to Nurudeen's father speaking to him that way, as though, for once, he were an equal. He even suspected, somewhere in the distant reaches of his mind, that he might have hoped for their success had they approached him in an honorable way, without all this trickery. As it was, of course, he was only biding his time, understanding the enemy so that he could better defeat him when the time came.

Smart, however, seemed to view Jerry's thoughtful pause as consideration and he said, "No, listen. If we had not set that fire it would have happened sooner or later anyway, and they would have gotten away with it, just as corrupt officials always do. But to bring you into it brings in the outside world, which is precisely what we need to allow us to move. And if we succeed then we will admit this small duplicity later, that much we promise, though most Nigerians won't believe us even when we say it."

Jerry had intended to remain cool, but he turned on Smart, raising his voice. "Small duplicity? You call it small when you have committed such acts as these? What about the secretary? What about what you've done to my life?" He remembered the slow-moving elevator and the chance he'd had to escape, to be away from these people and on his own, and he held up his hands, as if surrendering everything he'd just said. If he got another chance he wouldn't pass it up, so there was nothing to be gained by speaking so directly.

He looked at Pamela. "Anyway, this is it?" he asked. "After this there are no more surprises?"

Pamela nodded, but at that moment Nurudeen's father spoke again.

"Do not ask the tail what the head is thinking," he said. It was such a stunning remark. Jerry was about to say, "I am asking the person that I think most trustworthy," but he quickly thought better of it, saying instead, "All right, I'm asking you." It would have felt good to speak curtly in the face of such astounding arrogance, but he did not want to cut himself off from any information. And up until now he hadn't had a single thought that he'd kept to himself. He'd have to remedy that.

Nurudeen's father's expression was drawn across his face like a machete slash on the side of a coconut. "Look at it this way," he said. "The military, four or five army generals to be precise, is about to stage a coup d'état. If that happens things will be predictable. The new ruling generals will announce that civilian elections will be held after stability has been achieved, say in five or six years. During the tenure of their administration there will then be a series of other coup attempts, and if any of these attempts succeed then another announcement of civilian elections will be made, for some date even further down the line. In other words, if there is a military coup it will be years, perhaps decades, before we can try democracy again. We are attempting to avoid all

that. Believe me, I know these generals and I have their ear.
Maybe we have made mistakes, but the heart of the matter
is as I've just stated it, and it is a good heart."

Nurudeen's father's coconut face was pained by the vision
of how long it would be before civilians ran the country
again and he stopped speaking for a moment. He then offhandedly added, "Surely you realize by now that Nigeria is
really nothing like the West."

It was a surprising comment, and one that made Jerry suddenly see that, despite what he thought he knew, there was
still a gap. Maybe they could succeed. He really didn't understand the man or the country or the situation at all. Smart,
however, took away the chance for him to bridge that gap by
speaking practically again.

"The agreement we have with those generals really is a re-
liable one. Even they want civilian rule to work if Beany is
in charge. So if we can stage our coup during your trial, the
army will give us one good year, and by that time we will
have the best men everywhere—I'm talking about the ones
who are truly corruption-free, the ones with Beany's idea of
discipline within them.

"And so your trial is pivotal," Nurudeen's dad continued.
"To have an outsider involved was a dangerous idea all
along, but one we had to try. The international press will
now be on hand, don't you see? The international community will now take an interest in what is going on. And if we
can proceed correctly, then the military boys will have more
reason than ever to remember their promise because the
whole world will be watching them."

Jerry wanted to say that he didn't think the whole world
gave a damn, that he was sure, in fact, that his trial would
get only slight notice in the American press, but he held his
tongue. And since everyone else did too, the meeting seemed
to be coming to an end. After a moment Nurudeen's dad
looked at his bodyguard and said, "Phone down now. Tell
them I will be along."

Though no one had called him, Louis opened the outside

door just then, and Nurudeen's father walked halfway to it before stopping in front of Jerry Neal.

"No doubt you feel used," he said sadly, "but we had hoped you would take the long view, perhaps even understand it as some kind of privilege, a chance to expand yourself, broaden your horizons, so to speak."

"Some privilege," Jerry said.

Nurudeen's father was quiet for a time, standing there leaning against his cane. He then said, "I wanted to play a part in this myself; that is why I allowed my younger son to become involved, that is why I came to your school, and that is why I ordered his mother to visit you as she did. I believed that an American, full of the democratic tradition, would be moved by what we are trying to do, by such a long shot, by such grand nerve."

"But you didn't ask me," said Jerry. "All you did was set me up."

Nurudeen's father nodded and said, "It is certainly true that you have to open your eyes wide if you are ever to see what is before you here. I guess that must be it."

Smart was standing too, and both men were about to pass through the door when Jerry once again saw the form of the minister's secretary in his mind's eye, her swollen face, her body partially covered by those forlorn little pieces of cardboard. He said, "If I don't do it no one is going to talk about the secretary, isn't that right?"

"Her death was an accident," said Smart. "When the fire began she was asleep at her desk. Who would think that she would fail to awaken, what with the alarms and the sound of the flames. . . ."

Was that enough for them? To say that it was an accident, to say that her sloth had caused her death? Jerry looked at Parker and Pamela. Surely one of them shared his outrage, his opinion that what had been said was not nearly enough. But though he looked at them he couldn't read them. Pamela's face was bemused, and Parker seemed not to have been listening at all.

Nurudeen's father was at the door, but he turned fully around. Jerry was sure that he was on the verge of mentioning the woman, on the verge, perhaps, of saying something profound, but after a long moment he turned back again and passed through the doorway, out of sight and into the hall, Smart and his bodyguard soon joining him there.

Louis ran ahead then, to get the elevator, but Jerry knew that the elevator would not be impressed by what had gone on. In the elevator, at least, Nurudeen's father would get a slow ride. And though it was clear that they looked at things differently, Jerry could not help believing that the secretary would be riding down in the elevator with the man, that she would accompany him, in fact, everywhere he went. At first Jerry liked that thought a good deal. Later, however, he didn't get any pleasure from it at all.

It was daybreak by the time they got back to Smart's place, with its silly refrigerator walls. Smart's "gang," as Jerry thought of them, seemed now more like his family, a tired group of people who wanted only to find their dank room and sleep.

"I've told Elwood to awaken us at noon," Smart said. He then went into his private room and closed the door. It was left to Parker and Louis to sleep at the tops of the metal hallways again, to raise the alarm should anyone try to enter or leave.

"Nurudeen's at home alone," said Pamela. "I really need to go to him."

"It is morning," Jerry told her. "It seems to me that if there was danger it would have come at night."

The mats they'd used earlier were as they had left them, one here, one over there, an arm's reach away. Jerry sat down on one of them and removed his shoes. He'd been wearing the same clothing for three days, but that, somehow, hadn't bothered him much. When he thought of his shower and his solitary meals with Jules standing by his side he couldn't concentrate, as if those activities were a part of a dream or a past life that had ended long ago. He thought of Charlotte for a moment but he quickly left her alone as well. To think of her now seemed foreign and uncomfortable.

Pamela stood in the dim room playing with her car keys and watching Jerry stretch out. "It's been a long night," she said. "There has been a lot to take in."

"Tell me how you could have married such a man," Jerry said. "He's too old for you and he is too strange."

"He is Nigerian," Pamela said.

She spoke as if such a statement answered everything but Jerry asked, "How long were you together?"

"We were never together, really." Pamela came over and knelt on the mat. "He is not a Western man, nor does he pretend to be, but he is a great man, and he could be great for Nigeria if this thing works. He is not corrupt, he has dignity and honor, but he isn't Western, that's all."

"You are still tied to him then?" Jerry asked, and Pamela shrugged. "My house in Anthony Village belongs to him. Nurudeen's school fees and my study in America were paid by him. When he comes to the house occasionally I am always there."

Jerry wanted it to be beyond him to understand how such a smart and beautiful woman could involve herself in something like this, but the truth was he could picture her easily now, waiting for Nurudeen's dad, perhaps asleep and hearing his key in the door.

Jerry reached over and took Pamela's car keys from her. He put the keys on the floor beside him and then took off his shirt and placed it over them. He could not see Pamela's expression but when he sat up a little and reached over to touch her he could feel an exhaling and a movement in his direction. His fingers worked the buttons of her blouse well, as if they belonged to another, and when the blouse was open and her dark shape was there, he moved up next to her and felt her breasts against the exposed skin of his chest. Though it felt wonderful, however, it did not feel right. It felt, after all, like a bleak kind of payment, and it was suddenly beyond Jerry to continue, to go further with the idea.

Pamela, with her clothing removed, came onto the mat next to him, settling first on her side, facing him. She had not read his mood and asked, "Are you doing this only because Nurudeen's father can?"

Her face was inches from his own, her eyes nocturnal.

Jerry touched her breast again, feeling the nipple rise, and thinking, momentarily, that he might try, until he noticed the reaction of his own body, which was soft where it should have been hard, uninvolved from his chest to the tops of his knees. The idea that he would want this woman because Nurudeen's father could have her sat in his mind like a tumor.

Though Pamela misread it all, she nevertheless tried to come to his aid by saying, "Perhaps it is only because it has been too long."

Her voice was matter-of-fact, but after she said it she made no move for her clothing, as Jerry feared she might. Instead she came closer, aligning her body evenly with his, as if settled in for the night.

Jerry was immensely pleased with that and felt something good filling his chest. He felt it in his lower back too, and then in his legs and finally in the binding muscles of his neck and shoulders. He did not feel it in his groin, but Pamela's steady breathing told him that she knew he wouldn't find it there, even with such closeness, at least not now, at least not this time, and he thought, what a good woman she is after all.

When they finally slept it was six a.m., though real sleep came only to Pamela, with Jerry waking often, to lift the sheet that covered her and let a shaft of dim light shoot down across her breasts and belly. It was strange, but what he felt as he looked at her was not desire, nor even a sense of wonder at being where he had never been before. What he felt was rather a kind of detached curiosity, an unencumbered focusing of attention, and a great pleasure too, though he understood perfectly well that this was the final portion of Pamela's job. After having coaxed him and cajoled him and straightened his spine, she had now been ordered to fold her legs around him in order to give him a wonderful reason not to want to leave. And somehow Jerry knew that in his understanding of all of that and in his refusal to do it, he had wiped the slate clean. He believed that Pamela knew it too and he had the clear idea that, if things were only different, he and Pamela would surely be able to start again.

Jerry stayed that way, awake and watching Pamela, until around nine, when he slipped from the bed and soundlessly got back into his clothes. Pamela had woven the web around him that Beany had assumed he would be unable to break. Yet while she slept he did break it, walking up the hallway and past the sleeping figure of Louis, who was dead to the world but a little back from the door. Jerry had Pamela's car keys with him. He held them tightly because he did not want them to make a sound, and because the feel of them digging into his hand kept him alert, intent on finally getting away, and kept his fatigue at bay. It was Christmas morning, 1983, and he was about to save himself, though Beany Abubakar and the people sleeping down below would have him believe that, with his help, they could save their whole world.

PANEL NUMBER TWO

February 25, 1984, a.m.

Though he was expected in a week, the artist did not come back to the school until over two weeks had passed, by which time the first panel had been viewed by everyone and was covered by a thin Plexiglas sheet, something the school board said would protect it, but which also made it hard to see.

The second panel was delivered on a Saturday. The artist came alone in his truck but found Joseph and his crew and asked them to help him unload it and secure it to the wall. Luckily, the crew was on hand. It was the morning of the school's main fund-raising event, the annual auction, so they were preparing the central courtyard. The artist too would come again that night to pound out panel number three in public, thus bringing his obligation to the school to an end.

This second panel was larger than the first; though less active it was broader in scope. After that hectic beginning the artist needed the extra space to accent some of the nuances of the story, its softer middle, the stranger manifestations of its asides. He wasn't unhappy with panel number one, but he thought of it as essentially a foreign tale, an entry, while the second panel seemed truly African, unembarrassed by its Nigerian center, unflinching in the things it told.

135

Since the artist had promised that by the night of the auction all three panels would be done, he ran home in order to
get ready to come back that night, and when he was gone Joseph's crew stood looking. They all agreed that it was easier
to look at this second panel, not only because it was larger
than the first, but because it was not yet under glass.

By the time the woman and the boy arrived, the custodi-
ans had finished their work and were resting in the shade,
watching as the woman and the boy stood in front of the
second panel, listening while the woman looked at the boy,
asking him what he thought.

"It is all too difficult," he said. "I don't like it very much."

The woman then said that she thought the second panel
looked vulnerable next to the first, but really not difficult at
all. Although neither the boy nor the maintenance crew understood what she meant by that, the boy nodded, staring at
the panel again. He wanted to accommodate his mother in
this, but he didn't know how. In the second panel everything
seemed in congress—at least he might have said that. But he
really didn't like such things very much, so though he kept
his head fixed in an attentive pose, what he was actually
doing was watching his mother, out of the corner of his eye,
as she absorbed herself in the artist's version, so primitive yet
so modern, of what had taken place when the story took its
African turn.

One

Christmas Day, 1983

Pamela's Peugeot wouldn't start, so Jerry Neal sat in it, listening to the engine try to turn over, in front of a growing number of interested passersby. He turned the key and watched the gauges and turned the key again, but though the battery seemed strong and the fuel tank was full, the car wouldn't start.

It was a hot morning, the Peugeot was already an oven, and Jerry could see smoke coming from the mountain of garbage that sat behind him. He put his head in his hands and rested his elbows on the steering wheel. He then rolled the window down and looked at those who stood there looking at him. There were perhaps twenty of them now and they were all men. Jerry could see that they did not know him, that they had no expectations at all.

"Excuse please, Oga," said a voice.

He had been so intently concentrating on the driver's side of the car that he'd ignored those standing to his right, but it suddenly came to him that this thin voice had been calling to him for some time. Jerry thought for a moment that he'd get out and run, but then he sat back and prepared himself, hoping only that when he turned his head he would not find

137

someone holding a newspaper up, pointing at his passport picture on the front page.

"Excuse please, Oga, but you forget sometin' small," said the voice. "In our everyday haste sometime such forgetting takes place."

The closed car window kept the voice distant, but the face was familiar, and in a moment Jerry realized that it was the ironing-board boy, who was cupping his hands to see in.

Jerry opened the passenger door.

"Get in," he said, "hurry up about it."

The boy was surprised, but happy with the prospect. He quickly jumped in and closed the door, saying, "You will laugh when I say, Oga, but you forget de immobilizer. Dis Peugeot got one underneath de floor mat on you own side."

It was true. Jerry's car had an immobilizer too, a device meant to slow thieves down. When he took the key from the ignition he saw a smaller key on the ring next to it, and when he pushed the rubber floor mat aside he was able to quickly disengage the immobilizer, and just as quickly start the car.

The ironing-board boy was delighted. "Nevermin', Oga," he said. "Once in a time every man forget like dis. Even myself, I do that."

Jerry had been careful leaving Smart's hideout and it had not been easy. He'd had to summon the will to break away from Pamela, to take his life into his own hands once again. It had been his first purposeful act since all of this began, but now, only moments later, he was sitting in Pamela's Peugeot with the ironing-board boy, slowed by a device designed to slow thieves. And before he could move again the back door opened and Pamela got in. She looked at the ironing-board boy and smiled. "Hello, Bramwell," she said.

"Hello, Miss," said the ironing-board boy.

It is at times like these that men don't know whether vertigo is a physical or a mental thing, whether the world truly turns, or whether the turning is in a delicate balance thrown awry, the inner ear on strike against the absurdity of the words it hears. Jerry held the steering wheel and pinched his eyes shut, but when he opened them again she was still there, smiling slightly in the rearview mirror. She shrugged when she saw the look on his face. "It *is* his name," she said. "If you don't like it blame his father."

Jerry's mind flipped like his inner ear had just done, but he suddenly understood something without having to be told. This ironing-board boy was another one of Beany's sons, Nurudeen's older half-brother by another mom.

The car had somehow put itself into gear so Jerry let out the clutch, giving them a slow roll away from the other parked Peugeots, down the rutted path to a roundabout that would get them back up on the highway again.

"Where are we going?" Pamela asked. "I gather nothing you heard last night made you want to stay?"

To have smooth pavement under the car was reassuring, and for the moment Jerry didn't answer. To be above Lagos like this, coasting along in the morning traffic, made him breathe easier. Harmattan had diminished since last he'd noticed. The tops of buildings were sharp against the sky.

When he looked at the boy next to him he somehow saw, now, as if the magic of his name had done it, an altered boy, a boy with better posture and more intelligence in his face than the ironing-board boy had had. "Well, Bramwell," Jerry said, "where do you keep coming up with these ironing boards?"

Bramwell smiled. "I buy them in the market," he said. "I get them for around eighteen naira each."

Jerry nodded. He knew he had paid too much. He thought of Sunday and then of Jules, ironing away on a board that was too high. "I don't know what I thought of what I heard last night," he finally said, looking, again, at Pamela, "but I am going home and take a shower. I want a change of clothes."

"Good idea," said Pamela. "With Christmas at hand no one will be around."

Jerry knew that was true. The flats would be empty and the entire school property would have that quiet feeling that he liked so much. He had changed lanes and was approaching the school cutoff when Pamela said, "But let me direct

you to another place first. I have ordered you a Christmas
gift but it is too cumbersome for me to carry, so I left it with
its maker."

Jerry felt stung. If Pamela was lying then nothing had
changed since the night before, the catharsis he had had
while lodged against her sleeping body had been a totally private one and it had been wrong. He wanted her to have feelings for him as a man, not just as a pawn in Beany's plan. But
he also knew, of course, that she was twenty years his junior,
so why would she look at him with anything other than a
calculating eye? No, he would drive to the school, drive past
the security guard, and go into his flat for a shower and a
change of clothing. After that he would go to the American
ambassador's house, where he would demand an audience
with the ambassador himself. But of course it was Christmas
Day and likely that the ambassador was out of town. Everyone left Lagos over the holidays. What if there was no one
for him to see? Even Lee Logar could be gone.

Pamela said, "I know you don't believe me, you don't think
I have a Christmas gift waiting for you, but I do. It is something
I had commissioned, and it does not involve Beany or any of
these others, but is from me alone. It's a very long drive, but it's
safer there than in Lagos. Why not take a chance?"

Jerry knew there would be no gift, didn't he? He knew, of
course, that she would only direct him into some further
complication, to another obscure hotel, perhaps, or to someone else's underground house. Pamela was a smart and
charming woman but she had the disease of the others, she
believed that because Nurudeen's father was at its head, this
ridiculous coup idea, this wildly improbable scheme, had
some chance of success, and Jerry felt she would say anything
to keep him tied to it. That was true, wasn't it? She would
do that, would she not?

Jerry looked at Bramwell. "What do you think of your father's plan?" he asked. "Do you think a new Nigeria will
spring from such a group as his?"

Though there was too much sarcasm in Jerry's tone,

Bramwell answered sincerely. "I do believe it, sir," he said. "My father is a great man. Every Nigerian knows it. Nigeria can be a wonderful place under him and I believe that he will easily succeed."

The boy spoke softly, moving his hands in front of him in the cooling air, and Jerry looked at Pamela again.

"Is he a great man, Pamela? Most boys think their fathers are great, but do you think so too?"

Pamela gave Jerry a wry smile but then answered just as well as Bramwell had, and with the same calmness, the same quiet tone. "Of course I believe it," she said. "Why else would I be involved? We took you to the hotel last night because we were all quite sure that you would begin to see it too. That you did not is our biggest surprise so far. That his greatness isn't obvious to everyone, however, is a good lesson for us to have learned."

Jerry slowed the car as he headed across the Marina toward Victoria Island. He remembered the events of the night before as well as anyone and what he remembered was that he had been in the presence of idle talk and vanity, the kind of weak intellectualism that he'd always disliked and easily put down. Perhaps Nurudeen's father had spoken well, but Jerry saw him only as a man of words.

Jerry looked at Pamela and slowly said, "What if you are inventing this Christmas gift of mine? What if you are making it up right now, what then?"

"If there is no Christmas gift, that would be the last straw," she said. "If there is no Christmas gift you will know that I am not sincere, you will know that I am hollow and that my admiration for you is a sham. If there is no Christmas gift you may dismiss me after that."

Jerry drove on for a while but he was too pleased with the words Pamela had used to continue. He stopped the car and turned to ask Pamela which road would lead him to the place where the gift was waiting.

"It will take some hours," she said, "and we are going in the wrong direction even now."

The gift was near Onitsha, a provincial town in the east, and by the time they reached Benin City, three hours had passed and Bramwell was asleep. Though Jerry marveled at the distance they had gone, he thought of the trip as a Christmas cleansing, and he did not begrudge the decision he had made. Pamela had said she had admiration for him, and he had to believe that that was true. Also since he was driving, he was in control and could always turn around.

Onitsha was a market town on the far side of the Niger River. A huge and decrepit bridge took them into the town, but Pamela directed them right back out of it again, along a lonely road at the base of a shallow hill. "It isn't far," she said. "Everything, now, will be close at hand."

They had been quiet for most of the trip and were quiet again, until Pamela found the gate she was looking for. This gate was unpainted and orange rust ran down from its top like an orange map of Africa. The number 11 was painted in the orange, but the number was poorly done and looked rather like two trees scorched by fire. The gate had been built against the edge of the road and when Pamela reached over and sounded the horn, Jerry jumped, looking into the rearview mirror for traffic coming from behind.

No one responded to the horn, but Bramwell was awakened by it, so he got out to pound on the gate with his hand. He then reached through a hole and opened the gate from the inside, closing it again after Jerry drove through.

This was an odd estate, with a grim and woodsy yard.

When Jerry and Pamela got out of the car, Bramwell stepped back. A thin man was standing at the base of a nearby palm tree. He had a hard and owlish expression on his face, but when Pamela said, "Oh good, LeRoY, come meet Jerry Neal," the man's demeanor changed. He approached laughing, his right hand way out in front of him.

"Good day, Jerry Neal," he said. "Good day and welcome!"

The man's exuberance was a pleasant surprise, and his smile transformed him. "I've been working jus' now," he said. He pointed over the top of the car toward the front door of a highly peaked and whitewashed house. His name was stenciled on both sides of the door. LeRoY BaLoGuN. Every other letter was capitalized, and when Jerry went over to look at it LeRoY said, "I understand the pure affectation of such a thing, but I like it, don't you? It makes my name look like a difficult journey with success at its end."

Jerry smiled but took a moment to look around before following LeRoY inside. There were rusted farm tools on the porch of this house, with live chickens walking carefully around them. At the side of the yard there was an old car, orange like the gate, and under the palm tree was a card table and two broken chairs.

LeRoY was not only thin, but he was also bald, with only a little white fuzz above his ears. Jerry thought he was perhaps sixty-five, though he seemed to have the energy of a younger man. LeRoY wore dark glasses and he wasn't a very tall man, the top of his head coming just to the area of Jerry's chest.

"Pamela tells me that you are interested in Nigerian art," LeRoY said. "If that is so then this is a good spot for you to have come."

"I like masks," Jerry said. It was the truth, but he was surprised at having said so.

"Ah yes, masks," said LeRoY BaLoGuN, "Nigeria's great disguise."

LeRoY led them into the house and then into a large,

well-lit room with high ceilings. He said that there were six such rooms in the house, though what could be seen from the hallway was only the mazelike passage between them.

"This is my workshop," LeRoY said. "Let me show you the work that I do."

LeRoY BaLoGuN's name was stenciled all around the walls of his workshop, an ostentatious display. Jerry really felt that if a man's name ballooned before others it should be from deeds done, not from its physical presence on walls, but he nevertheless liked the man. He tried to think of his own name written like that—JeRrY NeAl—but it didn't lend itself to the effort the way LeRoY's did. LeRoY's name looked staunch and successful, while JeRrY's was suspicious and squeezed together. It seemed to change him into WrY Al, and he didn't like that at all.

In LeRoY's workshop there were several long tables, with more workbenches lined against the wall.

"I began as a painter," LeRoY said, "but I soon wandered into sculpture, and then into all these copper panels that I do now. In them I can find the thrill I got from painting, but I get to build things as well. It's the construction of it that I like, for then your work has depth. You can look into its valleys and up at its peaks."

LeRoY's voice was softer in his workshop than it had been outside, and it somehow made Jerry say, "You speak good English. Did you learn it in the U.S.A.?"

It was a strange thing to have said, and he surprised himself by saying it. Bramwell, however, saved him from embarrassment by asking LeRoY a question about a drawing on the table nearest them.

"I guess this is the beginning," Bramwell said. "Next must come the depth, is that right?"

"Oh yes," LeRoY said. "Wen de dep' come den we go understan' more 'bout de serious business o life. Before de dep' dem can know only de shallow aspec', but life be deep, Brammy, das de point o art. Das de point o dep' too."

Jerry had certainly not meant to offend the man with his

comment on the good quality of his English. Now, though, he was beginning to feel offended himself, and he said, "What's wrong with thinking that you studied abroad?" He had assumed that most Nigerians were proud of it and he said so.

"Of course they are," said LeRoY. "And somehow that is integral to everything we are going through right now. If a man always looks to others, then his eyes will forever be turned away."

LeRoY paused a moment, but then chuckled and looked hard at Bramwell. "My God, Brammy, das it," he said. "When you daddy come les tell 'im. Is like pidjin become Nigeria an standard English de outside worl'. Les' make 'im for speak dat point in 'is firs' speech, make 'im speak in pidgin, Brammy, set de proper tone-o."

LeRoY's face was lively, the energy in his eyes pouring through his glasses and bouncing around the room. "I go fin' paper," he said. "Make dem sketch while dis be fresh in my min'. Is rich, Brammy. Always don' forget, de simple idea be de bes' idea. I know in art das true."

LeRoY put a hand on Jerry's arm and squeezed it. Then he was off to the far end of his studio. Jerry watched him go and then looked at Pamela. "Where the hell is my Christmas present?" he said.

Pamela led Jerry and Bramwell down the long corridor of the house, but she didn't stop to visit any of the other artists who might have been working there. Rather, she took them out back where another building stood. This building was low and narrow, with many doors facing out. "Here is where they all sleep," she said.

The building reminded Jerry of the one Jules lived in in Moroko. He knew from where he stood that these doors led to single rooms, that only a few were connected by internal doorways, forming double rooms for extended families.

"I love it here," Pamela said. "I love the work they do, the mood of the place when they do it."

Jerry asked how many artists lived in the house and how she had found them in the first place, but as soon as he asked it he shook himself loose from such a comradely question. He still had to try to contain himself, to be concerned with what to do next. He had agreed to come for his Christmas gift, so far as he could tell, for three good reasons. First, because to discover that there was no gift would, in a bad sort of way, finally set him free, and second because he had suddenly got the idea that the police would be waiting for him in his flat, ready to rush him back to jail before he could take his shower. He was beginning to understand, however, that the third reason had to do with Bramwell, with the shock of seeing the ironing-board boy transformed into a real person before his eyes. When he looked at Bramwell now he could see individual features, a friendly face, intelligent eyes, but had he been asked to, he could not have described the ironing-board boy at all. In his mind's eye the ironing-board boy was featureless, a mask, as much represented by the warped tops of his ironing boards as by eyes and a nose and a mouth.

Jerry was about to grasp it, about to understand something, when Pamela answered his questions, bringing him away again. "I don't quite know how many artists there are," she said, "and we were brought here first by Beany, of course, by Nurudeen and Bramwell's dad."

They had walked to the middle of the yard, and as Pamela spoke she pointed to the low bench, suggesting that they sit a while. Jerry, however, was still looking at Bramwell. "If I ask you where you studied will you stop speaking well?" he asked.

"I was first at St. Savior's, then at King's College, then in the U.K.," said the boy. "Maybe Nurudeen will go there too."

If Bramwell was that much older than Nurudeen, then he was ready to enter the university, and Jerry pointedly asked if he would do that abroad.

"If my father is successful I will stay here, study in Nigeria, help to make things right," he said.

Jerry thought he knew that if Bramwell's father's plans were unsuccessful there was little chance that he would study anywhere, but for the moment he wanted to hear Bramwell talk, to better understand how he felt about his father. He was about to speak again when a tall man came out of the main house and walked off to the side where there was a stack of short logs piled under a tree. These logs were thick but the man moved them around easily, choosing one near the stack's middle, then tucking it under his arm and starting back the way he had come. He put the log down in order to open the door again, picking the loose bark from his clothing.

Now that the man's shirt was clean he seemed not to want to wrap his arms around the log again, and the log was too heavy for him to hold at arm's length. There was a screen door too, and though the main back door stayed open, the screen door wanted to swing shut on its spring. Jerry couldn't remember having seen a screen door in Africa before, but the way it had banged shut when the man came out had startled him, taking him all the way back to summers in Oregon, where screen doors banged all the time.

Pamela said, "Let's give him a hand," and when they walked over to the man, she held the screen door while Jerry and Bramwell helped him bully the log through the door and into his workshop. They put the log up on a long table, letting it roll into a worn groove.

Though the man had seemed large before, he now looked thin and muscular, like the laborers and janitors at the school. He was bald, like LeRoY BaLoGuN, but where LeRoY had a smile that changed him completely, this man's mouth fell naturally down. His room was smaller than LeRoY's, but it was as busy. Wood sculptures stood along the floor and hanging on the walls were several chain saws, gas operated and rusty as the outside gate.

Pamela spoke with a scolding tone in her voice. "This is it, isn't it, Ben?" she said. She pointed to the log they had just carried in. "It was today you were supposed to finish but it is today that you are going to begin."

Pamela turned to Jerry. "There it is," she said. "Inside that log somewhere is your Christmas gift."

Though Pamela was upset, Jerry felt pleased. There really was a Christmas gift; she hadn't lied. He wondered when she had arranged the gift, and he worried that perhaps she truly hadn't done it on her own, but he said, "I don't mind waiting, either here or in Lagos if it takes too long."

Jerry took a closer look at the finished sculptures that stood at the edges of the room. Some were like totem poles, some trees of life, while others looked like traffic accidents in the Lagos night, abstract tragedies that made something inside him ache. They were all quite fine and he wanted one of his own.

The artist watched him as he looked, finally saying, "I like to split my wood roughly so that the early cuts are accidental. Like the Europeans did when chopping up Africa. I like to echo that in my work."

This was political art, and as Jerry looked at it he imagined a chain saw making its cuts, pieces falling out, chips flying away. Most of the finished work was highly abstract. Some of it looked vaguely human, but the one he was most drawn to resembled the roots of a tree, as if the roots were in the log and the artist's job was only to expose them, to cut away the surrounding wood until the roots were visible again.

Jerry looked at the uncut log on the table. "When will mine be done?" he asked, but before the man could answer LeRoY stuck his head into the room.

"It's time for dinner," he said. Pamela and Bramwell left the room quickly then, but Jerry stayed a while with Ben. He wanted to examine the log, but he was also disturbed by the fact that when LeRoY had spoken, he had thought, for an instant, that it was Jules. And his first impulse had been to scold, to say that dinner could wait and that Jules could wait too, standing by the dining table in the other room.

It was time for dinner all right, but it wasn't served as Jules would have served it. Since the whole house was given over to artists' workshops, there was no proper kitchen, so they all followed LeRoY out the front gate and onto the country road again.

By this time it had grown utterly dark. There wasn't a Christmas moon, and once the gate was closed there were no lights coming from the compound. They could hear a chain saw, though, starting out loud and then lowering its voice as it burped into the uncut wood.

"Eating here is haphazard under any circumstances," LeRoY said, "but this is an occasion. When we have guests we try to do it well."

LeRoY was walking fast, and Pamela took Jerry's sleeve, pulling him into the darkness in front of Bramwell, who took up the rear. "I forgot my torch," LeRoY said, but in a minute they saw candlelight coming from the side of the road, the wider glow of a camp lantern at the bottom of a gentle hill. There was a building there too, with an awning and a few tables in front of it. Off to the side was the firefly flicker of a neighborhood, small lights here and there, like tears in the black blanket of a sky.

"This is the People's Canteen," said LeRoY, "and there, behind it, is Beany's own home village, the one he came out of to put things right."

By the time they had descended to the People's Canteen, they could see quite well. And though it had been quiet on the road, music was now easy to hear, a poorly recorded kind of Afro-pop coming from the single speaker of a tape player.

Beneath the People's Canteen awning, next to a scarred old chalkboard with the menu written on it, a couple of tables had been pushed together. Two men and two women sat at the tables, and three more women, employees of the People's Canteen, were swaying around, sashaying in a kind of embarrassed greeting, in time to the music that they heard. There were other customers too, peering in from tables difficult to see, dotting the dirt at the edges of the awning and off into the dark.

"It was either here or the Club One," LeRoY said. "They are eating fish at the Club One tonight."

At the People's Canteen they were eating chicken-and-pepper soup, and those waiting at their table had already ordered for everybody. Three of the other artists from the house were there as well as an ancient-looking woman from the nearby town.

Once they were seated LeRoY ordered beer, calling out the names of Nigerian beers as if he were bidding on something at an auction. "Gulder, Star, Harp, Gold." Pamela ordered a shandy for herself and for Bramwell a Coke. The old woman held a glass of palm wine in her hand.

When the drinks came the waitress opened everyone's beer, then placed the caps back on the bottles to guard against flies getting in, and as she did so Jerry looked at those sitting around him at the table. One man was a painter and another worked with bronze, he had been told that much. The only woman among them was a fabric dyer, a worker in batiks, who was dressed wonderfully well, her beautiful face smiling out from under a headwrap of indigos and blue. But what else? Were these the country's leading artists sitting here, and were they somehow attached to Beany and his plan? And what was there about this strange Christmas Day that continued to keep Jerry at odds with his own plan to pick up his Christmas gift and then get away?

Jerry was seated next to the old woman, whom no one had

introduced, but who nevertheless sat easily among them, her hands wrapped around that palm wine glass. Pamela and the fabric dyer were sitting on her other side. They were both beautiful women, both young and well poised. Jerry was terribly drawn to Pamela, but he liked the look of this fabric dyer too. The old woman, however, was a visual roadblock between them, and seeing her made him think about the passage of time. He was fifty-seven, Charlotte was long dead, and these young women would become like this old one in the bat of an eye.

Jerry wondered if the old woman had once been beautiful. Her eyes were wide and clear even now, but her skin, though smooth about her forehead and nose, was so wrinkled around her cheeks and chin that she looked like two women stuck together, an old one and a younger one mixed, age creeping up from below. Also her hair seemed planted backward, black at its roots but white where the strands all met to form a frosty forest at the top.

"I've never tried palm wine," Jerry said. He had leaned over and was trying to speak to the old woman. "I've seen men tapping the trees but I've never tasted the stuff myself."

When he spoke the woman let her eyes rest on him in an incurious way. "Are you my brother?" she asked.

Pamela, who was closest on the woman's other side, put a hand on her arm. "No, dear," she said, "this man is white. Your brothers are all black."

LeRoY, who was on his left, touched Jerry's arm the way Pamela had the woman's. "She likes to sit quietly," he said, "it is best to let her do it."

"But who is she?" Jerry asked, and though the fabric dyer was three seats away, it was she who answered his question. "This is the great man's mother," she said, "Bramwell's grandmom. Nurudeen's too."

LeRoY had wanted the meal to be an occasion, but the old woman's presence was making everything tentative. It was she who owned the house in which they all worked, but she didn't live there and she rarely came to the People's Can-

teen, so they didn't see her often. She had another house in
the village and she liked to stay there better, to hold a kind
of crazy court in front of the house, to receive her son there
whenever he came to call.

"I have a son who will lead Nigeria one day," the woman
told Jerry. "Do you know him?"

Jerry said that he did, but just then the food came and
soon thereafter the music got louder, so it was difficult to
talk. When the beer was finished LeRoY ordered more, and
when Jerry's food was only about half gone the fabric dyer
surprised him greatly by coming around behind him and asking him to dance. He had a mouth full of chicken but he
looked around. "I don't see any place to dance," he said.

The fabric dyer pointed to a space over by the People's
Canteen's main door. Someone had placed a piece of lino-
leum down on the dirt there, an American-style kitchen
floor. "With music like this I can't sit still," she said.

Jerry had been enjoying his food and didn't want to let it
get cold, but he nevertheless soon found himself standing
and actually walking away with this girl, who was swaying
like the waitresses, the indigo bunch of her skirt already
rhythmic as she walked.

Had Jerry been asked to do so, he would have called the
music they were dancing to "reggae," but in truth it was not.
The specific tune was called the "Lagos Jump," and it probably belonged under the general musical heading of High
Life. It was an up-tempo, cheerful tune, and at the chorus,
which was "Lagos, Lagos jump!" Jerry found himself following the fabric dyer up into the air in a kind of hop. Soon the
bronze man was on his feet with Pamela, Lagos-jumping his
way over to the kitchen floor, and soon after that other
Lagos-jumpers came out of the shadows, men and women
from the village, perhaps, or from Onitsha, which was only
a few miles away.

Jerry was amazed at himself but quickly came to believe
that dancing made his troubles, the real difficulty of his life,
seem distant, and he understood that as much as anything he

needed a psychological break, a hiatus from the constant worry of his recent days. Just as quickly, however, he began to tire and to jump badly, a gangly kind of North American jump. And as he got worse, the fabric dyer got better. He could see her body moving under her dress like a tongue inside a cheek, her round parts coming out and then receding, showing themselves and then falling back again.

The old woman came onto the dance floor by herself. She wasn't jumping, but began coasting among the dancers, her clear eyes and smooth forehead bobbing up and down. Perhaps Jerry was affected by the fabric dyer's body beneath her dress or by constantly dwelling on Pamela, but the sagging portion of the old woman's face, her sloshing jowls and chin, soon began coming up over the smooth parts, and he was reminded of the head of a penis, covered and uncovered by the folds of its foreskin. Even her hair, dark at its roots the way it was, seemed in favor of it, accepting her head in a pubic sort of way and making Jerry turn away in wild embarrassment.

Mercifully, the song ended then. The fabric dyer fell briefly against Jerry's chest, then pushed herself away. "You are a good Lagos-jumper," she said. "When I asked you I was certain that you would refuse."

Jerry wanted to speak to her pleasantly, but the old woman was quickly next to them, surprising them both by placing a hand over the fabric dyer's where it rested on Jerry's arm. She pulled herself up and blew a steady stream of air onto Jerry's face and neck. Her eyes were contorted when she blew, and the fabric dyer jumped back out of the way of the older woman's wind.

Jerry was suddenly so sure that this old woman knew the thoughts he'd had about the look of her face and head that he began to apologize, though the image was so bizarre that he could barely acknowledge having had it himself. But just then another song started, this time real reggae, and the old woman suddenly floated off again. As soon as she was gone the fabric dyer—Sondra was her name—reclaimed Jerry's arm. She smiled up at him nervously and said, "I think she was trying to make you disappear."

Pamela and the bronze man had already resumed dancing. This time, since the tune was slow, the dancers touched, and as Jerry watched the bronze man put his arm around Pamela, he felt the fabric dyer, he felt Sondra, put her arms around him. "Perhaps I will make you a shirt," she said. She then leaned into him and they were quiet for the remaining three or four minutes of the song.

Back at the table the pepper soup was cold, but the chicken was still tasty, so Jerry continued eating while the others listened to the old woman talk in a language he couldn't understand.

Jerry felt a little proprietary about Pamela. The bronze man had changed chairs after the dance, was now sitting next to Pamela where Sondra had previously been. LeRoY was in Jerry's old chair, presumably so that he could listen to the old woman, and Jerry was in LeRoY's chair, with Sondra now on his other side. It was complicated, but since Sondra was the only Nigerian too far away from the conversation to join in, Jerry tried to talk to her. He nodded toward the old woman. "If she's Beany's mother why is she living here?" he asked. "Why isn't she living in Lagos with her son?"

Sondra gave him a look that said, "Who would want to live in Lagos if they could live here?" but what she finally did say was a good deal more interesting than that. "This is her home," she said, "and she lives here like a queen. She is the juju mistress of the entire region—everyone comes to her with their problems."

Juju mistress? Jerry thought. He had not forgotten the complicated problems of his own life, but to be sitting here watching a juju mistress argue with a bunch of artists had its own draw, and he remembered the fetishes he had bought, those strange things hanging from the walls of his flat like

stale works of art. He was eating pepper soup and seeing penis heads dance about, and these two women, first Pamela
and now Sondra, seemed to have captured a certain
unexercised portion of his brain.

"I would like to see your work before I go," he told
Sondra, but Sondra held a hand up, shushing him so that she
could hear what was being said. "They are now discussing
the color of your skin," she said.

It was hard for Jerry to allow that there was any "they" in
the discussion. The old woman had been holding court.
Sondra, however, began letting him know what was going
on.

"This is how it started," she said. "She claims that when
she came up to us during our dance she wasn't making you
disappear, but trying to do you a favor by altering the color
of your skin. She is upset now because we all thought her intent was malicious when it was not, and she is saying that we
don't want to see your color changed because we enjoy looking down on you. LeRoY's telling her that's absurd and Pam
is saying that in America it is the dark-skinned people who
are looked down upon."

Just then the old woman laughed and the others stopped
talking, turning to look at him carefully. The old woman's
jowls moved a little and a sound came out. "She wants to
know whether you would like it or whether you would not?"
Sondra said.

"Like what?" Jerry asked.

There was a pause but this time it was Pamela who spoke.
She leaned toward him and smiled and casually said, "She is
offering to turn you into a black man. If you would truly like
her to, that is. She says it will make your days easier, that it
will improve your life."

"I think she's right," said LeRoY.

Jerry looked at the old woman. "Thanks," he slowly said.
He had meant to say "Thanks but I'm fine the way I am," or
"Thanks but I think I'll pass," but he had paused too long
and the old woman thought he was finished.

"Very well then," she said in good English. "But it cannot be done as I attempted tonight. Tomorrow I will come to the house and we will do it properly."

She stood then, holding her hand between herself and Jerry as if commanding him not to speak. She told Bramwell to come with her and the two of them stepped into the shadows and were gone.

To himself Jerry said, "Holy shit." Along with everything else he certainly was not about to get involved with Beany's mom, but all he said to the quiet group was, "I had meant to decline."

A waitress took two of the chairs away and the rest of them slid close together, but they were subdued now. The bronze man was frowning deeply and LeRoY was too. Pamela's expression hadn't changed much but when Sondra began speaking again, chattering really, it was in a way that Jerry felt was meant to do something like give him courage in the face of what tomorrow might bring.

In a moment, however, Jerry yawned and said that though the company had been good and the conversation interesting, he really did need to get some sleep.

"Ah," said Pamela, "my God, me too."

They all stood then, LeRoY signing something for the People's Canteen. On the road again, Pamela took one of Jerry's arms and Sondra the other. The men walked closely ahead, but were not visible, and when they got to the house they all walked through it and out the back door to the sleeping quarters without slowing down.

"Good night," Jerry said, but the others only nodded. Sondra and Pamela brought him to the door of a room and opened it for him, Pamela standing a little away but Sondra staying very close. He truly had been tired, but he began to wake up a little then. When the door was wide and he stepped into the room, however, Sondra stepped back and both women nodded at him, finally saying good night and closing the door.

The room was as dark as the road had been. Jerry had to

feel his way around to discover that there was no light and that the place was small and that there was a mat of some kind, and a blanket, on the floor. He tried waiting for his eyes to adjust, but the particles of light were too few.

Jerry sat on the mat and removed his clothing. His fingers could not find a pillow but he lay down anyway, pulling the blanket around him even while he wondered what it looked like and whether it was clean. There was nothing to see any-where. He thought of the old woman and held his hand be-fore his face and looked at it, but it was invisible too, as black, right then, as the surrounding night.

Jerry closed his eyes and tried to find something to watch inside his head. His hand was up there, balanced in front of his face, but it fell down and awakened him slightly when he settled into sleep.

When Jerry awoke it was midmorning and Charlotte was on his mind. He was surprised at how little he had thought of Charlotte over the last days. Before all his trouble began she'd been with him always, her photograph on his nightstand, her memory popping up unexpectedly, like something he'd forgotten to do. So why should he forget her now after remembering her for so long? Was it because in the early dark hours of Christmas morning he'd considered forswearing his celibacy with Pamela or because he'd been drawn to Sondra on Christmas night? He had always considered his celibacy a tribute to Charlotte, a badge of some kind, but now that he was in trouble, desire was finding a foothold in him. He had wanted two other women in the course of a single day. Where was his singlemindedness? Where was Charlotte when he most needed her by his side?

As Jerry sat in the small room thinking such thoughts, he noticed a dull light seeping from under the outside door. He could see, now, a low table with a candle on it, and he watched the hairy thickness of his arm as it touched the candle and then explored the table around the candle's base. He could see clothing hung from nails around the walls, a stack of books in the corner, the dark shapes of sketches taped here and there, an artist's idea remembered during the night and recorded by the light of this candle.

Jerry's fingers felt the smooth rectangular coolness of a lighter, a Zippo, he knew it instantly. He gave the lighter to his other hand and flipped it open with the sureness and simplicity of his teenage years, and as he heard that click the lighter lit and the room was all aquiver with the flame's dance, which he applied to the candle, whose wick seemed to reach a little toward it. This was the kind of sureness Jerry missed, the feeling that all the movements of the world could be contained in the opening of a lighter.

Now that the candle was lit he could see that the room was orderly. Though there was a chain-saw sculpture in one corner, Jerry immediately knew that this was LeRoY's room, the drawings on the wall told him that. They showed people in congress, leaning together as if blown by an even and democratic wind. To be sure, these were drawings of abstract people—their necks stretched ropelike off their shoulders, their knees bent backward at the angles of breaks—but they were orderly and attractive as well.

Jerry pinched his eyes, rubbing at the bridge of his nose. It was hard to look at such sketches in candlelight, but the sketches were everywhere, marching around the walls without a stopping or a starting place. It was as if the stories that the sketches told were circular, a never-ending idea that made him pause.

When Jerry finally blew the candle out it was afternoon, and when he opened the door the sun hit him through the spindly branches of a nearby mango tree. There was no more harmattan in the air, but the porch of the sleeping house seemed longer than it had the night before, with more rooms than he thought there could be. Now everything was visible in the outside air. There were old tools lying about, and a few more chickens, giving the place the feeling of a farm.

Though Jerry was surely the last one up, he could find no evidence of anyone else. Perhaps they were working inside the main building, but when he listened he could hear nothing of the industry of making art. Nevertheless, he was hungry; the food of the night before had not begun to fill him up, so he walked across the yard and opened the back door to the main house. He let the screen door bang behind him again, and when he did so two things happened: he remembered his summers in Oregon one more time and Sondra came out of the nearest room, the one across from the chain-saw man's.

"Ah, good," Sondra said. "You remembered that I wanted to show you some of my designs."

What Jerry thought he remembered Sondra saying was that she wanted to make him a shirt, but he smiled and said, "I seem to have overslept."

"What better activity for a Monday morning," said Sondra. "Start the week off as if it were the week's end, what could be better than that?"

"Where is everyone?" Jerry asked. "I don't see evidence of anyone working around here."

Instead of answering him, however, Sondra stepped away from her door and invited him inside. He realized when he saw the mess of the room that he had expected this one to be the neatest, but there were pots boiling on burners and many pieces of material hanging from lines. Jerry had to lower his head to follow her around, and when they got to the spot where Sondra wanted to stop, he was strangely out of breath. Though everything about the room was foreign to him it was made familiar and unpleasant by the smell, which was without question that of cooked cabbage, a smell he remembered from his youth.

"It's hard to see what the finished product will look like from this stage of things," Sondra said, "but you'll be surprised."

The odor was so oppressive and the hanging material so low down, that Jerry wanted to bolt, to get back at least as far as the hall, but Sondra drew him into the place, into a smaller room at the side. Here a small air conditioner coughed away, making Jerry feel better.

"Lord," he said, "how do you work in there?"

"Oh, it's quite easy," Sondra told him, but by then Jerry had begun to take stock of this new room. He turned in the center of it, amazed at what he saw.

"My God," he said and Sondra laughed. "My God, nawao," she said, imitating his surprise.

Sondra worked entirely in hues of indigo and blue. Each piece of dyed material was stretched on a frame, and the frames absolutely filled the room. The one nearest them seemed to depict the yawning blue mouth of a snapdragon, the colors of its throat deepening, nudging right up against black as they went down. It was a beautiful thing, open and enticing and it made Jerry want to step in. He tried to look at some others, indeed, he did look at them, but the snapdragon kept calling him and when he came back to stand before it for the third time Sondra said, "Very well, then, you have made your choice, and it is a good one. It is too sensual for a man like you but it is yours, my Christmas gift given to you before Pamela could give you hers."

Jerry was surprised at himself, but he absolutely loved the snapdragon, though of course there was plenty of evidence that it wasn't a snapdragon at all. Sondra was standing between Jerry and her gift to him and he noticed that the material of her dress, the same one she'd worn the night before, seemed an extension of the yawning snapdragon on the wall.

"But I don't have a gift for you," he said. "I don't have Christmas gifts for anyone this year."

"Come," said Sondra. She led him through the first room again, where the soggy stalactites still hung down. Though the night before Jerry had thought Sondra to be about Pamela's age, he believed now that she was younger, and when they stepped back into the hall he thanked her again. His first intention was give her a hug to let her know how much he liked the gift, his second to give her a fatherly little kiss, on the forehead or on the tip of the nose. But when he leaned forward Sondra leaned forward too. She was a tall girl and she didn't hesitate in moving her lips to where her forehead had been so that when Jerry got there her lips met his and his fatherly little kiss was soon deep.

When they parted Sondra's eyes were misty but her expression was self-assured. "That's what I love about American boys," she said. "They could teach these Nigerians a thing or two about kissing."

For his part Jerry laid a hand against the wall, hoping Sondra wouldn't notice the bending of his knees.

"Are you hungry?" she asked him. "I know I am. And I think this morning they've got something special in mind."

From inside Sondra's workshop the rest of the house had seemed inactive, but as they walked down the hall they were met not only by the sounds of working artists, but by the smell of freshly baked bread, which came from LeRoY's room.

"Good," Sondra said, "I was right." When they entered the room there was food on the table and good cheer everywhere, as if Christmas had come a day late.

"Ah, hello," LeRoY said. "Ah, good afternoon!"

Pamela was there, as was the bronze man and Bramwell and the painter. Jerry was pleased with the sense of occasion, though he somehow didn't want to show it. He looked at Pamela in a guilty way and said, "I guess I slept too long."

Pamela took his arm, leading him away from the doorway where Sondra still stood. "Never mind that," she said. "Last night we ate village food so today we're trying Western."

There was a wonderful loaf of thick bread on LeRoY's table, and though it was oddly shaped, its smell was unmistakable. The bronze man had somehow baked it in the same oven that he used for his bronze.

They tore the bread without further comment, but just as Jerry was tearing his piece away, the chain-saw man came through the door carrying a large bundle and followed by the old woman from the night before, Beany's juju mom, whose head still bobbed as she walked behind him.

The chain-saw man put his bundle down by the bread. This was to have been the central moment of the day, the presentation of Pamela's gift, but the old woman took everyone's attention away. She was wearing heavy black clothes and had a critical cast about her eyes that quickly made everyone subdued.

"I am late for having trouble finding all my ingredients," she said.

The old woman had a bundle too, a smaller one than the chain-saw man's, and when she put it down she began pulling at its knots, slowly drawing the strands apart. Jerry stepped up to her when she asked him to, but tentatively, and the bronze man tried to offer her some bread that she waved away.

Jerry wanted to do something to alter the change of emphasis, the swing away from the moment of Pamela's gift, but when he was next to her the old woman reached up and quickly pulled a fistful of hair out of his head. "Ouch!" he shouted. She had two dozen strands of his hair in her hand, and she laid them down in a small and shallow saucer, a juju petri dish.

Though the woman's bundle was untied, a flap of it still covered what was inside, and when she threw that flap back the reaction from the others made Jerry so nervous that he tried to step away. There was a thorn carving in the bundle. The carving was large as thorn carvings go, and it was of a man standing next to a table on which several bundles could be seen. Thorn carvings were everywhere in Nigeria—Jerry had a dozen of them in his flat—but in his carvings dark wood was used for people and blond wood for clothing. In this carving, however, the reverse was true; the skin of the man was blond and his coat and pants were carved darkly. He was a tall figure, gangly even, and he was peering down at the tabletop before him, just as Jerry was now. It was quite spooky. On the tabletop that the carved man looked at there was a smaller version of the same carving once again, with yet another blond-skinned man looking down at yet another tabletop. And as Jerry bent forward, to see how many replicas he could see, he got the idea that the carved men were bending forward too, in the progressively smaller versions before him.

Jerry was as astounded as everyone else. Though its intent made him nervous it was a wonderful carving, a terrific carving, and what he wanted to do was buy it. When he looked at the woman she was not, however, looking at him. Rather she was busy stacking material around the thorn carving's base.

"Now," she said softly. "Maybe you don' know it, but a man's hair contains all of the color of de whole worl', and dis one . . ."—she pointed at the carved figure and looked up at Jerry for a moment—"dis one represen' de all-alone white man always lookin' roun' out of his one pitiful face. Everywhere he look is de black world lookin' back at 'im, everyone he see is de black man walkin' by. . . ."

Though it had not been the night before, the woman's language was now easy for Jerry to follow. Also, the act of speaking to him seemed to soften her a bit. She was explicit, like one of the good teachers at his school.

"Look careful at dis man standin' here," she said. She pointed to the carving and waited until Jerry got close to it with his face. "Do you see here aroun' where de eyes is set? In dat part of de face de whiteness is mos' prominent, do you see how dat is true?"

Jerry peered at the eyes of the figure, whose face, aside from its white-wood skin, really looked like all the other thorn-carving faces he had seen, but quite suddenly the skin around the eyes did look lighter, as if the carver had lightly bleached it there. And as he looked he began to see crow's-feet coming from the corners of those eyes, giving the figure age. He remembered that his own crow's-feet were a part of him that Charlotte had always noticed and had not liked. She had sometimes even rubbed lotion there, with the idea that his wrinkles might diminish under the constant pressure of her hand.

"I see it," Jerry let the woman know.

"Dat is good," she said. While she had been speaking she'd been placing other items, all of them unrecognizable to Jerry, in the little pile around the thorn carving's base, and now she pulled the petri dish closer, laying Jerry's two dozen or so hairs on top of the pile. "Now I tol' you about how all de color of de world be lock into de hair of every man, but you don' really believe dat is true." She had completed whatever she was doing and had shifted her attention fully to Jerry.

"Turn aroun' one time," she said. "Look into de face of you' fellow man." She pointed at the others in the room, all of whom were dead serious and standing away. "Look at dem face, firs' de female face, den de male ones, an' don' hurry up. When you look at 'em, look at 'em deep, notice 'em, I mean, like you just finish noticing dis carving here."

Though Jerry was uncomfortable doing what the woman told him to do, he also found it quite beyond him to actually protest, so he simply let his gaze fall on the two women that he liked. Pamela and Sondra were leaning together, their heads touching at the temples, their eyes wide. The skin on both women was smooth, Sondra's more youthful, perhaps, but Pamela's covering a finer bone structure, a slightly more beautiful face. Sondra's expression, however, was readier than Pamela's, the muscles beneath her skin poised to more quickly respond to the outside world. She was more easily knowable than Pamela was, Jerry could see that now, she was readier to react, whereas Pamela was more judgmental, cautious, and more refined. The more he looked the more he saw. Sondra's cheekbones turned into a rounder smile, her entire face a seduction, while Pamela's carried the weight of her past and was more directly attached to her mind, her forehead expressing alternatives, the possible ways that things could go. And they were not the same color, the two women that he watched. Though both of them carried slightly reddish tints, Sondra's skin was darker, really a brown turning gray, like the last dusk of hazy day.

Minutes passed and Jerry eventually noticed that he was no longer looking at the women, but at the men. He could not remember altering his glance, but when he awoke to himself he understood that two of these men, LeRoY and, ironically, the bronze man, really did seem black to him. Both of them had tribal markings on their faces and, because of these, perhaps, their skin seemed impenetrable, not layered like the women's. The tribal markings, different one face to another, seemed like small ladders leading upward from the center of their faces, and Jerry imagined that the world sometimes climbed those ladders, ideas for art slipping over their cheekbones and into their eyes.

He turned to look at Bramwell but by that time the woman was calling him back, pleased that he had taken such care in following her instructions, but ready to get on with it as well. For his part Jerry was surprised. He could not have imagined, before, that the mere act of looking at people could offer such rewards. He still wasn't looking forward to the rest of the woman's act, but he had found a strange kind of solace in what, thus far, she had told him to do.

"Now here come de hard part," she said. "In de worl' a man can choose 'is color, jus' like he can choose 'is name. If a man carry de name Bolagi, for example, den people will look at 'im in one certain way. If he carry de name James den de look he get will be Jameslike, you understan'? It de same wit' everyting. Not only wit color but wit quality o voice an' strength of arm too."

The woman paused, perhaps she had finished, perhaps not, but Jerry discovered that he was involved again, following what she had been saying so closely that he thought he saw some truth in it, though when he tried to focus on that truth it went away.

The woman shook him slightly, pointing back down at the thorn carving and the pile of odd materials at its base.

"Do you have a match?" she asked, and without pausing Jerry pulled the Zippo lighter out of his pocket. Though he'd been unaware of it, he had taken the lighter from LeRoY's room and had been clutching it the whole time. He flipped it open and watched the flame dance up, smiling when he saw the old woman's surprise. Though he wanted to believe that everything he'd seen was a harmless exercise, he had found it terribly interesting, and he was pleased that when he held the lighter out to her she handled it gingerly, two fingers on its bottom, ready to flick it away if it felt too hot.

She held the lighter in one hand and put her other hand

on Jerry's elbow, pushing him around until he stood just like the thorn-carving man did, both of them looking down. Then she touched the Zippo to the edge of the table, about a foot from the carving but against a trail of what Jerry could only imagine was some kind of fuse. There was a sharp snapping sound while the flame shot across the table, and there was the mildest of explosions when it hit the main body of the bonfire she had built, leaping from the carving's base and engulfing the figure of the man and sending the putrid smell of burning hair into the room at the same time. Surely he imagined it, but Jerry thought he felt the sting of the flames too, and when he looked to the place where the sting was strongest he noticed the presence of a rash on his arm, unknown to him before, but thriving, from his elbow onto the back of his hand. He lost a little of his disbelief then and tried to step back to the edge of the room with the others.

The awful smell of the burning hair was accompanied by so much smoke that for a moment the figure on the table was difficult to see. But in a minute the old woman took the last item from her bundle, an African cap, and before things got worse she placed the cap over the entire fire, making everything die quickly down and, rather miraculously, making that putrid smell go away too. When she removed the cap she held her hand out to the thorn carving and everyone could see that, indeed, the carved man was now black.

"The body of a living man is larger than dis one, so wit you it will take longer," she said. After that she pulled Jerry toward her and put the smoky cap on his head and told him not to take it off.

The old woman packed up and left then, and when she was gone LeRoY went to the wall and turned on his air conditioner, sending a rattling sound into the room long before the cool air came. The others seemed relieved that she was gone, but they were still subdued, so Jerry used the time to go over next to LeRoY and put his arm against the air conditioner so that when the cool air did finally come it would flow across that newly discovered rash of his before jetting out into the room.

After Bramwell's grandmother left, the bread was passed around again, and then the bronze man brought in a course of eggs and rice, and by the time they had all finished eating, the pleasantness of their earlier mood had sufficiently returned for Pamela to bring Jerry back to the bundle that sat on the far edge of LeRoY's table, her Christmas gift to him, the original reason for their visit here.

"My arm really hurts," Jerry said. "Do you suppose I'm allergic to something that she put on that fire? It feels almost like a bee sting." As he spoke he tried to remove his cap, but everyone told him to leave it on.

Sondra took his arm, holding it up to the light. "Maybe it is a coincidence," she said, "maybe it's a bite." She pointed to a welt about midway between Jerry's wrist and elbow. The redness seemed to emanate from the welt and a certain swelling was evident directly under it.

For a small moment everyone looked for signs of red ants, but Jerry could feel the falseness of their search. The old woman had done something to him and he'd been stupid enough to let it happen. Now, on top of everything else, he'd probably have to find a doctor. Jerry was irritated, and a little worried, but pretty soon they were all grouped around the gift again, so he let his irritation go. The chain-saw man had worked through the night on Jerry's gift, but whoever had wrapped it had done a poor job. Most of the wrapping was newsprint, some of it an advertisement for Nigerian toilet tissue. Jerry could see the flat depiction of a blond baby girl staring up at him from the bottom of the gift.

Pamela put her hand on Jerry's sore arm, making him flinch. "Open it," she said. "I think that you will like what you find."

At first Jerry tried to untape the gift carefully but the taping job was too random for such intricate work. So in the end he tore the wrapping away, pausing only briefly to see whether or not there were articles about him in the newspapers that had been used.

Though Jerry had not understood it when he'd seen the chain-saw man start work on his gift the day before, the log he'd used was ebony and the darkness of the wood gleamed at him as the paper came loose in his hands. He had expected something rough, something that carried a chain saw's legacy, something, perhaps, like the redwood tabletops he remembered seeing in northern California when he and Charlotte took their yearly vacations, but what he got was nothing like that. What he got was nearly a filigree. The log had been hollowed out without breaking the continuity of its outside inch or two, and then that outside inch or two had been worked so finely, cut so beautifully, that Jerry thought it must have been done with the best and most intricate hand tools. He looked at the chain-saw man and then at Pamela and then back at the cuts in the wood. The ebony log had been worked into a tree of life, with men and animals carved so cleverly into it that they seemed to dance around like the figures on a carousel. There were men climbing toward the top and monkeys swinging from one cut to another with such realism that Jerry felt sure that the ebony would break the moment the monkeys released their hands. When he looked really closely at the figures he could see that the contours of their bodies were not smooth, but beveled, and he imagined a chain saw the size of scissors, the sounds of its motor muffled in the artist's big hands.

"This is wonderful," he said. He wanted to say something better, but he could not take his eyes off the tree of life, which seemed to him to depict what he was doing now, climbing toward the top, trying to get into the sunlight again.

"This is a terrific gift," Jerry finally said, and though it was Sondra who gave him the smile he wanted, Pamela nodded gravely, as if to say she knew it was.

By this time, though everyone had treated it as a special day, the day that Christmas should have been, the others seemed ready to get back to work. So Bramwell helped Pamela carry the tree of life while Jerry picked up the charred thorn carving on his way out of the room. Though the carving had been burned, it had looked solid enough, but as he stepped into the hallway it fell apart in his hands, its ash turning his arms really black, and small pieces of it falling to the floor. While Jerry bent to clean up the mess, LeRoY swept his tabletop, pushing the residue of the juju fire out the door after them.

Sondra and the chain-saw man were going along the hallway toward their respective rooms, and when Jerry paused, Sondra called to him. "I will bring you my gift before you go," she said. "I will take it from its frame."

Jerry looked at her and nodded, somehow not wanting to speak. But when Pamela and Bramwell went through the screen door, the banging of it shocked him again, this time not conjuring summers in America but making him stop anyway, as if there were something else that should have come to mind. This time the door's cracking sound seemed like a warning, and though he was completely at a loss as to what the warning might be, he could not take his eyes off his arm.

Though by late the next morning it looked as though the swelling on Jerry's arm had gone down, the redness and itching continued, so Pamela suggested that they walk into the village and try to find something that would take the itching away. There was a chemist's shop. Bramwell was going with them and knew where it was. Jerry wanted to mention going back to Lagos again, but he found it strangely easier to concentrate on his itching arm.

During the previous two days Jerry had marveled at Bramwell's metamorphosis, he had dwelled on it, and he was beginning, now, to find it impossible to remember Bramwell as the ironing-board boy at all. It was as if the ironing-board boy really had been someone else, a kind of Good Samaritan, a simple boy who had come to his aid when Pamela's Peugeot would not start and had then disappeared into the ambiance of the car.

The ironing-board boy had been a product of Bramwell's father's mind, a creation of Bramwell's own ingenuity and of Jerry's imagination too, but at fifty-seven years of age Jerry had to believe that he was not like Bramwell. At fifty-seven, surely long before that age, the real Jerry Neal had emerged and real life had been continually lived. Despite that belief, however, Bramwell had become a kind of metaphor for Jerry, making him think that there were other men within us all, alter egos knocking at the inner walls, a universe of ironing-board boys waiting to come out.

The day was hot but the sky and the air were clear when they started into town. They cut down a trail that turned behind the People's Canteen, letting Jerry see that the restaurant's backside abutted the crumbling clay back of another building.

"Ah yes," said Pamela, "this is the village school."

They walked to the front of the building, which was really one of three such buildings in a small compound. At the center of the compound was a dirt yard, one that Jerry imagined the students used for play and that made him think of the courtyard at the International School. This school, like his own, was closed for winter break, but when it became clear that there was activity in one of the rooms, Pamela took his arm and walked him over.

"This is the office," she said. "The man inside is the headmaster."

When Jerry looked through the window he saw a man in a dark suit working at a small desk. He at first supposed he would speak to the man, but as he stood there looking, he began to concentrate on his own reflection in the glass of the window. He still wore the old woman's African cap, but in addition to that his clothing looked slept in and his posture was bad. And when he looked down at his hands they seemed still covered with the ash of the burned thorn carving of the day before. How, then, could he speak to a fellow educator, telling him hello and that he was a principal too?

They stepped away from the headmaster's window and walked quickly around the school, looking into a half-dozen unpainted rooms, but by the time they left the school grounds Jerry felt so at odds with himself that he took hold of Pamela's sleeve, as if, like Scrooge, he were helplessly following the ghost of some other Christmastime.

They were in the village proper almost immediately after leaving the school, but since the pathways were twisted and the growth along them was lush, it was difficult to see very far ahead. As they walked, however, the kinds of buildings that they passed didn't change much. Most of them were small and facing the street, their sides made of brown clay, a material that looked like adobe but that had fallen down in places, exposing chicken wire. Jerry tried to see into some of the houses, but the interiors were invariably dark.

The village appeared to be built pinwheel-style, with paths meandering off a main square and intersecting haphazardly, like the twisting tails of snakes. There were children in the village, but Jerry was pleased that for once they did not seem interested in following him about or shouting at him like Lagos children often did.

When they got to the end of their path they found a tree with benches under it. Across from where they stood there was an asphalt road, one wide enough to accommodate a bus, but though this was without question the village square, apparently the center of things, it seemed as though they had just come from the center and were now standing at the edge. A man in a badly made suit was there, as were three well-dressed young women, all of whom seemed to be waiting for a bus.

Across the square next to the bus stop was the chemist's shop, though since the sign was down Pamela had to detect it by stepping over to see what items were inside. She seemed relieved and said, "We can get what we need for your arm. Perhaps we can buy something to drink and sit for a while under the tree as well."

Both Bramwell and Jerry felt thirsty then, but when they tried to follow Pamela back across the square the three styl-ishly dressed women stepped up to them and so did the man in the suit. This man was an albino, and his countenance frightened Jerry. He was like the man in the thorn carving, but he had no crow's-feet next to his eyes. "O brudder," said the man, "let dem chemist alone. I can fashion you symptom away wit dis what resides in my case."

"He can do dat, is true," said one of the girls.

Jerry had not intended to respond to the man, he'd had

more than enough magic with the grandmother, so he surprised himself by saying, "My arm itches. I just want to get
a lotion or something."

"Famous las' words," said the man. "Lemme see de arm in
question. Give it here."

The arm in question was Jerry's left, and when he held it
up the man grabbed it. "My, my," he said, "dis rash need one
quick treatment like de chemist don' have."

All three of the well-dressed girls were smiling at Jerry
now, and Pamela, who had come back to listen, smiled too.
The albino man saw her and said, "Every person come for
look at dis rash." He had let go of Jerry's arm in order to
squat down in the dust and open his case. "You don' know
'bout Power 99 yet, do you, brudder?" he said.

The three girls had formed a tight half-circle around the
man and echoed what he said, "The man don' know 'bout
Power 99." It was incredible but they sang it, their tight harmony bringing more bystanders over to look.

"Really," said Jerry, "I just want to buy something in the
chemist's shop, I don't want you messing around with that
stuff."

But the man ignored him, saying, "Das all right, brudder,
don' be o shame. Power 99 don' have its wide reputation yet,
das all. A wide reputation is often slow to come."

He stood up quickly then, a thin plastic bottle in his hand.
The bottle was round and white, with "Power 99" written on
it in big black letters. Because of the growing crowd
Bramwell and Pamela had been pushed up closer to Jerry,
and Pamela said, "If you asked me I'd say let's go inside."

Jerry wanted to agree with her, but the crowd was keeping
him pressed in. He knew, of course, that he had been chosen
as this man's shill, yet he felt that there was nothing personal
in it. The man had simply been waiting for someone to try
to enter the chemist's shop so that he could gather a crowd
and sell. Jerry felt a certain chill. Surely this man would want
a black man for his target, surely he wouldn't want to choose
someone who was white.

The Power 99 man held the bottle above his head and spoke loudly. "Folks, dis my brudder here foun' him lucky day. Because I wan' show every person 'bout Power 99 I darefore will work de rash out his arm for free. It won' cost 'im a naira. It won' cost 'im a kobo too."

The girls sang "Work de rash—out for free." Their harmony was perfection and when they smiled at the crowd the crowd smiled back.

"Now hold it," said the man. "Firs' I wan' every someone to cas' 'is eye on de rash in question. Dis ain' no easy rash."

He looked quickly at the girls—he didn't want them singing this time—and then he pushed Jerry's unwilling arm above the crowd.

"Is a bad red rash, and one wit some small swelling on de underneath side," the man said.

"And it itches," Pamela told him, "don't forget that."

The man looked quickly at Pamela, but he couldn't find the facetiousness he thought he heard, so he said, "Das correc', madam, an' tank you for de remin'. I forget 'bout de itchy which been drivin' our poor brudder to distraction all dese long weeks."

He looked at Jerry then, realizing that he might have gone too far, but Jerry only said, "All these long days," and the man repeated it, as if his only purpose was to get things right.

Jerry's arm and the Power 99 bottle were equal partners in the salesman's outstretched hands. "Come close now," he told everybody. "Les begin."

This time, though the girls were quiet, they were supposed to have sung "Let's begin," and since they hadn't done it he had to repeat everything, shaking Jerry's arm so hard that Jerry thought it might rattle for the crowd.

"Come close now, come close," he said, and now the girls were ready. They sang "Les begin" really beautifully. They were like the Andrews Sisters, and though Jerry hoped that later they might sing an entire song, when the man opened the bottle of Power 99 he had finally had enough. Bramwell and Pamela pressed up next to Jerry. "Are you going to let him touch you with that stuff?" Pamela asked.

Jerry was about to say that of course he was not when the Power 99, which he had assumed would be slow out of the bottle, a lotion or a salve of some kind, came splashing down like water from the tap, spilling over his arm and down the front of his shirt and pants, where it dried away to nothing right away.

"Wow," said the salesman.

The liquid had been cool but as it evaporated the stinging on his arm got worse, for Power 99 was alcohol. The smell of it was in the air and nothing else could disappear like that. Jerry shook his arm, hopping around a little in the small amount of room that he had. "Ouch," he said and to even the salesman's surprise the girls sang, "Ooouuch—Oh, Oouch." Their harmony was still good but the salesman was irritated. And just then a bus came down the road, stopping at the place where the man and the girls had originally been waiting.

"We got to go," said the man. He put the cap on the bottle and shoved it back into his sample case, where other bottles were waiting to be sold. This man knew what he was doing. It appeared that most of the people in the crowd had been waiting for the bus, and by the time he got his things together the girls were in line. "OK," the salesman said. "Les get on board an' sell dis stuff."

Bramwell and Pamela and Jerry stood in the center of the village square watching them go. They waved at the bus, and as it turned and went back up the road the three girls waved back. The Power 99 man, they could easily see, was standing in the aisle.

When the bus was gone the village square seemed to blend back into the hot tiredness of the day. There were still a few people around but they were slumped back against things, as if they hadn't seen the Power 99 man at all.

"That was something," Pamela said. She had spoken to Jerry, but Bramwell answered her back.

"My grandmother hates men like that one," he said. "She says they give folk medicine a bad name."

Pamela went into the chemist's shop and when Jerry reached her she was already telling the chemist that they were looking for a salve. This man wore a white medical shirt, the kind with tight buttons at the side of the neck, so though Jerry was tired of displaying his arm, he put it on the counter, turning it so that the rash would show.

None of them had actually looked at Jerry's arm since the Power 99 man had treated it, but they did now, and what they saw was a surprise. The redness was gone and the rash had receded too. Under the rash, however, there now appeared to be a bruise, an ominous darkening that looked as though it should hurt quite a lot.

The chemist took several bottles from the wall behind him, lining them up so that Pamela could read what the labels said. In Nigeria drugs can be purchased without prescription, but though Pamela was examining something dark, when Jerry saw the calamine lotion he picked it up.

"This one," he said. "When I was a child it worked well for poison oak." Jerry shook the bottle, opened it, and poured so much calamine lotion onto his arm that he was reminded of the Power 99 man again. The calamine lotion, however, felt good, and though it also dried quickly the itching was soon gone and his arm was an even and dull-looking pink. Pamela paid for the lotion but when they went back onto the street the sun seemed hotter, though it was getting late in the day. "Do you want to go back now?" she asked. "Have you seen enough or do you want to prowl around a bit more?"

Jerry hadn't felt normal in weeks. He could not, in fact, remember when he had last taken a walk or looked at something with plain curiosity, unself-conscious about his movements, and he said that by all means he did not want to go back. If he went back, he would surely have to go all the way back to Lagos, and he was beginning to understand that that was something he was reluctant to do.

"Let's go up this way," said Bramwell.

There were a dozen paths leading from the square. The village was larger than it had seemed from the road, and Jerry, had he been asked to, would not have been able to say which of the paths they had come by.

"Bramwell wants us to visit his grandmother," Pamela said. "When he sees her at her house she is calmer. She's usually kinder too."

Jerry didn't want to see the old lady again but Bramwell walked away so quickly that there wasn't any choice but to follow him. The path was wide enough for Pamela and Jerry to walk on together, but Pamela nevertheless stepped in front of him, calling after Bramwell once in a while, but never catching up. When she turned at intersecting paths, Jerry followed her, and though he had the feeling that the path wound down, when he glanced back he did not have the corresponding feeling of looking up.

Around one bend, though he expected nothing of the kind, Jerry found Pamela and Bramwell waiting for him beside a fast-moving stream. There were women washing in the stream and Jerry somehow felt his spirits lift. He walked past Bramwell and Pamela and down to the edge of the water, where one of the women was filling a jug with stream water.

"How much do you want for that jug?" Jerry asked the woman. He'd had no idea he was going to ask such a question but he was suddenly able to see the jug so clearly, an artifact standing in the corner of his living room, next to the rest of his art.

The woman looked up at him. Her skin was as black as andirons and crinkled around her eyes. She said something that he didn't understand.

"That jug," Jerry said. He remembered as he spoke that his clothing was filthy and his pockets were empty of cash, but the woman suddenly stood up and nodded, holding the jug out to him. "Drink," she said.

Jerry was about to say that he wasn't telling her he was thirsty, but suddenly he was. He took the jug and tipped it back

and drank deeply from it, for an instant seeing himself reflected
as the sun flashed over the water in front of his eyes.

The woman took the jug back and dipped it into the
stream, replacing the bit of water that he had drunk. She
then laughed a little and walked down to a series of rocks in
the stream, crossing over to the other side and moving out
into the fields.

Jerry felt his forehead with the back of his hand, then
looked at the calamine lotion on his arm. Down where the
woman had crossed it the stream was a silver ribbon, and
even in the shadows the water was phosphorescent. He
thought of nighttime smelt fishing on the Oregon coast, the
way the sides of the fishes flashed in the light of the moon.
Suddenly Jerry took his shirt off and, kneeling in the stream,
washed himself in the clean water. He washed his face and
under his arms and he let the water fall nicely across his
chest, wetting his pants but feeling wonderful just the same.

Jerry thought to take his hat off and wash his hair, but when
he turned back toward Pamela and Bramwell, to see how they
would react to such an event, it was now Nurudeen who stood
by his mother's side. Directly behind them was a small house,
its front toward the path they had come on, its back up against
the stream. How in the world had he missed seeing the house
before? Jerry wondered. The old woman came out of it with
Bramwell and stood behind Pamela and Nurudeen.

"Good afternoon," she said.

"Hi," said Jerry Neal.

Nurudeen looked small and young now that he stood next
to his brother. It seemed impossible that this was the boy
who had stolen the copy-machine toner, more impossible
still that any father would misuse his son so. Jerry asked
Nurudeen how long he had been staying in the little house.

"Several days, sir," said the boy. "I often come here during
school holidays."

Jerry suddenly thought to embarrass the old woman by
holding his arm in front of Nurudeen and actually asking the
boy to tell him what color he saw. But when he looked at the

old woman she too appeared to be changed. Where before she had been aggressive, now she seemed only grandmotherly, her odd-looking face joining its components in a smile. When she spoke, however, though her voice was gentle, her words weren't connected to that smile.

"You don' believe anyting," she said, "dat's de problem here. Soon as somebody mention a thing you take de position of 'I don' believe it.' Is that a common problem where you come from?"

The old woman had come forward as she spoke, letting Jerry see that she was carrying a low-cut three-legged stool. Amazingly, the others had stools too, and soon they all sat in a circle, in the shade of the house and next to the stream. Someone had carried an extra stool for Jerry and he felt his body drying quickly as he sat down.

When they were settled, though he was beginning to feel like an acolyte in a monastery, Jerry spoke first. He had been oddly hurt by the grandmother's opening remark and he said, "I believe a great many things. Where I come from most people do."

"No you don'," said the grandmother. "You don' believe dat every person see you differen' now, you don' believe anyting 'bout dat."

She was right, but Jerry said, "I thought you were talking about serious beliefs, the ones that form your character, that make up the kind of person you are."

The old woman waved her hand and asked, "If people don' see you differen' now, den why you don' get special attention dis day in our village? What for de children don' come roun' you anymore calling little names?"

It was true that he'd been walking around easily, but the day was hot and the village, he remembered, had been nearly empty.

"I *was* singled out by one man," Jerry said. "A guy trying to sell medicine."

The grandmother hadn't understood so Pamela said it again and she laughed. "Dat proves my point," she said. "De travelin' medicine man don' never talk to de white man. De travelin' medicine man know de white man gone be de firs' to laugh at 'im, so he stick to 'is own kind, sell where de selling is good."

The grandmother's house provided such good shade and the spot where they sat was so cool and peaceful that Jerry had felt little tension, but the woman had said exactly what he'd been thinking before, namely, why would the Power 99 man expose himself to the ridicule that he'd surely get from most white men? If he looked, though, Jerry could see that his skin was white, so the whole thing was ridiculous. He considered for a moment simply asking Pamela or one of the boys again, to make them tell the old lady what they saw, but he didn't do that. Whatever power the old woman held in the family might not hold up under direct questioning, and he needed to bide his time. The old woman, however, seemed to understand it all and said, "Das fine. Pamela, tell de man how 'e look today."

Pamela shifted a little but quietly said, "Today he looks like everybody else I've seen. Not African, really, but like everyone else just the same."

The grandmother looked at her grandsons until they nodded, all three of them easy with their lies, their eyes clear and their bodies relaxed in their postures on the stools. Jerry too was feeling so fine that he thought he'd let it drop. If Pamela's semantics had allowed her to speak truthfully without upsetting Beany's mom, then so much the better for Pamela. But something made him hold his hand out one more time. "Then why is it that when I look at myself I see only what I've always seen?" he asked. "Why do I look the same to me?"

"I tol' you," the old woman patiently said. "Is because you got de 'I-don'-believe-it' disease, and dat disease make its home in de eyes. Don' dat make sense? If de eyes is sick den how can you trust 'em?"

"My eyes would see black if there was black to see," said Jerry, "just like they see the house behind us and the river to our side."

"If dat is true den de eyes is de boss," said the grandmother, "an' das bad because de eyes don' have a brain and de eyes don' have a heart. De eyes, de ears, de nose, and de mouth. Dem tings are servants but you give 'em de job as boss. You got to control dem tings wit discipline, jus' like Beany says. Beany wants it for de country but you got to have it for de eyes an' ears firs' of all."

Jerry was quiet after that, calm and with little inclination to continue talking. When Pamela smiled at him he felt so good and settled that he was happy just to watch the river for a while, never mind what the grandmother said. He had been too tired over the last days and he liked it here. It was peaceful and the itch was gone from his arm, and he had found a way to keep his long legs out of the way while he sat upon the stool.

It was, however, getting late. The sun was casting a weaker shadow across the ground, its angle turning the river ordinary again. And though something in Jerry wanted to gather enough energy for him to speak again, that something wasn't gathering its energy well. They just stayed there, quiet and calm, only Nurudeen standing once to go back into the house to bring his grandmother a shawl.

At seven o'clock they were as still as they had been at five, and at eight, when Pamela stood, helping Jerry unfold his legs from around the bottom of the stool, it was not the hour that moved her but the fact that someone had come down the trail and was standing behind them, just at the edge of the path.

It was LeRoY and he said, "There is a message at the house. Someone has driven in from Lagos."

Jerry looked at Pamela and then at the old woman who had stood up too.

"What kin' car day drive?" she gruffly asked.

"It is a Mercedes-Benz," said LeRoY, "a black one."

"Dat would be Beany's car," said the grandmother. "Les go. That car belongs to Beany who is my son."

For reasons of his own, LeRoY chose not to say that though Beany's car had arrived, Beany wasn't on board. Smart and Louis had brought the car, with Elwood at the wheel and with news that though things were moving smoothly toward Jerry's trial, the senior military officers were now worried about the junior men staging a coup of their own. Beany, in fact, felt that the senior officers' promise to stay out of the coup might be a promise they could not now keep. And if the military took over, one of the first things they might do would be to find Jerry and spirit him out of the country, thus canceling the trial and destroying the entire civilian plan.

"We should therefore keep him moving," Smart said, "make him harder to find."

Smart's news was bad news for everyone but Jerry, who understood that if the senior military men took over the government then his ordeal would surely end. He didn't think they'd be interested in making him leave the country; he thought, in fact, that they'd just give him the proper visas and let him stay. The deflated looks of the others, however, made him hold his tongue.

With the exception of Sondra, they all ate at the People's Canteen again that night, but the mood wasn't celebratory. Again the place was dimly lit and again no one paid much attention to Jerry. People at the other tables didn't look at him, and his companions seemed content to eat and then go home, the old woman back to the village—this time with both her grandsons—the rest of them back to the house.

When they got home, however, though Pamela and the others went into LeRoY's room to make plans, Jerry headed back
toward the sleeping quarters. He had just opened the screen
door, had nearly passed through it and was looking forward
to hearing it slam, when Sondra called him from the doorway of her studio. "Hello, Snapdragon," she softly said.

"Ah," said Jerry. He reached up and touched the edge of
the cap that he wore. "Tell me," he asked. "When you look
at me what colors do you see?"

Sondra laid a long index finger up under her eye. "Well,
you are green with envy and I might say that you are white
with fear, but that would be the same thing as calling you
yellow. I believe that you are really quite blue about everything that has happened but that means that your mood is
primarily indigo. I also think that if I keep this up you'll be
seeing red. So I would say that you are the presence of all
color and that makes you black, your greatest fear realized,
I'm afraid."

Jerry was shocked by her reply. He had been through too
much, the rash on his arm had no doubt been caused by the
grandmother, he'd let that snake-oil man touch him, the
grandmother had lectured him all afternoon by the stream,
and now Sondra, though in a charming and flirtatious way,
was telling him that she saw him as black too. He only
asked, however, "Where have you been all day?"

"I've been working, of course," Sondra said. "Since I gave
away my snapdragon I had to replace it with something really
extraordinary. Would you like to see?"

Jerry said that he would and when he entered her studio,
there was his snapdragon, unmoved from its place on the
wall, its mouth wide, the sides of its inner channel calling
him. He wanted to stay by it, to walk up closer with his hand
out, but Sondra drew him past the cooked-cabbage smell and
deeper into the room, making him look up at a fresh frame
on the wall above her workbench. This new project was
smaller than anything else in her studio, perhaps only one
foot square. It was an African Chagall, the stylized depiction

of a man, his face cubist, his body trailing after it as a string
follows a balloon.

"It's Beany Abubakar," Jerry said.

"It is and it is not," Sondra told him. "Look again."

It was startling, but as Sondra spoke Jerry was able to see
himself in a part of the abstract face that beveled away from
Beany, in the backward slant behind Beany's ear, in the inner
rectangle of his forehead. It was as if slices of himself had
been placed there, as if he were a thought, an idea born out
of Beany's mind. And all of this was done with dyes. "How
did you do that?" he asked.

"I really don't know," Sondra said. "It came out in the
wash, you might say. I never try to put living people in my
work, but Beany has appeared before. It's really quite magical, and who would have guessed that you and Beany would
be tied up in such a way."

Jerry could see that it was magical; it was a Mobius strip
with him and Beany turning into each other, like deep pur-
ple Siamese twins. "Why do you insist on such darkness?" he
asked. "What is it about all these shades of blue?"

As soon as he spoke he thought of the question as beside
the point, but Sondra answered it well. "It is because I am
color blind, don't you know? I love my indigos because I can
see them. My color blindness is all around those hues but it
isn't in them. And since they are the ones I can see I feel it
is my duty to see them well. I think I see the shades of blue
better than anyone alive, though I'm blind to the colors that
others see."

As Sondra spoke Jerry looked down again at the dirty skin
on his arm. The calamine lotion was old by then, but still
visibly pink across the otherwise beige background of his
forearm. The light in this back room wasn't good but he nevertheless pushed his arm under the hanging bulb and per-
sisted, asking her what shades she saw in it. Sondra sighed
but stared at the lotion and the surrounding skin. She
touched the arm and peered at it as if she were peering into
a crystal ball; she rubbed the skin as if she were moving an

intervening fog out of the way. "Let me see," she said. "It is . . . Now it is coming clear, yes, it is . . . indigo!"

Jerry had thought they were having a serious moment, and he gave Sondra a little shove, but she came back teasing. "I jus' tol' you, mon, you are talkin' to a girl for whom de whole worl' be indigo yet you spec' your arm be differen' from de whole world. Das foolishness, brudder, you de same color as de worl', don' you know?"

Sondra's playfulness was fine but Jerry had another question in mind. "What about shades?" he asked. "Are there gradations in what you see, are there light indigos and dark ones when you look at things?"

Sondra took his arm again but she didn't look at it, and she wouldn't go back to speaking normally. "Of course dere be shades," she said, "indigo come in all de shades. An indigo life be de richest one, das what I believe."

Jerry hadn't meant to draw so much away from Sondra's amazing new work, but when he looked back at it this time he was suddenly able to see it twice. It was all indigo, no question about that, but now he could see color gradations, too, between the part of the work that was Beany and the part that was himself. And within the angles of the two faces, at the bevel or at the departure, where one face moved into another, he thought he could see the reds of the ministry fire and the awful yellow of the dead secretary's dress. He couldn't hold these colors—if he blinked everything turned indigo again—but in his sidelong glance there was first green, then the orange of a burning Lagos sky. And between everything, where the molecules of color stood like soldiers so tightly ranked, he could even see white, the space between the dyes, the original color of the cloth before Sondra turned it blue. Was this the absence of color or the blank face of a work of art not yet made?

"I love this," Jerry said. "I love my snapdragon, but I love this new one too."

"That's good, but it won't do you any good to hint,"

Sondra said. "I have given you my best work. I'm not giving you my newest too."

Jerry said he wanted to wash his arm, to get the lotion off and see whether it was still inflamed, so Sondra took him to her sink, its porcelain sides as deeply dyed as anything else in the room. She washed his arm for him, soaping it and then flaking the last of the calamine lotion away with the fingernails of her right hand. It was ridiculous but Jerry felt aroused by the action, by the way her fingernails kept after the last dried flakes of the lotion, by the way they left soapy furrows of their own, indigo veins along his nondescript arm. Sondra's leg was next to his, touching him from knee to pelvis, and he pressed a little into her hoping that she wouldn't notice the altered rhythm in his breath. She not only noticed it, however, but she turned into him, pulling the washed arm to her breasts and looking into his eyes. "Indigo man," she quietly said.

Jerry nearly spoke—his impulse was to apologize, to say that it was really Pamela that wandered about in his mind—but just then his body took over, shutting his mouth and tightening the muscles from his solar plexus to his knees. It was a feeling he hadn't experienced in years, and as he fell into it he threw Sondra off balance and up against the edges of the sink. "Oh my," she said.

Sondra's face had lost its smile but it wasn't critical. Her jaw had locked into its serious mode, and she pulled him toward her, pressing into him down low and throwing her arms around his neck.

The floors in this house were wooden, and Sondra's were disorderly, littered with rags, with tossed-out failures, with the soft-looking sides of cardboard boxes upon which she sometimes drew preliminary designs. When Jerry first thought of the floor he rejected it, looking instead toward the outer room and then around the walls, hoping to find a cot. It did not occur to him to take Sondra to the sleeping quarters, but he did think of those still chatting in LeRoY's room, of Pamela and the others. He knew that there was something happening between Pamela and himself but now what was he to believe? Here he was with Sondra, his knees buckling toward the floor even as his eyes kept a lookout for that cot.

"My working room is a virgin," Sondra said. They were down on top of the cardboard now, stiff edges sticking them before gruffly bending aside. Sondra's indigo dress seemed to flee of itself, falling among the dyed rags. She wore only white panties under that dress and the sight of them nearly killed Jerry, the way they weren't indigo, the way their whiteness seemed luminescent, like a call to come home from a dark, dark world. He thought for a moment that he would have to stop, that such excitement might make him ill, but just at that moment Sondra did the stopping, pushing herself away.

"Wait one second," she said.

Jerry's clothing was askew too, his pants down around his knees, his shirt unbuttoned and gone. Thank God he had washed in that creek, he thought. His shoes were still on him and he flung them away, kicking out of his pants while Sondra rummaged around somewhere on the other side of the room. He supposed they had been making too much noise, for now the house seemed quiet. He was sure that those down the hall had stopped talking to listen.

Sondra spoke from across the room. "I can't find a condom," she said. "I thought I saw one in this drawer but it is gone. I'll get one from LeRoY—be right back."

"Wait!" Jerry hissed, but Sondra had left the room, pulling a robe from a hook as she went. He could hear her footsteps, could feel the weight of her movement in the portions of the boards on which he lay.

Jerry's body sank back, his blood receding like a speedy tide. She was actually going down into that room again, the one in which Pamela sat, to ask LeRoY if he had a condom she could borrow. God, he would never understand these people. He tried to imagine Sondra whispering her request into LeRoY's ear, LeRoY finding the condom quietly, maybe slipping it to her without the others seeing, but his imagination wasn't good enough for that. When he strained his ears, however, he now believed he could actually hear her making her request, and his imagination was certainly good enough to see everyone else in the room turning their heads toward her while LeRoY searched around, first in his pockets, then across the surfaces of his worktable, perhaps in the pockets of the sweater he had hanging by the door.

My God, what would Pamela think? If not for Pamela Jerry would have extracted himself from everything easily and earlier on, he would never have come anywhere near this artists' house. But if he had gotten into everything so deeply because of Pamela, then what was he doing with Sondra, his pants down around his knees?

Jerry had found his clothing again, had most of it back on when Sondra returned.

"He keeps them in his sleeping room," she said. "I should have thought of that."

"Ah well," Jerry said. He would have said that it was late, that sleep was what he needed if he was to face the rigors of tomorrow, but Sondra had brought back something bigger than a condom. She brought Jerry's Christmas gift from Pamela, the circular ebony carving, the tree of life.

"This is really quite good," she told him.

Sondra's voice did not betray anything, but the fact that he was dressed and standing had certainly registered somewhere. She brought the sculpture to him and then led him back into her main room and took the snapdragon down from its place on the wall. It had been stapled across a thin wooden frame and she pulled the staples expertly out. "You may iron this," she said, "but do it lightly."

Jerry felt he had offended Sondra, but he wasn't sure how. Surely not by getting dressed or by his embarrassment over her nonchalant trip down the hall, that tell-all condom search of hers. He took the snapdragon, holding it against the tree of life, which really did look quite wonderful now, with its delicate filigree, its evolutionary movement of climb-

ing animals and men. Though he was somehow beginning to
hate the idea of it, he could easily imagine his living room,
the snapdragon professionally framed, the tree of life below it
and playing off of it in the angles of light, black and indigo
in the afternoon sun and against his beige walls.

"Look," he said. "I'm sorry about this." He was surprised at
himself for speaking, it was much more like him to simply
leave, and as he looked at her he could tell that Sondra was
surprised too.

"I have not been with a man since I came here," she said,
"and I am reminded now of how they are."

Jerry had no idea what to say. He didn't know how men
were or how women were either, and as a consequence of
that he had always believed that silence was the best rule,
keeping one's own counsel. He looked at Sondra but in the
end he only asked, "How long have you been here then?"

"I came on my thirty-fifth birthday," Sondra said, "in Oc-
tober, just last year."

My God, he thought, she doesn't look thirty-five. But
something about the fact of her age made him happy, bringing a little of that other feeling back. He was old enough to
be her father, perhaps, but not old enough to be her grandfather. "Would you come with me?" he asked. "Back to
LeRoY's room?"

Sondra looked at him carefully then. His rumpled clothing
made him look like a gardener. He had his two pieces of art
in his hands, his cap pushed firmly down on his head. "The
moment is past, I think," she said. She cast her eyes back toward the floor by her sink and he remembered the feeling of
the cardboard getting out of his way, the loss of breath, the
buckling of his knees.

Sondra came closer, pushing his artwork up against his
chest and giving him a kiss over the top of it. "I will work
a while longer tonight," she said. He thought of the work in
progress, the indigo collage of Beany and himself, beveled together like glass.

"Well, good night then," he said.

"Yes," said Sondra, "good night."

There wasn't an actual door on her studio but when Jerry was in the hall again the dim light did not allow him to see her anymore. He could hear the voices of the others, down in LeRoY's room, and for a moment his impulse was to go that way, to join them, to walk in casually so that he could gauge how much they knew about what had transpired. But though he took a step in that direction, he soon stopped. He could hear laughter, Smart's voice on the top of it, but the voices of the others too, and in Pamela's he could not hear any tension or any sense either that she was offended or that she was calling him, sirenlike, to sit beside her in that room.

So Jerry went out the back of the main house, letting the screen door slam. He could see the rusted farm tools and the coops in which the skinny chickens slept. There was a full moon but clouds were in front of it, diffusing its light. Before going into the sleeping house he stopped to tuck his snap-dragon under his arm and to hold his sculpture up, looking through its filigree at the moon-lit clouds. It was strange but that soft white light made the sculpture's carousel quality stronger, and when he got the idea to turn it he could see the figures of the sculpture climbing, foot to shoulder, as if in co-operative flight, a communal effort to let just one of them reach the top, jumping away into the night.

In the morning things had changed. Jerry was up early, perhaps by seven, but the others had already eaten and were in LeRoY's room again, arranged in much the same configuration as the night before. As soon as Jerry came in Smart told him to sit down. Late the night before, Smart said, he had had Elwood take Beany's car back to Lagos, the darkened windows not letting anyone see who was inside. "We know now that the senior military men will go back on their pledge," he said.

Jerry felt refreshed by his sleep, not in the mood to be solemn, but he tried to adjust himself to the heavy faces in the room. He got the feeling that though his ordeal might be coming to an end, theirs was just beginning.

"Why?" he asked. "Whatever gives you that idea?"

"Someone shot at Beany's car," Pamela told him. "We just got word."

It had happened on a dark stretch of road, somewhere between Benin City and Lagos. Elwood had not been injured in the attack—he had, in fact, sped past the attackers and reached Lagos without further incident, and Jerry said, "Maybe they were just highwaymen. Even I know that that road is famous for thieves."

But Smart said no. "Elwood saw their uniforms. They were junior military officers. Elwood wouldn't make a mistake about a thing like that."

"And if it *was* the junior boys, then the senior men won't

wait for us," said Pamela. "In Africa low-ranking officers stage preemptive coups all the time. Look what happened in Ghana."

Jerry was surprised and irritated. Always before, though the plan of which he had become a part had seemed farfetched, he'd had the idea that its organizers were prepared to face opposition should opposition arise. Now, though, they appeared to be ready to cut and run and he felt a little grouchy about it. It seemed to devalue his personal loss.

"Beany should get to the senior officers today," he said. "He should reestablish his lines of communication, extract the promises again, move his timetable up if necessary. . . ."

Jerry certainly had not before been of a mind to offer political advice, but if they were going through with this thing, then he thought they should go through with it properly.

"Beany is in Lagos now," Smart said, "and that is what he is trying to do. He called this morning with our change of plans."

"What change of plans?" Jerry asked. "What plans did you have in the first place?"

"Beany feels that if the junior officers took the chance of attacking the car, they might come here," said Pamela. "He wants us to leave quickly, going back to Lagos slowly by bus. He says we should get lost for a few days, giving him a chance to straighten things out."

It was December 28 and by nine in the morning everything was decided. Some of them would ride with Jerry on the bus, but in sequence, one from the beginning, another from Onitsha, another from Benin City where the bus made its last intermittent stop. Pamela's Peugeot would follow the bus, dropping his escorts in the towns along the way. LeRoY and the other artists would continue working and if the soldiers came they would say that though the group had visited they didn't know where they had gone. In the end all that was left was to wait until late afternoon, when the bus was expected to depart from the village square.

It wasn't a surprise to anyone when, at the last minute, Sondra ran out to the Peugeot, saying that she too would like to go along.

Two

Before they could take a bus from the village square, two more days had passed and, though the military hadn't come, the idea of going on the bus, though at first unpleasant to Jerry, had taken on an odd sort of appeal. He would use the time to think. From now on he would bring himself to the events that awaited him as a full-fledged player, no longer a pawn.

But the bus that had not arrived at all since Wednesday was late again, and when it came into the square it was full. Smart bought the tickets from a man who stood outside the chemist's shop, and when they got on the bus there was barely any room in the aisle.

Jerry turned around and found that directly above his head was a vent, a place where the ceiling of the bus bent upward into a square eight inches higher than the ordinary ceiling. By putting his head into the vent he could stand straight, but it was then nearly impossible to keep the sides of his head from banging against the vent's walls at each bump in the road. It was intolerable and he ducked quickly down again, kneeling next to Smart, a bundle containing his tree of life and his snapdragon beside him in the aisle.

Jerry still felt shy with Smart, still tentative with the man, and when Smart didn't speak Jerry kept quiet too and began to look around. The bus was packed with market women, their bundles taking up as much space as their bodies. These were big women, and their demeanor was serious. Jerry had seen them on airplanes a time or two, flying up to Abidjan to shop, bringing goods back to sell in markets like the one they were heading for in Onitsha or in Jankara, where this man kneeling next to him lived. When Jerry looked at Smart, Smart said, "I will accompany you for the shortest leg of your journey; from Onitsha I will be returning to my car."

Jerry wanted to say that it was Pamela's car but he did not. Instead, though it wasn't a place in which one could speak freely, when the bus rhythms had lulled the nearby passengers, he said, "Tell me something more about Beany." Jerry had been trying to understand the phenomenon of Beany for days, and he knew that Smart was a devotee. When he asked his question, however, it seemed like the whole bus came alive.

"Say again?" asked the nearest market woman.

Smart rolled his eyes, but Jerry looked at the woman evenly and repeated himself. "I was asking why it is that everyone loves Beany Abubakar so? He seems an ordinary man to me."

A moment before the people around him had seemed as inanimate as pieces on a chess board. Jerry was sure that they had been asleep, surer still that he had spoken softly, but now a half-dozen people were looking down on him from the nearby seats.

"Oh, brudder," one man said, "where you get dat hat? Dat hat tell us sometin'. You dumb question tell us de res'."

The man, stuffed into a seat with two of the market women, made everyone laugh and Jerry smiled too. He reached up to take the hat off, but Smart stopped him, so he simply said, "I'm not from around here, I'm not even Nigerian," and they all laughed again. "Tell us sometin' we don' already know," the first woman said.

Passengers from up toward the front of the bus were craning their necks, smiling back at the conversation, and Jerry felt himself relax. There was a sweetness to the group that made him comfortable even kneeling in the aisle. The thin man had opened a window and a nice breeze came in, increasing his comfort and letting him say, "Since I've been here, though, I've been hearing Beany's name. I just wondered about him, that's all."

He expected more general comment but it didn't come. Rather, the thin man looked at him seriously. "Where you come from in de firs' place," he asked, "an' what business Beany of yours?"

"He's none of my business," Jerry said. "I've just heard his name a lot, that's all."

The man was about to speak again but the woman put a hand up. "Beany a local man," she said, "but he live in Lagos now. Beany a man o de people, das all. His own one mudder is a frien' o mine."

"If Nigeria ever come together Beany be de glue," the thin man said.

This comment brought a rush of agreeing voices, but then Smart spoke, asking the people, "Is there one anodder man we can trus' like Beany? One anodder man who ain' tribalistic, lookin' to his own folk firs'?"

To Jerry's mind Smart was too obviously a shill, but the people shouted, "No, dare ain't!" and the thin man glared at Jerry. "So don' come here speakin' bad 'bout Beany!" he said.

The man was angry but the woman poked him and said, "You got to listen better, my frien'. He don' say nothin' bad 'bout Beany but only ask 'bout Beany like he don' know 'bout 'im and wan' find out."

The man glared a second longer, but then nodded. "Das good," he said.

After that the people settled into the ride again, some looking forward, others closing their eyes. When Jerry looked at Smart, Smart smiled at him, but he didn't want to speak. The bus had been making good time, they were already entering Onitsha, the first stop. Jerry looked forward to standing, to possibly getting one of the seats, but when he glanced up to see who might be leaving, the thin man caught his eye. "So," the man said, "where do you come from anyhow?"

The man rubbed his hands together as though he were about to make a guess, then he thought for a while, staring into Jerry's face. Out the windows behind the man Jerry could see that the buildings of Onitsha were passing by, he could feel the bus turning and slowing down. The man looked at him for a long while but then sat back and conferred with the two women who were his seat mates. Finally it was one of the women who spoke again. "We have only one idea," she said. "You are from Ethiopia, are you not?"

The bus was stopping, the people at the front already heading toward the door. Smart stood, then reached down to pull Jerry to his feet.

There had been a clear question in the woman's voice, but just then she picked up her bundle and began bumping the thin man along toward the door, disallowing any chance for Jerry to answer, taking away his chance to make up his mind, to tell them whether he was Ethiopian or was not.

As it turned out the bus they took into Onitsha was not the same bus they would take out of it, so though Jerry had slipped into an unoccupied seat, he soon found himself standing again and following the others out the door, his bulky bundle by his side.

"It is good," said Smart. "It looks like an ordinary Onitsha day."

The river was off to their left and closer by, running along its side, were scores of merchants' stalls. Smart took a turn around the area and came back to tell Jerry that the next bus wouldn't leave until ten. That meant Jerry would have nearly a five-hour wait. Smart held out his hand and when Jerry took it Smart passed him a few crumpled bank notes. "We are here but we must not be seen," he said. "Come back later and you will find your next companion."

It was only as Smart prepared to leave that Jerry got a little miffed. No one had mentioned the change of bus or the long delay. "What am I supposed to do now?" he asked. "How will I spend my time?"

Smart shrugged and then glanced at the money in Jerry's hand. The other passengers had gone and the driver was coming down, pulling the doors closed behind him, when they saw the front of Pamela's Peugeot edging off the road. "Now," said Smart, "don't speak to strangers." He turned and walked back up toward the car, which was parked about fifty meters away.

Jerry looked down at the money in his hand and then to-

ward the river, which was wide and brown and busy. This was
the Niger, its slow mass striking through West Africa. He
had been intending to see the Niger ever since his arrival all
those years before so he sighed and told himself that he
would, at least, accomplish that much during his five-hour
wait. He would see the river. He'd imagine himself on vacation and try to take some joy from standing along its old and
muddy banks.

Jerry walked away from the bus stop, but before he got to
the first of the merchants' stalls he came to a store selling
glass, and he stepped inside. Unusual for the area, this was a
completely closed shop, a four-walled building with windows
that were covered by bars. There was no one in the shop, but
as he stood there Jerry understood that what had drawn him
was a far wall lined entirely with mirrors, which he had
dimly seen from the outside. He walked toward the mirrors
carefully for he hadn't seen himself in days and the old lady's
machinations had made him a little afraid. Before he could
look into the mirrors, however, a voice called to him from
the far side of the store, forcing him to turn that way. "You
are interested in a mirror of quality?" the voice wanted to
know, "a nice gilded one perhaps?"

The man was Indian and had been there all along, sitting
down low behind a counter. When he stood and came forward, though, his manner changed, his smile falling down.
"Ah, but surely not," he said.

"I only wanted to look into one of them," Jerry said, but
he soon got the idea that if he wanted to do even that much
he would have to hurry, for the merchant was pointing toward the door. "My mirrors are not for looking," he said.

The man placed his body between Jerry and the mirrors so
that when Jerry looked over the man he could see only his
own face and the proprietor's head and shoulders, a hunched
and cancerous-looking gargoyle stuck below his own chin.
He could see a pained expression on his face, anger at not
being allowed a moment to look at himself in a mirror, but
other than that he saw only enough to be pleased at finding

that the workmanship of these mirrors was flawed. There was not enough light in them, and the image of both himself and the proprietor's back was gray and grainy-looking, like the image in the window of a car. Only the vision of Jerry's cap was crisp, and as the man shoved him roughly from the door even that seemed in danger of coming off.

Jerry was cast into the street, and when he looked back at the man, half his size and fat to boot, his first impulse was to jump up and strike him, to knock him over the head with his tree of life. But the man had receded into his shop, and when the door closed between them the event was over. Jerry stepped back close to the shop when a truck came too quickly by, and he tried to see himself in the store's windows, hoping to irritate the man, but in the window, too, only the elements of his hat and his filthy shirt were clear. His hands, when he held them up, were easier to see through than they were to see, and when he tried to concentrate on his face he too easily saw what was inside the shop as well.

Jerry sighed and stepped into the dust that was left by the passing truck. Now he would have to wander around this town for hours, waiting for the next bus to leave. His mood was bad, but it improved when he remembered his original idea and left the shop to walk down past the merchants' stalls to the river. This was, after all, the Niger. How many rivers in Africa were as famous as this one?

He found a stump to sit on that let him watch the low boats as they carried passengers around. This river was used for commerce, of course, but Jerry's interest, quite suddenly, was in the low boats, the ones whose sides floated just above the water. In his Lagos flat Jerry had thorn carvings of such boats, boats full of women with babies, of men in short pants sailing off to look for work. In one of his carvings there were prisoners in the boat, and he thought of himself as being transported somewhere in chains.

Jerry stirred on his stump when one of the real boats came ashore just below where he sat. This boat was no more than sixteen feet long, but Jerry counted twenty people getting off, not including the babies. It was the river's version of the bus he had just been on.

Once the passengers were gone the two boatmen came onto higher ground to stand near Jerry and smoke. These were hard-bodied men, and though their postures and muscle tone did not denote much difference in age, Jerry somehow knew that they were father and son. They were very near him but they didn't acknowledge him, nor did they speak together. Jerry thought of his thorn carvings and quite suddenly decided to hire the men, to ride in their boat across the river, to get to the other side.

"How much to go across?" he asked, and both men jumped. Only after he stood did Jerry notice that a group of people were lined up by the boat, their bundles already placed in the boat's center to keep them dry.

"Naira fifty," said the younger man, and Jerry took out one of his crumpled bills. "I don't have change," he said.

The man did not take the money but pointed toward the boat and then hurried off, with Jerry following him down the bank.

At the boat the younger man took the other passengers' money, but it was not a naira fifty. Instead, each rider handed the man fifty kobo, one third the price that Jerry had been told. When it was his turn Jerry surrendered his five naira and then waited while the man counted out his change.

"Where you come from?" the younger man asked. He had handed back three naira fifty but Jerry stayed his hand, hoping to get another naira back. "Ethiopia," he said, "East Africa, long way from here."

The young man looked at Jerry and then at his father. The boat was already nearly full, the father working its nose off the riverbank once again, when the younger man nodded and handed Jerry back the rest of his change.

Jerry sat in the boat's middle, his bundle on his lap, and facing a woman who might have been one of the women on the bus. But the passengers on the boat were not talking among themselves, nor did there seem to be the potential for it that there had been on the bus. The woman stared at Jerry, but perhaps only out of a need for somewhere to rest her eyes, and the others looked into the brown water, at the ships and ferries that plowed past them without regard.

The boat landing on the far side of the Niger was identical to the one on the near side. There was a low bank, then a slightly higher one. There was even a stump on which a man might sit, looking back over to where he'd sat before. But when Jerry got to the stump he did not sit down. Rather he waited for the woman, then followed her past a line of merchants' stalls that also seemed a mirror image of what he had seen on the river's other side.

Jerry liked the idea of being Ethiopian, but the truth of the matter was that he had slowly begun to think of himself not as Ethiopian but as invisible to those who passed him by. He knew, of course, that he was not invisible, but the fact was that ever since Beany's mother had burned his hair and shoved this cap down on his head, he had been primarily ignored by other people. Only when he forced the issue, as in the glass store and with the two boatmen, as he somehow had with the passengers on the bus, did people respond to him at all.

Jerry suddenly remembered Parker Akintola, letting Parker's prison voice echo in his head: ". . . in de night you mus' exis' wit' quietude, like only de night go by. In de day you mus' blen' in, become de man anodder man don' see, like de invisible man. Dat is how to get by during de day."

It had been one of the first things Parker had said to him and the memory of it stopped Jerry in his tracks. He was surprised when the woman he was following stopped too, turning to face him down.

"Wha's goin' on?" she asked. "You in need o sometin' down dis way?"

The woman wasn't smiling. What's more, she had taken her bundles from her head and placed them on the path, herself between the bundles and Jerry.

"I'm sorry," Jerry said. "I'm just wasting time, waiting for the bus to leave."

"Bus leave from de other side," said the woman, "don' ask me why."

It was true that Jerry had followed the woman, but it had been an aimless following, an exercise. What he was doing was just moving along, staying in the shadow of her size, letting her movement dictate the speed and direction of his own. "I'm just looking around," he weakly said.

Slight as his answer was, it seemed enough. She picked one bundle up, and though she had immediately placed it back on her head, she somehow looked down at the other one. "Give a hand," she said. "My shop ain' far."

The woman then turned and walked on. The bundle she left was tied in red cloth and was about the size of the stump Jerry'd been sitting on. Though he had his own bundle to carry, he reached down, lifted this other one by its knot, and walked along behind her. The bundle wasn't heavy but its contents had sharp points and he got the idea that if he wasn't careful something might break. He carried the bundle at his side for a while but finally grasped the knot more tightly and lifted it to his head, where it settled onto his cap perfectly, as if it belonged there.

Perhaps the woman's shop wasn't far, but by the time they got there the river was no longer in view. They had crossed several streets, cut down several pathways, and had come to a broader, better-looking road, where, somehow, the river could be seen again.

"Thank you," said the woman. "Wait please, jus' one moment more."

Her shop was made of plywood and reminded Jerry of an American fireworks stand. She unlocked two big padlocks and swung the shutters up, laying them flat along the shop's roof. She then picked up both bundles and set them inside.

The shop was on a rise of good ground, its western exposure lighting it just a little as the sun went down. This was a shop that sold thorn carvings, of all things, and though it didn't seem to be located in a tourist spot, the carvings that Jerry could see, the ones that were already arranged on shelves, looked superior to the ones in his flat, those he had been thinking about all day.

"I thought only tourists bought these things," he said. He had picked up a carving of a man in a palm tree. He had one like it in his office, but this one was better, the man's face had more dimension to it, more expression by far.

The woman unpacked her bundles, both of which contained more thorn carvings of the same superior quality as the one in Jerry's hand. One thing Jerry knew about thorn carvings was that they were fragile, but though these had not been packed particularly well, they were coming out of the bundles unharmed. And the subject matter was astounding: a wide variety of daily life was carved out and arrayed before him.

The woman put the new carvings on a low shelf against the back of her shop, and then stood straight. "OK brudder, tell me now, who you be an' why you followin' me along in dis way?"

She looked at him steadily as she spoke. At first Jerry thought to say that he was Ethiopian, but that seemed a tired response. When he didn't say anything, however, the woman stepped nearer and peered at him, first at his face, then at his filthy and wrinkled clothes. She said, "Befo' I tink you a high-tone man but now I ain' so sure. You got a bad look. Are you not feeling fine?"

She took his hand as she spoke to him, so Jerry finally said, "I am, in fact, an American. I come from the United States."

The woman shook her head. She seemed grieved to hear it. "You know my one husban' Clarke, he come from dere," she said. "Dat's why you look familiar, you look 'bout like Clarke, I suppose."

By this time the sun had nearly left the store, sinking into the faraway trees and making the muddy river red, but letting Jerry see one particular thorn carving in the last corner of its light. This carving sat at the edge of the woman's highest shelf. Jerry had noticed it earlier, when the sun was democratic, but then it had remained subdued. Now, though, when Jerry picked it up the woman said, "Das de one for you. I was waitin' for you to get 'roun to findin' it youself."

The carving, which was surrounded by carvings of boats and mammy wagons and men on motor bikes, was of a building on fire. It was a tall building, and from one of its windows up high a woman was leaning out and screaming, blond wood flames surrounding her face and hair and yellow dress.

"My God," said Jerry Neal. He felt as if he were about to fall, and, in fact, he nearly sat on his tree of life before letting the woman direct him to a chair.

"Yes," the woman said, "I tink 'My God' too, when I see dis one sometime."

Jerry asked about the artist, and then about what specific event the woman thought was depicted there, but she held up her hands.

"I dunno de carver or anyting else. Mos'ly I know but for this one I don'," she said. "My frien' work for me de day it come an now my frien' long time gone, so I dunno."

"I want it," Jerry said. "How much do you need?"

"Is de bes' in my shop," said the woman.

He could see himself reflected in the woman's eyes and he knew that if this carving were for sale in Lagos it would be a hundred naira, many more. He'd had five five-naira notes in his pocket and he had spent fifty kobo of that. And he would need another fifty kobo to travel back to the river's other side.

"I'll give you ten naira for it," Jerry said.

The woman laughed. "Please," she said. "Make las' price firs'. Don' wais' my time."

The woman stood between Jerry and that other woman, the carved one screaming from the window of the burning building. In Lagos he would have feigned disinterest—he knew how to deal with traders—but he couldn't walk away. "I don't have much money," he said. "Make it fifteen."

The woman looked at him and said, "Why you wan' make insult dis way? Now you soun' like Clarke for sure. Don' you know de price is high? I can get forty naira. I don' have hurry in my min'."

"I know," said Jerry, "but I don't have forty naira. Look . . ." He shoved his ashen hands into his pockets and pulled them inside out. When his rumpled money fell to the ground the woman picked it up and counted it. "Twenty-four naira fifty kobo," she said. The tone of her voice was not that of one counting, but of one finalizing a deal. "OK," she said. "Sol'."

Jerry wanted to agree, but he needed fifty kobo to get back across the river. "Let me keep boat money," he said, "and maybe another two naira for food."

The woman had taken the carving from its place on her shelf, but she set it back down. "Twenty-four naira fifty kobo," she said. "Don' change de price when de bargaining done."

So though it was absurd, though his situation demanded nothing so much as the conservation of his resources and the clearness of his mind, Jerry Neal, filthy and hungry, lost in Onitsha and on the wrong side of the river as well, gave this woman all his money for a thorn carving of a woman screaming from the side of the building that housed the Ministry of Internal Affairs.

Jerry had been keeping his bundle close beside him, the folded snapdragon inside the tree of life inside a tied-up piece of Sondra's discarded cloth, and he watched as the woman untied it and put his new carving down in there too, slipping the snapdragon around it for padding.

"Is nice," she offhandedly said, "a man like you keep his fine collection no matter what."

Before he left the shop Jerry asked for water and when it came he dipped his hands into it, washing his face and arms. After that he left quickly, not concerned with finding the way he had come but simply keeping the river in view and making his way toward it.

When he got to the river he was happy to see that stump again and to sit upon it, his eyes on the water, hoping to be able to discern the same boat. There was less traffic now than there had been earlier, but from many of the boats Jerry could hear the good-humored chatter of people at the end of their day.

When the boat arrived, Jerry got up and walked down toward it, his bundle in his hands. He would ask the boatmen to take him on good faith, promising to pay twofold the cost of the trip when he got to the other side. But at the edge of the water, with the two boatmen facing him, he spoke these words instead: "I am traveling alone and without resources; Beany Abubakar is my friend."

He had not meant to say any such thing but when the words came out the older boatman nodded and the younger one helped him step inside, holding his elbow until he was safely sitting down. It was such an odd thing to have said, and so unpremeditated, yet the words had worked like a code, a mantra even, and to be used only once in a while.

The evening was peaceful, the river calm, and perhaps rush hour was over, for as the boatmen paddled away Jerry noticed that the boat was not nearly so full. He had his bundle by him and he thought of its contents: the tree of life, feet on shoulders and heads, men climbing toward the top; his snapdragon, an invitation, a soft abstractness, a female inner life; and that astounding thorn carving, proof of the existence of evil in the world. These were his possessions, all that he had, and for the duration of the boat ride he could not rid himself of the feeling that he was a traveling monk of some kind, the keys to the meaning of things tied up in a piece of cloth and sitting by his side.

When the journey was over Jerry stepped from the boat easily, but when he turned to thank the boatmen they seemed not to hear him, and when he walked toward the bus stop he did not greet those who did not greet him in return. It was not as late as it needed to be for the bus to depart, but when Jerry got to the bus stop the first person he saw was Sondra, dressed in indigo and leaning into the velvet night.

"Hi," she said. "Where in the world have you been?"

He would have told her but in fact he did not know. And while he was searching for something to say, Sondra waved her hand in the air.

"Never mind that, let's eat," she said. "I'm starving and we've plenty of time."

Sondra had money in her purse and when she dug for it she found the bus tickets and handed them to Jerry. "If you really want to know what I think," she said, "I think all of this is silly, unnecessary to say the least."

She meant, of course, the intrigue, the cautionary travel, the idea that soldiers would actually be searching them out. When she spoke, however, Jerry momentarily got the idea that she was talking about life itself, and he nodded his head, though Sondra wasn't watching and though it was apparent that no one else was paying any attention to his movements at all.

Sondra and Jerry got seats in the middle of the bus, and though Sondra was supposed to sit alone, she moved in next to Jerry anyway, by the window, making herself look small against the glass. It was ten forty-five before the driver got on and the bus lurched away. "Benin City," he loudly said.

But though the bus was late, after the first half hour most of the potholes moved over to the side of the road and everyone slept. Jerry and Sondra leaned into each other, unknown men and women found ways of sharing common ground, and far in the back those who didn't have seats slept on luggage or between the sacks of merchandise that took up the rest of the space.

Jerry's sleep was deep, but troubled. As he slept he felt Sondra's softness next to him, yet he wanted that softness, now, only for the sake of comfort, for the sake of rest. He wanted to think that he had disconnected himself from Sondra because of Pamela, but he remembered that he and Charlotte, too, though they'd sometimes caught a glimpse of passion's coattails, had rarely looked into the longing depth of its eyes. And now it was as if what he had felt with Sondra, those three nights before, was of the same fleeting quality. In other words, though he had wanted Sondra then, he did not want her now, and that realization gave his sleep a certain sadness that he brought with him when the bus stopped along a length of straight road and the driver woke everyone up. "Some small trouble wit de engine," he said. "Dis be Agbor. Everybody get down small."

Jerry awoke more slowly than the others, but when he looked out the window he could not see Agbor, and when the others, many of them complaining about the stop, finally got down to stretch their legs, he found himself alone on the bus. Where had Sondra gone? How had she slipped so easily past his knees?

Jerry stood, then squatted in the aisle, trying to shake his melancholy mood. Out the window to his right he could see the passengers standing in the road, behind them now the outlines of a few miserable buildings, darker rooftops against the lighter sky. To his left were fields as flat as someone's Oregon lawn, and across the fields another few houses stood.

There was a palaver starting up on the road and when he finally stepped down from the bus a few of the market ladies were yelling at one another, bursts of explosive language bothering the nearby houses and causing low-down lights to go on.

"What's wrong?" Jerry asked. He had found Sondra, looking fresh and wonderful against the nighttime sky.

"These ladies do not believe we have engine trouble," she said. "If there is a problem they want to know why the bonnet is still shut. Also, they can't locate our driver. He has disappeared, it seems."

It was true. Though the passengers stood in a rough circle near the door of the bus, the driver wasn't among them. One Yoruba woman was screaming by this time, winning the war of indignation and quieting the others with the force of her shriek. "This one's just discovered that Agbor is our driver's hometown," Sondra said. "She thinks he's faking the breakdown so that he can stop at his house."

The passengers had awakened in stages, the Yoruba woman leading them, but the others getting into the spirit of it too. Though the bus had stopped very near a group of houses, the passengers didn't worry about waking the residents of the town. They were in fact yelling, shouting for the driver to come back, but causing instead the appearance of a growing circle of kerosene lamps, carried by the citizenry as it came out to see what was going on.

Though Jerry's little sleep had been troubled, it had still somehow refreshed him, and he soon got interested in watching this event unfold. The leader, the Yoruba woman, seemed to be as angry at the other passengers as she was at the driver. Words leapt from her like machine-gun fire, outbursts so fiercely delivered that Jerry thought there might soon be blows. Sondra pulled him away as the residents began shouting too, unhappy with the invasion of their town and telling the passengers to go away. The circle of kerosene lamps closed upon the passengers who immediately joined forces, turning on the townspeople and telling them to shut up, to mind their own business and go back to bed.

Luckily for everyone, just then the driver came back. Both the passengers and the townspeople were mad at him, but he was carrying a tool box and that seemed to quiet them down. "He's been with a woman," the Yoruba woman said, "look at the way he carries that tool box in front of him, he's covering a stain." A few people laughed, but when the driver got to work on the bus the palaver ended. Some of the passengers found their seats again, others peered past him at the engine to see what the matter really was.

And something definitely was wrong with the bus. All his life Jerry had worked on cars, but it didn't take an expert to understand from the smell that wires had burned. It was lucky that they had gotten as far as Agbor without a fire. He came up close to watch the way the driver pulled the burned wires loose and then he found Sondra again, back where the remaining residents stood. He was about to speak to her, but the people standing nearest them drew his attention. Three women and a man were watching him. Jerry at first thought that the man was white but in the next instant he knew, one more time, that he was wrong.

"Hello," the man said. "Fancy dis, ladies. Here come our man from up de way. De ol' rash man who help us out dat one las' time!"

The Power 99 man seemed terrifically glad to see Jerry. The Andrews Sisters, however, were ambivalent.

"Hi," said Jerry Neal.

"Oh hi, yes hi," said the Power 99 man, and when he nudged the girls they chimed in. "Hi," they sang. Their harmony was still tight though they were obviously sleepy.

"We take dis bus often our own self," the Power 99 man said. "Fancy it breakin' down in Agbor, our own hometown."

"It's the bus driver's hometown too," said Sondra.

The smell of burned wire had convinced them that the bus wasn't going anywhere very soon. Some of the passengers were still interested in watching the driver work, but when the Power 99 man said, "Come to our place," there didn't seem to be much reason to argue. "Don' worry," he said. "We stay close, can hear de bus if she try to get away."

The Power 99 man had a lantern and walked away quickly so that he could clean up. The four of them did live very close to where the bus had stopped, in two rooms of a building similar to the one in back of the artists' house. The front room, the one the Power 99 man was cleaning, contained so many cases of Power 99 that the usable space was greatly reduced, and the back room, into which he had thrown everything, was closed from view. Jerry put his bundle of art down on top of a case of Power 99.

"It ain' much," said the salesman.

Jerry couldn't argue with that. It was a dismal place. The room seemed to sag in on itself and the walls were bare on three sides. When he turned to look behind him, though, he was surprised to see two paintings hanging there. One of them was of an albino Jesus, his face bloodless, his head wearing an unusually thorny crown. It was a haunting Jesus, even a frightening one, but Jerry's eyes were more strongly drawn to the painting next to it, which was of Beany Abubakar. Beany was wearing tribal clothing and was every bit as powerful as Jesus. The paintings were of equal size, both of them too large for the room, and the two figures seemed to be staring at each other. For the first time Jerry saw something in Beany to admire. Maybe he *was* a man of the people, like the albino Jesus, a symbol of life to come.

Jerry looked at the paintings for a long time before making his voice light and saying, "Look, there's Beany." He turned Sondra toward the picture, but all she said was, "Oh, yes, that one, I haven't seen that one in a very long time."

The Power 99 man smiled. "You ain' seen it because is a collector's item," he said. "All over Agbor dis de only Beany of is kin'. Other people got de new Beany wit' him wearin' de business suit, but dis one go back to 'is regional days. In fac' dis one de firs' Beany to catch on."

They leaned against crates of Power 99, admiring the collector's-item portrait of Beany until Jerry broke the silence by pointing to the crates and asking, "How's business? It doesn't look like you're about to run out of stock."

The Andrews Sisters looked like kittens sitting around a proud tomcat, and when Jerry spoke the Power 99 man smiled again. "This is all new stuff," he said.

Indeed, the walls of the boxes looked strong and sharp compared with the walls of the room, and Jerry understood that the boxes alone, even empty of the magic cure-all, would be worth something on the street.

The Power 99 man opened the box nearest him and pulled a bottle out, passing it across the small expanse of room. "Here," he said. "Take one along, my gift."

The Power 99 bottle Jerry remembered from before had been round, with soft sides and no proper label on its front. This new Power 99, however, was much more substantially packaged. The bottle was square, and though it was the same white color as before, there was now a large label stuck on its front. Perhaps he shouldn't have been, but Jerry was surprised to see the collector's-item portrait of Beany embossed on the label. "Power 99!!" was nicely written below the portrait and in a cartoon balloon, as if it were coming from Beany's mouth, was the slogan, "The War Against Indiscipline Starts with Good Health."

"My," Jerry said, "did Beany really say that?"

"Course 'e did," the Power 99 man said. "Dat one is Beany's motto. He always say sometin' 'bout it in 'is speech."

Jerry sat up straighter. If he wanted to talk more about Beany, now was his chance. If Beany was a man of the people, then who would be better than the Power 99 man to tell him what such a thing meant. Before he could speak, however, Sondra put her hand on his arm. And when he looked to where she pointed he saw that the Andrews Sisters were asleep.

"What time is it?" he asked. "I wonder what's going on with that bus."

It was two A.M.; Sondra had a watch, and after she told him so she too slipped down a little on the floor. Jerry and the Power 99 man tried to listen again, to hear the outside noises of the irate townspeople, but it was now quiet, both inside and outside the room.

"Let's go see," Jerry said. "I hope the bus hasn't left without us."

"Spen' de night in Agbor," said the Power 99 man. "Travel when de new day come."

When the two men stood the four women took up all the space on the floor. Jerry put the square bottle of Power 99 under Sondra's head as a pillow, but once outside, though he really had been worried about the bus, the bright moon and the way it played off the Power 99 man's face somehow made him calm. If they missed this bus there would be another.

When they walked the short distance to where the bus stood, however, it wasn't gone. And though the hood was still up, no one was working on it. The bus was as quiet as the surrounding town had become, and when Jerry stepped onto it, he saw that most of the passengers were sleeping in their seats. The Yoruba woman was there, sleeping as soundly as the Andrews Sisters were.

When he got back off the bus the Power 99 man told him that Agbor had mechanics who could fix the bus in the morning, and then he suggested that they walk in the cooling air. "Is my favorite time o day," he said.

Jerry followed the man away from the bus and, so far as he could tell, away from the sleeping women as well. He had never heard of Agbor before, and though he had thought that it was small, as they walked he saw a large town opening before him, spreading out in the quiet night.

Jerry knew that African moons could be terrific, but the one they walked under was magnificent. Though it was smaller than it had been earlier in the night, it was brighter, and it cast an odd color about the town, letting Jerry see everything in its light, broken chairs in the doorways that they passed, chicken wire showing through the walls.

The Power 99 man was wearing the same black suit and white shirt and thin black tie that he always wore, but he walked slowly now, with his hands in his pockets, the salesman's hype gone from his face. Jerry had been avoiding looking at that face. The man had pink eyes, and though his skin color was roughly the same as Jerry's, it was unsettling to look at it for very long. Jerry let the word "albino" fall from his mind, landing on his tongue in a quiet sort of way. Was it a word he had used before? He delved into his past but no albinos came forward to stand beside the word he had formed.

Jerry vaguely thought that they might be stopped by the police, walking so late at night, but until the moment they turned between two roads and came out next to an open field, they hadn't seen another soul. The Power 99 man pointed at the field and said, "Les walk out a distance. I like to sit down dere sometime, where I don' see my town at all."

The Power 99 man didn't wait, so Jerry followed him onto a path that field-workers used during the day. It was impossible, at night at least, to tell what grew beside the path, but it was a low-growth harvest. Foliage was only knee high on both sides of them, and though the leaves were probably green, the silver moon and the albino's face and Jerry's own dark countenance kept the green at bay.

The path was narrow so Jerry walked behind the Power 99 man, his eyes on the back of his head. This man wasn't wear-

ing a cap, as Jerry, of course, still was, and the color of his
hair in the surrounding air made him difficult to see. *"When
it be night no man can see me in de shadow of de bush or tree."*
Jerry remembered Louis's words and Parker's reply: *"Properly
in de night you mus' exis' wit' quietude, like only de night itself
go by."*

Up around a bend in the path, perhaps two hundred meters off the main road, the Power 99 man sat under a leafy
mango tree, the only one in sight and sprouting from the
ground around it like a fountain from a windy evening sea.
There was an expanse of hard dirt under the tree, and a
makeshift bench or two.

"This place is fine," the Power 99 man said. "Some people
come here for talk small when de day get hot. In Agbor this
is a well-known tree."

Though the Power 99 man sat on the ground, Jerry chose
a low bench and let his weight come down slowly, his legs
out before him. The mango tree had taken the moon to
highlight its highest branches so it was darker where they sat
than it was in the fields around them. Jerry didn't know the
geography of this region but he had a feeling that he was
looking down the long floor of a valley. Yet though the land
looked lush, he thought he knew that much of it was fallow.
Nigeria was importing too much food, and he had an image
of villagers abandoning rural life for the decrepit lure of Lagos.

"What does Beany really care about the people?" Jerry suddenly asked. "What real evidence is there that he cares
about anyone other than himself?"

The Power 99 man laughed softly. "Das a very ignorant
question," he said. "Dat question mean I got to start from de
beginning."

The Power 99 man's face was a small moon lighting up the
area that the real moon didn't hit. He looked at Jerry and
sighed, but soon he said, "Beany de pied piper for village
folk; when he play 'is flute dey follow 'im aroun'."

Now it was Jerry's turn to sigh. He wanted hard talk, not

parables. In the morning, or whenever the bus was fixed, he'd be on his way back into everything, and he wanted to know what the man who'd been instrumental in dismantling his life was about.

Jerry leaned forward and tried again. "Tell me something that Beany has actually done," he said. "Has he built a road or has he arranged for student scholarships—what has he done for people?"

The Power 99 man laughed again. "Oh no," he said, "de road aroun' here need work right now, an' de student got to fin' 'is own school fee. Beany don' do work like that. Beany ain' on de practical side. School fee for de chil' of annoder ain' Beany's forte at all."

"Well then, what is his forte?" Jerry asked. "I've been trying to discover that for two weeks and no one can tell me. So far as I can tell he doesn't have a forte."

"Course he does," said the Power 99 man. "He is a man of de people. His forte be exac'ly dat."

The conversation was a joke and Jerry laughed. It was three A.M., he was sitting with a weird albino salesman under a mango tree far out in an African field, and he was trying to discover the essence of a man whom he didn't know or like at all. He tried, however, one last time. "What people?" he asked. "If Beany is a man of the people, what people is Beany a man of?"

"All of 'em," said the Power 99 man. "Dat's de point."

"He's a man of all the people?"

"Yes, you see, wit Beany it ain' tribal. He's a man of all de people, a pied piper for 'em. Even in de nort' you can fin' 'is likeness on de wall o some man home, jus' like in my very own. Even in de eas', even de Ibo tink to follow Beany widout mistrust. An de Yoruba tink so too, das de big surprise. Beany de I-don'-mistrust-'im man for de Yoruba too. Dat wha' importan' 'bout Beany."

Jerry remembered his visit to Beany's mother. She had told him he had the I-don't-believe-it disease, and now he was confronted with the I-don't-mistrust-him man. These were hyphenated lessons he was learning but he pursued them anyway. "Just tell me one thing that Beany has done, one thing that he tells people, even, that they can believe."

"OK," said the Power 99 man. "Beany tell 'em 'bout discipline, just like it say on de new bottle, 'bout gettin' de senses in order to see tings right."

That, too, had a familiar ring to it. Someone had recently told Jerry that he should begin disciplining his eyes and ears, training them as to what to see and hear.

"I'm not unfamiliar with discipline," Jerry said, "but I think it has to do with habits, with working hard and fulfilling one's duties well. Isn't that a better definition of discipline than telling people to get their senses in order, to retrain their eyes?"

"Yes, das a good one all right, I know it too. When I go for selling I got jus' dat kin' o discipline in my own min'. Workin' hard is my ethics an' I do it even when I don' feel like doin' it, so I know what you mean."

"Well then," Jerry said, "how can that kind of discipline take a backseat to the kind of stuff Beany tries to pull? If he were supporting a work ethic like yours and mine I could understand it a lot better, couldn't you?"

Jerry hoped he didn't sound patronizing, but the Power 99 man simply said, "No, my discipline an' your discipline is fine but Beany got de better one. Beany discipline ain' got no tribalism in it; we trainin' our eyes to see pas' de tribalism, trainin' our ears too, not to hear de soun' o Ibo or Hausa, but jus' to hear what de words say. Beany de one-Nigeria-man, he say les take Nigeria de way de British cut 'er up and make sometin' good out of 'er anyway."

Jerry stopped trying to argue. Beany was the one-Nigeria-man and the I-don't-mistrust-him man, while he was stuck with I-don't-believe-it. It was true, of course, that he did not believe it, but just then, and just for an instant, he'd had a sense that maybe he was wrong. What was tribalism, after all, and what did he know about it? He wanted to ask the Power 99 man what tribe he came from and also to which tribe

Beany belonged, but in the face of what he'd just heard such
a question seemed a violation.

"I always thought it was a question of religion," Jerry said.
"I mean, I read in the papers that Nigerian politics revolves
around a Christian–Muslim thing more than it does around
tribes."

"Oh, yes," the Power 99 man said, "you can tell sometin'
'bout Nigeria from dem papers. But Beany say we can' jus'
have our discipline 'bout tribes. We got to have it 'bout religion too. I was jus' usin' dem tribes as my example. If a man
listen to Beany too long it get complicated."

Jerry was sure that was true, but he nevertheless felt
strangely satisfied by what he had heard. That Beany was a
man of the people didn't sound so absurd to him now. Jerry
stood up from the bench and leaned against the trunk of the
mango tree, closing his eyes. He then reached up and removed Beany's mother's cap from his head. He had been
wearing the cap for four days now and making himself comfortable with the idea that nobody he ran across could truly
see him because of it. He opened his eyes again and found
the Power 99 man stretched out on the ground. He leaned
away from the tree, trying to get a little under the moon's
waning light, then he ran his fingers through his hair,
scratching and rubbing the place where the cap had been. It
felt good but as he rubbed he began to smell the awful odor
of his body, which he hadn't noticed since he'd washed it in
the creek, but which was suddenly so terrible and overpow-
ering that he nearly retched. When he looked at the Power
99 man he could see that he too had watering eyes. It was a
rancid, horrible smell, and on impulse, as if he were corking
a bottle, Jerry put his cap back on. Almost immediately the
smell went away.

Jerry looked quickly at the Power 99 man, who hadn't
moved from his place on the ground. Surely the smell had
come from the nearby field, brought to them by a coincidental breeze, just at the moment he'd removed his cap. "What

was that?" he asked, but the Power 99 man was breathing steadily again and he did not respond.

Jerry closed his eyes then, sliding down the trunk of the tree until his back was on the ground, his cap pressed firmly to his head. He felt freer than he had in a long while, and certainly more at ease. Perhaps hearing something good about Beany made him feel that way, but whatever the reason, sleep came before he could think about it too much. And he did not move again until a dozen field-workers found him in the late morning, awakening him with irritating claims that only Agbor people could sleep under this tree, and that at the very least he owed a small and proper fee.

The Yoruba woman was wrong to believe that the driver had only pretended his bus had broken down so that he could spend the night in Agbor, but the fact of the matter was that the driver had slept at home that night while the passengers were restless in the uncomfortable bus. When Jerry and the Power 99 man returned from the field they could still see them there, necks crooked at odd angles, mouths wide.

Back at the Power 99 man's house the women were awake and the door was open. Sondra had placed Jerry's bottle of Power 99, her pillow from the night before, inside his bundle of art, and the room had been swept clean, an activity that made it seem larger in the morning air. Though the women hadn't slept much longer than the men, they were cheerful and hungry, and since the Andrews Sisters knew that they would not have to sell Power 99 again until the first of the week, until the new year, they decided that they'd all go on the bus with Sondra and Jerry, at least as far as Benin City, where they had family.

"It will provide us with good cover," Sondra told Jerry. "If we pretend we are selling something everyone will naturally want to stay away."

Since Sondra was the only one among them with money, they all hung back, waiting for her to decide what it was she wanted to do about breakfast. The Power 99 man had food in his back room, but the Andrews Sisters wanted to go out to eat. There were good restaurants in Agbor, and the idea of air-conditioning and a proper washroom made Jerry tell Sondra that he wanted to go too.

"How 'bout de Loaves and Fishes Hotel?" the Power 99
man said. "De place be new but I hear is fine."

By the time they left the room again it was after ten, the
day was getting hot, and Jerry felt, once more, like he hadn't
slept or bathed in weeks. He could see readily enough that
his clothing was filthy, but the idea that his body odor was
bad hadn't occurred to him until that moment in the field.
When he looked at his companions, however, he was amazed
to see that they appeared fresh and comfortable as they
walked along. Sondra's indigo gown still seemed clean, and
the Andrews Sisters, though they always wore black, looked
as if they were on their way to church. Even the Power 99
man seemed to have affected a way of looking comfortable in
the same old clothes that he wore.

At first sight the Loaves and Fishes was a disappointment. It
was low-built where Jerry expected something high, and it did
not look new. Inside, however, the place was cool and quiet,
there were seven or eight tables with white cloths on them,
and, though there were no other customers, there were about
fifteen waiters. The restaurant was closed off from the rest of
the hotel by a single heavy door, and once that door was shut
even the street noise seemed to die away. They sat at a table
in the room's center. The linen was starched and the waiters
were wearing uniforms that were starched too. Even the walls
of the place looked as if they had been washed the previous
day. It was more than Jerry could take and as soon as they were
settled he excused himself and went into the washroom.

Here, a little surprisingly, he could see the outside world
again; through a little window he could see the normal activity of the Agbor streets. The bus was there, though the driver
was not, and he could hear the voice of the Yoruba woman
from the night before.

There was soap in the washroom and there were paper tow-
els, but though there was also a white porcelain sink, no water
came from its tap, so Jerry had to decide whether or not to use
the water that sat in a bucket at the sink's side. He could see
the bottom of the bucket through the water, but he had no

idea whether or not it was clean. There was a stopper on a chain wound around one of the unworking faucets, so Jerry plugged the sink with it and poured some of the water in. It was clear and odorless stuff, and the sink's white bottom called him, so he pushed his face into the water until he could feel its wetness under his chin and into his hairline at the base of his cap. He opened his eyes and saw the white sink's bottom and pushed his face farther in until the water entered his ears, casting away, once again, the outside city's sound.

Jerry hadn't taken a breath before putting his face in the water but he felt no need to breathe while he was there. It was like one of those dreams he used to have and it was an encapsulation, for what the water seemed to do, as if it had been waiting in that washroom bucket just to do it, was to wash from the channels of his ears and the outside circumference of his eyes the last remnants of all the expectation, all the assumption that his lifelong view of the world had placed there. Jerry closed his eyes and opened them again, but the bottom of the sink was still white and breathing was still impossible, with water filling his nose and running into his now open mouth the way it was.

This was a moment that Jerry would forever after be unsure of, but when he finally pulled his face from the water it seemed to him that a great deal of time had passed and that things had irreversibly changed, though everything, of course, was absolutely the same. He picked up the soap and washed the dirt from his hands and arms and watched as the water, this time, took on the dark color of the dirt that ran off him, clouding the bottom of the sink and making it seem far away.

As he dried himself Jerry unplugged the sink and let the dirty water leave, though it went down the drain too slowly, reminding him of a flat and muddy tide moving out of its basin over the course of an entire day.

Did all of this, the reordering of his senses with their predispositions washed away, have anything to do with Beany? If it did, then though the war that Beany wished to wage was surely an impossible one, for every man's eyes were as clouded as Jerry's had been, it really was the kind of thing that men should follow. It could give them hope, Jerry could see that easily now.

When the last of the water was gone Jerry poured the remaining clean water into the sink, so that even the sheen of his previous disposition was gone, and then he stepped into the restaurant again. The room was still quiet, his companions still the only eaters. He had no idea how long he had been gone, but though they had ordered in his absence, no one seemed to think that he'd been gone too long. When he took his seat, the waiters placed a plate in front of him and on the plate were any number of little fish, smelt or herring or river fish of some kind. The others had fish too, and in the middle of the table were round loaves of bread, which his companions were pulling apart and on which they were placing pieces of the fish.

Jerry laughed then—the menu at the Loaves and Fishes was the same as its name—and he said, "Perhaps the age of miracles is upon us again, maybe that's what this is all about."

Sondra smiled at him. "You know," she mildly said, "no one like Beany has ever before risen so high. Among Nigeria's animists only Beany has been able to stretch so far."

Given the name of the restaurant and his experience in the washroom, Jerry was intent upon making some sort of serious Christian parallel, and he was taken aback.

"What animist?" he said. "I'm afraid I'm lost again."

Sondra leaned forward. "You like those pieces of art of yours because they have soul," she said, "that's all."

The Power 99 man and the Andrews Sisters were eating quietly, bread and fish coming to their mouths as if there were no end to it, and Sondra was staring at Jerry as if she had told him some truth that demanded a response. After he sat there long enough, though, Sondra took her eyes from him and began to eat again. And as she did so Jerry let himself look at the loaves at the center of the table, which were round and didn't seem particularly torn apart, weren't particularly diminished at all. He remembered Charlotte's Christian period and

he remembered his own. The parable of the loaves and fishes
had been a favorite of his, and as he watched the loaves on
the table in front of him now, their black tops like the far-off
roofs of mosques, he was suddenly a child again and could see
a patient Jesus standing in front of a long and orderly queue.
Jesus was a white man in his mind's eye, with blond hair and
a beard like D'Artagnan's from the Three Musketeers. The fish
were big ones, wrapped in tinfoil like Pacific salmon, but the
loaves were what brought him back to Beany once again. The
loaves were long and slender baguettes, cut down the center
like his mother used to do and laden with garlic butter so
thick that when he looked at the others he was certain that
the odor of it had invaded the room.

Jerry was silent for a while, though he too finally began to
eat again. Art and religion were now somehow inextricably
tied up with a new idea of discipline in his mind. It was the
five senses that made the world, that was all there was to it,
Beany was right about that.

By the time Jerry finished his meal he could somehow hear
the outside world again. First the sound of the room's air
conditioners came to him, then the sound of the waiters
clearing the plates away, then the sounds of the ordinary
Agbor passersby.

"It is time," the Power 99 man presently said. "Soon now
the bus will go."

Sondra paid for everything from a roll of bills that Smart
had given her, and when they went back onto the street Jerry
had to hurry to get his bundle while the others climbed on
board the already moving bus. They had to argue with the
driver and the other passengers, literally dragging their feet
until Jerry got there, out of breath but carrying his package
of art, the center of which was a tree of life, given to him by
Pamela and, even as they rode away, taking on additional
meaning in his hot but colorless hands.

Jerry really slept on the bus and when they got to Benin City he awoke only long enough to see Sondra and the others step down from the bus's front door and disappear with the departing crowd. Sondra and the Power 99 man waved to him and the Andrews Sisters seemed to sing a farewell, but sleep had such control of Jerry's faculties that if he waved back, it was only at the figures in his dream.

From Benin City to Lagos it was Louis Smith-Jones who accompanied him. Because the bus was so late it didn't stay long in Benin City, and though Louis wanted to wink at Jerry, to give him at least a cryptic nod, Jerry's exhaustion was such that he was unable to keep his eyes open and instead of nodding back he nodded off.

Jerry had always believed that too much introspection was bad for a man, but look how far he'd come. Not only had he stayed up all night, under the mango tree, listening to the speeches of the Power 99 man, but he'd reexamined the reliability of his senses and he'd even had a cathartic moment while submerging his face in the water of a bathroom sink. And all the while he'd been compulsively wearing this African cap, one he believed kept him safe from the scrutiny of others, letting him pass by as if only the breeze and the trees were there, as if only the night itself went by.

Jerry smiled as he slept and when he did so images from his past life came up to examine that smile, to press themselves against it like goldfish against the glass. When images of Charlotte came by, Jerry remembered her conversion, for a time, to a serious Christian belief. Charlotte had told him that if Jesus had truly risen from his grave then nobody had any other choice but to follow him. It was an idea that had kept Charlotte occupied for two years and Jerry remembered his surprise that she had not particularly clung to the idea during her final months, when the cancer, he should have thought, would have made her cling faster still. At the time he hadn't understood such abandonment but he understood it now. With death beside her in her bed, Charlotte had not so much given up on the resurrection of Christ as she had understood something about grasping, something about the nature of holding on.

Jerry awoke suddenly and reached up to touch his cap, as if its strong position on his head would let him continue to dream and to think as well as he was. The bus was bouncing wildly, at times nearly achieving free fall, and when he pulled himself up and let his hand come back down off the cap again he forgot his dream and looked, instead, out the window at the shadow of the bus flickering along in the grass. Had they been gone from Benin City for one hour or for three? His mind was clear now, but though he tried to formulate some sense of things, nothing came. The sky was blue, the bus was quiet, that was all he knew.

Since his seat mate had fallen nearly into the aisle, Jerry took a little extra space, bringing his bundle to his lap and unwrapping it. He felt his tree of life, like the ribs of a drum he felt the men that were carved there, letting his hands design their ascent, foot to shoulder, toward the top of the world. Inside the tree of life was his snapdragon batik. He unfolded it until its center was toward him, until he could feel the fertility of it with his hands. Jerry wanted to concentrate, to retrieve some of what he had learned in the restaurant, some of what he had recaptured in his dream, but when his hand fell down on that thorn carving he automatically brought it out, letting himself see the blond-wood thickness of the flames as they shot off the carved woman's head. He could not see her face very well but he could see everything that defined that face, the yellow dress, the yellow flames burning it away. He put the carving back inside the tree of life, beside the snapdragon once again, and when he did so he felt the last item in his possession, the last of his collection of oddities from this increasingly familiar world. It was the bottle of Power 99, the one he'd been given yesterday, the new square one with the Beany label, easy to squeeze. Jerry took the cap off the bottle but the odor was faint and didn't bring anything back. He took some of the liquid on his finger and rubbed it on his arm.

Suddenly Jerry's seat mate sat up and stared at him. "Where is Lagos?" the man asked. "Where do we belong?"

It was certainly a good question, and when Jerry told him he didn't know, the man took hold of his arm. When they got to Lagos it took Jerry a moment to pry the man's fingers away, a much longer moment to rouse him from his second and perennial sleep.

At Lagos, Louis Smith-Jones was the first one off the bus, pretending to disappear into the crowd and then doubling back. Because of his sleeping seat mate Jerry got off late. It was December 31. It was five p.m.

Perhaps it had something to do with an overriding sense of having been gone longer than he had, perhaps it was his change of mind, but even considering that it was New Year's Eve, Lagos seemed less crowded than it should have, less crowded than he'd ever seen it before. There were too few hawkers about, too few people pushing through the thinning crowd. Jerry saw Louis dodging about and walked over to him. Though they stood in the middle of the road, there was no one about to listen.

"Now what, Louis?" Jerry asked. "Here we are back in Lagos. Where do we go from here?"

"Shhh," said Louis Smith-Jones.

Jerry felt kindly toward Louis, he remembered the benefits he had received from having Louis as a cell mate, and he liked the bumbling quality of the man, but he said, "Didn't they give you instructions? Am I to change hands here? Are you supposed to take me someplace?"

"Smart say we mus' wait on Pamela," Louis replied.

The lack of a crowd on the street was unnerving Louis, and Jerry didn't like it either. The others from the bus had disappeared quickly, some boarding other buses, some getting into waiting cars.

"Dis ain' good," Louis said. "I feel like I got no where to stan'."

Jerry had his bundle but he didn't have any money. Still, his idea was to catch a cab, if they could find one, and take it to Jankara or perhaps even back to the school. It was too strange, but he suddenly felt quite free to do whatever he liked.

"How much money do you have?" Jerry asked.

Louis shrugged and had begun digging into his pockets when the air was suddenly filled with sound.

"Uh oh," Louis said. He took Jerry's arm and pulled him around the side of the nearest building, off the main street, which was immediately occupied by a troop truck, coming in from the other side. "Oh no," said Louis. "Dose men don' belong out here. Dis ain' dere day."

Louis was so pained by the appearance of the truck that he nearly stepped back into the road. Jerry, however, quickly grabbed him. "This way," he said. "Be quiet now."

The troop truck was full of men standing up, the tips of their rifles next to their heads. The truck was moving slowly enough for the men to jump from it, search a little, and then jump back on. Surely there had been a coup already, at the very least a military action of some kind, but if so why had there been no evidence of it in Onitsha or Benin City, no word among the passengers on the bus? Jerry worried about Pamela and about the others too. Where was Beany now that it was time for him to tell his followers what to do?

Jerry and Louis moved away from the advancing truck. They didn't know the roads here, but they tried each door, rattling handles against locks, hoping to get inside. None of the doors would open, not even those of the restaurants and bars. They did see people occasionally, a disappearing face from an upper window, a fleeting bit of color two blocks ahead, but that was all.

Suddenly, though, there was the sound of an engine, a light popping sound this time, and they stopped where they were, listening for its direction. "Hold it, hold it," Louis said.

The sound was not that of a truck, but that of a motorcycle, and before they could duck out of its way the motorcycle rounded the corner ahead of them, the rider's head coming first, to see if the coast was clear. The rider wore a beaten leather helmet too small for his head, but Louis understood right away that it was Parker. "Oh boy," he said. "Hey Parker! Come 'ere quick!"

Louis had stepped out of the doorway in which they stood, so Jerry did too, but carefully, looking back and listening for the sounds of the truck. Parker, though his motorcycle was making plenty of noise by itself, was as irritated as Jerry was at Louis's shouting. He coasted up to them. "Quiet, Louis," he said. "Don' say nothin' more. Get on, hurry up."

The bike was an old black Honda, a small one, and though there was only room for two, all three of them were on it quickly, Louis wedged tightly between the larger men. They were parked sideways in the road and before they could turn around the troop truck appeared, a hundred yards away, but facing them. They could hear shouts over the noise of the two engines and then they heard the popping sound of rifle fire.

"Oh, shit," Parker said. The bullets were in the air around them but the bike was quick. Even with three of them on it, it bucked up and took off, Louis's arms around Parker and Jerry's stretched all the way past the man in the middle, his bundle banging along at his side.

But though the first seconds of their ride were promising, Parker was not an expert driver. They managed to turn the corner nearest them, out of sight of the men in the truck, but after that they wobbled, and then they got their front wheel stuck in a grate. They could hear the truck approaching as they got off the motorcycle and tried to lift the front wheel free.

"I tol' 'em," Parker said. "I am no good at running dese ting!"

The grate had been sticking up, a part of the broken street, and three inches of motorcycle wheel were lodged in it, the tire and part of the rim squeezed so well that Jerry was quickly sure they would never get it out. "We can't stand here waiting," he said, "let's go."

But Parker and Louis were busy pulling, shoulders against the motorcycle's handlebars, feet against the stubborn grate. Their faces were grimaced and the noises they made were loud, so Jerry went back to the corner and peeked around it, trying to gauge how much time they had before the troop truck caught up.

"Push," said Parker, "don' let me do it all."

Jerry took care with his looking, and when he saw the truck he was at first relieved. It hadn't advanced nearly so far as it could have. On second glance, however, he realized that the truck was empty.

"Hurry up!" he said. "They're on foot now, watch out, let's go!"

He had run back to Parker and Louis, but the two men had given up trying to free the motorcycle; they were too exhausted to move, Parker holding up his hands, Louis laid out across the bike as if he were trying to push the wheel farther in.

It took Parker and Louis only a moment to revive themselves, but a moment proved to be too long, for as they ran around a nearby corner, Jerry and Louis following Parker's lead, they found three soldiers leaning against a building and smoking, their rifles leaning against the building too.

All six of them were surprised. Jerry and Louis and Parker fell back on their heels like cartoon runners, and the three soldiers at first threw their cigarettes down and jumped to attention, as if it were they who had been caught. But the three rifles soon broke the stalemate. Parker tried to reach for one but he only succeeded in knocking it toward its owner. And after that the soldiers' mood turned dark.

"Looters," said the one whose gun had come back to him first.

To Jerry's eye the soldiers all looked about Bramwell's age and his first impulse was to scold them, to tell them that a soldier's duty demanded something more than just lounging about. Before he could make such a serious mistake, however, the other two soldiers picked up their rifles and pointed them, sufficiently stifling his impulse.

"Wha' store you gone loot dis day, looters?" the first soldier asked. He pointed at the locked door next to him, and
then quickly banged the lock open with the butt of his gun.
"I tink dis one," he said. "Les step inside."

The store was dark and the situation was deadly. This was
an appliance store but it was completely unlike Smart's. In
here things were orderly and organized, small appliances on
shelves, larger ones standing in the middle of the floor and
around the sides. One of the soldiers found a tape player. He
pulled a tape from a nearby rack and popped it into the machine and immediately reggae music was everywhere. This
was Bob Marley, and the sound of it made Jerry look at
Parker. The tune was "Natural Mystic," and Parker said,
"Sellin' dem tickets was a big mistake."

Though the soldiers had no idea what Parker was talking
about, his tone nevertheless got their attention. "Ah, good,"
one of them said, "firs' come de confession, den de
punishmen' begin."

The other two soldiers nodded, but they were also listening to the music and wondering about getting that tape
player out of the store. When the first soldier turned the tape
machine off, though, the quiet was so overwhelming that his
words had too much power.

"Go down on de floor," he said. "Go onto you knees."

"Oh no," Jerry said, and Parker held up his hands. Louis,
however, was the last to lose his cheerful attitude. "We all
Nigerians here," he said, "les talk a while firs'."

But the soldiers' answer to that was to bang Louis across
the shoulders with a rifle butt until Louis's cheerful attitude
went away. Louis fell down onto his knees where Parker already was.

Jerry still stood, but only because he feared that if he got
down too, their time would be completely up. They were inside an appliance store. The soldiers could say they had
found them there.

Jerry looked at the man who seemed to be the leader and
said, "Tell us, at least, what has happened, what's going on

outside," and though he flinched in anticipation of the rifle blow, the soldier went ahead and told him.

"Nigeria experience military coup d'état right now," he said. "De generals has taken over de gov'men'."

The generals? Jerry remembered that Beany was worried about the junior men, so he asked the soldier if he was sure it was the generals, and the soldier said, "De generals move before de young mens fin' dere chance."

So in the end that was it. All of Beany's plans meant nothing. His negotiations with the military meant nothing too.

"We didn't know there was a curfew," Jerry said. "We just now got into town."

It was a chancy thing to say. Perhaps there wasn't a curfew. But why else was there no one on the streets, why else were they being detained? Jerry simply hoped for more talk, but this time the soldier put the barrel of his rifle under Jerry's chin. "Shuddup," he said. "Get down."

So though he felt strangely calm, Jerry got down on his knees. He was feeling otherworldly, like he'd felt with his face in the water of that porcelain sink at the Loaves and Fishes Hotel. This time, however, he didn't see it as a good sign at all.

The third soldier, the quietest of the three, told them to empty their pockets and put their hands behind their backs. Jerry's bundle was in front of him and when the same soldier tore at it he said, "That belongs to me. Leave it alone."

It was the wrong thing to say, for though the third soldier did leave the bundle alone, he hit Jerry quickly, slamming him hard across the chest with the shaft of his gun. The first soldier laughed and hit Louis across the shoulder blades again. Jerry felt pain roaring all the way through his body, but since he'd been hit in the front, he only hinged back until he was sitting on his feet. Louis, on the other hand, fell down hard, his face against the appliance store floor. A little blood came out of Louis's nose and flowed next to Jerry's bundle, darkening the already indigo cloth.

"We go catch three tiefman," said the soldier who had hit

Louis. "Les' no call for come de lorry. Les' go take care dem now."

He was talking about shooting them, but the pain in Jerry's chest was such that he couldn't think how to respond. He had been hit too hard. Louis didn't seem to be in much of a mood to speak either, so it was all up to Parker, who, as yet unharmed, had regained some of his nerve.

"You know de Bob Marley you play just now make remember me wha' Bob Marley his own self say 'bout Yoruba man." Parker had spoken clearly, using his best confidence man's voice, the one Jerry remembered clinging to those first days in their jail cell. Then Parker had known what he was doing, and Jerry prayed that he knew as much now. Had he mentioned Yoruba men because these guys were Yoruba or because they were not? Jerry thought he knew that Parker was Yoruba and that Louis was not. He had no idea at all what the soldiers were.

But the soldier who had hit Jerry knelt down in front of Parker. "What Bob Marley say?" he asked. His voice seemed completely free, for the moment, of any threat, and Parker gained strength. His powers to be confidential were fully back now and he said, "Lemme fin' somethin' from my possession dere."

Parker nodded at his wallet, which the soldiers still hadn't touched, and which was in front of him on the floor. "Lemme reach down small," he said.

The kneeling soldier looked at the others and then at Parker again. "Go small an' slow," he said, "don' touch nothin' else."

Jerry and Louis had regained themselves enough to be watching Parker now, though Louis was doing so from the floor. Parker's hand was calm and it did move slowly down, finally opening the leather wallet that was there. Jerry could see the corner of a twenty-naira bank note in the wallet and he feared the soldiers might kill them just for that. But Parker's hand deftly pulled the note out and flipped it away, and when it dug farther into the wallet it found what it was after.

Three tickets to the bogus Bob Marley concert, the one that
had landed Parker in jail in the first place.

"I wan' you take dese," Parker said, "I dash you small."
The tickets were in perfect shape, especially considering how
long they must have been tucked away in that wallet, and
when the kneeling soldier took them he smiled.

"Thank you very much," he said. "When Bob Marley
comin' to town?" It was a relief to see the smile but horrible
to understand that Parker was staking their lives on these
guys believing that Bob Marley was still alive. Hell, even
Jerry knew he was dead. But the other two soldiers had come
around to look at the tickets, at the good photograph of Bob
Marley embossed upon them, and one of them even picked
Louis up, getting him off of his face and back onto his knees.
For a moment everyone was smiling. "You can' buy 'em,"
Parker told the soldiers. "Dem ticket no fo' sale."

Though Jerry was sure that the bogus concert's date was
written somewhere on the tickets, things were looking up.
Parker had bought them time, and the sudden sound of the
troop truck and another motorcycle on the road outside had
probably bought them their lives. The soldiers had barely
tucked the tickets away before a sergeant walked in. All of
the appliances gleamed at him, and when he asked, "Wha's
de trouble hea'?" the three soldiers were like the Andrews
Sisters, all of them speaking at once. "Looters, sah!" they
said. "Lootin' an' fussin' aroun' inside de store."

The sergeant, who was nearly as young as the three soldiers were, read from a piece of paper in his hand. "Looters
are to be arrested or shot on sight." He then looked at the
soldiers and asked, "How come you don' shoot 'em on sight?"

"Don' know, sah," the three soldiers said.

Jerry could see through the window that other soldiers had
rounded up other civilians, had pushed them up into the
canvassed back of another truck.

"OK, take 'em outside," the sergeant said. His speech was
so matter-of-fact, businesslike even, that Jerry decided he
would try to speak to the man. He had been lifted to his feet

by two of the soldiers when he asked, "Who's in charge now? Who is leading Nigeria into its new era of prosperity?"

He hadn't meant to sound cynical, he'd only wanted to discover as much as he could about what was really going on, but the sergeant stopped short and looked at him.

"You don' believe we can fin' prosperity more den we got right now?" he asked.

"It would be hard to find less," Jerry said, and to his surprise the sergeant laughed.

"You a chancy man," he said. "I got de powa' to shoot you in de street. How come you wan' go loot like dis anyhow? Any man know de firs' hour o de coup mos' dangerous time of all. Dis ain' de time for lootin', later is."

"We didn't loot anything from the store," Jerry said.

Parker and Louis were looking at him like he was crazy, but the young sergeant kept his friendly face. "Save it for de judge," he said, but he held Jerry's arm, helping him out the door and up into the darkened back of the truck, before he got onto his own motorcycle and prepared to drive away.

Jerry would have been content to ride along, now that he knew he wasn't going to be shot, but as the truck started to move he suddenly remembered his bundle of art, which had remained inside on the appliance-store floor. The sergeant had ridden off somewhere but there were other soldiers in the truck, so he asked one of them if he could go back inside.

"I forgot my belongings," he said. "Just hold on a minute, I'll be right back."

He had smiled nicely at them, but when he stood up one of the soldiers yelled at him, "Don' move! Siddown!"

The soldier was more startled than angry but the truck was moving and Jerry was sure he wouldn't be able to find this appliance store again. "No, really," he said. "I'll hurry, I promise I won't be long."

Though they were seated somewhere near the middle of the truck, Jerry had managed to stand completely up and take a step toward the truck's open back before the soldier stood too, swinging at him with his rifle butt. It was dark in

the truck, but Jerry felt the blow coming and ducked, so all
the rifle did was knock his cap off.

"Crazy man!" the soldier yelled. He held his rifle up to swing
it again, this time squarely into Jerry's jaw, but right then something stopped him. He let the rifle slip and put a hand up to
his mouth. The others in the truck, too, began moaning so spe-
cifically that Jerry breathed through his nose, catching a little
of what he remembered from under that mango tree, at the side
of that field, the passing odor of a rancid world. Jerry found his
cap then, and, though they were retching too, he helped Parker
and Louis climb out of the truck.

"Get my bundle from the store!" he shouted. Parker and
Louis were on the ground now, still gagging but recovering
some, and Jerry kept his head pointed inside the truck where
the remaining soldiers and prisoners had actually begun
throwing up. Jerry could smell himself too, but in a defused
sort of way, like walking past an overflowing cesspool at a
distance of fifty feet or so.

When Louis and Parker came back with the bundle Jerry put
his cap on and the three of them ran past the appliance store
and around the nearest corner again. Louis ran fast, Parker
slower, and Jerry took up the rear. When they got to the
stranded motorcycle Parker jumped onto the grate while Louis
flung his shoulders against the handlebars with such force that,
this time, the tire popped easily away. The keys were still in the
ignition and when Parker started it they all got on.

"This is a crazy life," Parker said. He had turned the motorcycle around and eased off on the clutch, and they were
gliding quickly away from the truckload of recovering soldiers and the handful of looters they had caught, past the surprised young sergeant, whose own motorcycle was now stuck
at the side of the road. It *was* a crazy life, Jerry thought,
Parker was right about that, but it was a lucky life too, for
they were able to ride all the way to Jankara without running
into any more soldiers, all of them thankful that nothing
came up to give Jerry reason to take his cap off once again.

In Jankara things at first appeared to be unchanged. They had expected an extension of the closed stores they'd seen downtown, a neighborhood of shutters, but Jankara, though it wasn't particularly busy, was open and normal, people walking by as if Beany's plan were still a viable possibility in their lives.

Parker drove the motorcycle slowly past the auto-parts stalls and down narrow paths until they got to Smart's first green door. Louis knocked while Jerry held his bundle lightly. His chest was still sore and he was beginning to worry that maybe the soldier had broken something with the butt of his gun.

"I don' understan' dis," Louis said.

The door to Smart's place was always kept solidly locked, but this time it had swung open with the pounding of his hand. "Don' go in," said Parker. "Les go back an' wait a while."

Louis, however, had already stepped inside. "Oh, Elwood?" he called. "Oh, Smart?"

The metal corridor led darkly down, but now Parker and Jerry both told Louis to stop. "Maybe Smart is caught," Parker said, "maybe someone else down there."

Jerry worried about Pamela, who was supposed to have met the bus, and about the others too, Sondra and those who had shadowed the bus in Pamela's car, but Parker said it was they who had sent him on the motorcycle, that they'd been safe at Smart's place only a couple of hours before.

Was it best, then, to stay out, or to go down into the belly of this whale? Jerry could still hear the echoing footsteps of his first descent, the sound of himself stepping into this thing, but he said, "You guys ride around to the monkeys' side, I'll walk down here. If I don't come out soon then go away somewhere and hide."

The moment he spoke his idea seemed a little drastic to him, but Parker and Louis both nodded, backing away like leaving thieves and closing the green door behind them.

Jerry's bundle was in his hands, his cap on his head, so what else in the world did he need? He put his free hand out to touch the enamel walls of the hallway. It was dark down below and as he descended he tried to step silently, though by doing so he got the feeling that this time he was getting into something that he might not be able to get out of again simply by taking off his cap.

The hallway had an elbow in it, a sharp turn after which he'd be visible to anyone waiting for him in the main room, but when he stopped and listened, his eyes closed, there was only silence. When he opened his eyes again, however, he saw the white wall opposite him in the quickly gone beam of a flashlight. It was a keyhole view, but it told him that some-one was down there after all.

Jerry really did not know what to do. He might be shot if he stepped away from where he was, he might be wrestled to the ground and taken away again, put into a cell worse than the ones he'd been in before. But he saw the flashlight beam again and then he heard a voice. "Perhaps it was nothing," the voice said, and it was Pamela's.

Jerry felt the surprising lightness of joy and he said, "Why are you sitting in the dark like that? Why hasn't anyone turned on a lamp?"

There was movement in the room and then someone turned the flashlight on again, this time finding him instead of the wall. "You got here safely," Pamela said.

"Who's there with you?" Jerry asked. He shifted his bundle and walked into the room but he could not remember the layout of it very well, and he bumped into a chair, his bundle smacking the head of whoever it was who sat there. "Ouch," said a man's voice. This was the man who held the flashlight, and he shined it into Jerry's eyes. "Ha," he said, "they told me my mother had gotten to you."

"Beany!" Jerry shouted. He didn't know the man well enough for such informality, but suddenly the name fit, and just as suddenly, as if the sound of the name had done it, Beany became the man everyone else had said he was all along. It was a stranger moment than any of the others Jerry had had, but he knew quite clearly then that Beany could have done it, he could have saved everything, he could have made Nigeria whole, if only he'd been given the chance.

Beany told Pamela to put the lamp on and when she did so Jerry saw that there was no one else in the room, the others, Pamela said, were in the city at large, trying to find out what they could about what was really going on.

Pamela and Beany had been sitting close together, and the sight of them made Jerry ask, "How is Nurudeen? How is Bramwell too?"

"They are safe," Pamela told him. "They are still with their grandmother in the village."

Nurudeen's face came into Jerry's mind and he said, almost as if he were speaking to himself, "You put that boy to such bad use. Both of you should be ashamed."

Beany looked sharply up for a moment, but then he looked down again. "Sometimes there is a greater good," he said.

Jerry did not know how to face this man so he bent over to untie his bundle. His feelings toward both of these people were still in turmoil and he needed the time to look away. But though Jerry had undone his bundle with only that purpose in mind, when the knot was open he automatically reached into the tree of life and pulled out that thorn carving he'd bought, all wrapped up inside Sondra's indigo gift. And when he moved the snapdragon aside and touched the thorn carving directly he knew, finally, why he had had to have it. The thorn carving was hot against his hand, aggra-

vated by his touch. Never mind the bad purpose he'd put
Nurudeen to, never mind the altered state of Jerry's own life,
Beany's biggest crime was in this carving. Jerry brought it
into the insufficient light. "Look," he said. "This is what
you've finally done. Nothing was accomplished but this."

He'd had no intention of speaking so harshly; only a moment before, in fact, Beany's greatness had been clear to him.
But the unexpected sharpness of his voice crackled in the
room like kindling in a fire, making him put the thorn carving down on the bench beside Pamela. It was a wooden icon
on an altar of tin, and though the light was bad they could
all see perfectly the ebony woman leaning from her window
on the building's soft side. Now, however, the woman was
not looking down at an imagined crowd but seemed to be
looking up into Beany's eyes, which, when Jerry looked at
them too, appeared to be full of tears.

There was a long silence then, with Beany nodding and
the others watching his face, which was surprised and thankful, constant and forlorn, all at the same time. Pamela had
reacted to the thorn carving in a more subdued way than
Beany had. She, too, had stared at it, but her expression had
not changed. Now, though, when she looked at Jerry he
could see worry in her eyes. "Surely this could have waited,"
she whispered, and then she said, "A Nigerian would never
have brought this back here." She didn't speak again so Jerry
covered the thorn carving, letting Sondra's snapdragon fall in
such a way that its beckoning throat was projected toward
them by the burning building's top. He brought the Power 99
out from the center of the tree of life and held it in his
hands.

Jerry had bought the thorn carving because of the surprise
he'd felt at its existence, because he'd had to have it at the
time. But now, as he continued to watch Beany's face, he was
transformed. Who but a fool could have thought that such a
carving was made by accident, found by the accidental wan-
derings of a rootless man? It was true, a Nigerian, no matter
what his background, could never have believed such a

thing, and Jerry suddenly realized that the market lady, had she been forced to, would have given it to him for free.

"Burn it," Beany Abubakar said.

Jerry was confounded by his own ignorance, it was true, but he didn't want to burn the carving. It was superbly made, its joints and glued pieces invisible, its draw as haunting as anything he'd seen before.

Jerry took the snapdragon back off the carving and saw the woman's beveled face again, staring up in its clear and harrowing way. The thing was too strange to destroy and he said, "Let's keep her, she can serve as a reminder, a tribute to the real woman who died in that fire."

Jerry's voice was back to normal but it was hopelessly weak. Pamela took the snapdragon from him and folded it carefully, placing it back across his knees. "It isn't here to serve as a reminder," she softly said.

Pamela's eyes were lively and deep now, the worry gone, the expression on her face sympathetic but strong. And though Jerry had not noticed her move, she was suddenly on her knees beside him, looking up. Jerry knew Beany was watching too, that he'd be able to see Beany's face if he lifted his eyes.

Jerry sighed then and nodded, allowing Pamela to speak again.

"Let me use some of this," she said. She touched Jerry's left hand, and when he released his grip on it she took the Power 99 bottle, letting each of them share the sound that came from it as she cracked its cap. The aroma from the bottle seemed to brighten the glow of the kerosene lamp, making everyone's face jump in the uneven flame, but Pamela didn't wait. She squeezed Beany's face on the bottle and wet the thorn carving with the Power 99, watching as the wood darkened, as the woman's features took on an even grimmer look.

"That's medicine," Jerry said, "a remedy for ailments, rashes, and the like."

Pamela replaced the cap then and, reaching into a pocket

somewhere, surprised Jerry one more time by producing that Zippo lighter, the one he had taken from LeRoY's room. She held the lighter lightly, its silver case compact in her palm, and then she lifted Jerry's hands from his knees and put the lighter gently into one of them. "You do it," she said. "This part of it is in your domain."

Jerry felt the lighter's heat and weight, knowing, somehow, that she was right. He flipped the Zippo open and let its flame dance up as it always did, at one with the opening of the case, like a cobra from its basket, transparent at its base but yellow up where it licked at the uninspired air. Beany sat forward in his chair, Pamela back on her knees. "Do it," Beany Abubakar said.

When Jerry touched the flame to the back of the burning building nothing happened at first. The thorn carving had been dry, and the thought crossed his mind that it would have burned better had Pamela left it alone. Now it was simply wet wood, Power 99 its prophylactic rather than its fuel. Jerry even thought to look around for a can of copy-machine toner, but at that precise moment the entire flame from the Zippo transferred itself to the carving, a transparent blue fire with a yellow hat on, climbing up the building's sides and working its way around to the top.

The Power 99 bottle had spoken to them when the cap came off, and now the building did too. When the flames got around to the woman, the blond wood, those other carved flames, did a little dance with the real ones, and then the woman seemed to sigh, turning her head all around before, like the dead head of a large match, it drooped toward the floor and disappeared.

It was astounding, but though the reburning of the ministry building and the sighs of the long-dead woman seemed spooky and bothered Jerry badly, they were a gift of such profound proportions to Beany that they soon brought him out of the funk he was in and let him smile with sad serenity at the other two people in the room.

"In the end Nigeria is all theater," he finally said. "Perhaps the rest of the world is too."

Beany stood then, walking up the opposite corridor to where Jerry had told him Parker and Louis waited to come back inside. Jerry had thought to go for the men himself, but instead he just sat there, watching the fire burn down. Even when the woman was no longer visible at the window he watched, even when the roof was gone and the walls had crumbled and the base of the building had flattened out against the enamel of the wash bench on which it stood. Perhaps it was the influence of the Power 99 after all, but this thorn-carved building burned like that other carving had, it burned with the blue flame of the Zippo, it burned hot, and it burned completely away.

Jerry had just looked up at Pamela, was about to try to say something that might bring her back into his life one more time, when they both suddenly realized that Beany had been gone too long, that too much time had gone by.

"It only takes a minute to walk out of this place," Pamela said.

Jerry and Pamela stood then, rushing up the corridor so quickly that the sounds of their footsteps seemed to stay inside. And they were into the back of Smart's appliance store and had stepped through its main entrance into the outside world before they heard the voices, before they realized that they'd have done better to stay inside.

Louis and Parker were there, sitting on straight-backed chairs with their arms bound behind them, and Beany was there too, standing up but facing the young sergeant that Jerry and the others had faced at that other appliance shop downtown. The sergeant's motorcycle was beside him, the one he had used to follow along, to trail the three escapees deep into the heart of things.

"Oh no," said Jerry Neal.

Whether or not the young sergeant recognized Beany, whether or not he knew him by name, was a question that Jerry would ask himself many times later on, but it was clear from the way he was acting that he did not like having to confront such an important-looking man whether he knew him or not.

"Sorry, sah, but you mus' leave dem tie," he was saying as Jerry and Pamela came out.

Beany had a small knife in his hand, something he'd picked up from a merchant's table nearby, and he was standing by Louis and Parker, bending as if he was about to cut their ropes.

"They work for me," Beany let the sergeant know, "they were out here waiting for me to call them inside."

Beany's voice held a measured calm, and carried with it such authority that it made the young sergeant pause, though he held a small machine gun in his hands and would not, normally, have paused for anyone.

"Dem escapees, sah," he said, "looters too. I had 'em in my truck downtown."

Beany reached down and cut Louis's ropes. He did so easily and without letting any further tension build, but when Louis brought his hands around in front of him, holding them up and rubbing his wrists, there was tension in the air anyway.

"Don' cut de nex' man," the sergeant said. His voice seemed now to plead, as if he knew that, even with a machine gun in his hands, he wasn't equal to the situation, but Beany cut Parker's ropes too, without looking up. And when Parker rubbed his wrists, using the same motion that Louis had, the young sergeant fired, squeezing the machine gun's trigger in a nearly accidental way, but sending three quick sounds into the air, three quick bullets into the breast pocket of Beany Abubakar's shirt.

Jerry and Pamela had been frozen in the long moment that preceded the firing of the gun, but the sound seemed to release everyone. The sergeant dropped the machine gun on the ground, and when Louis stood out of his chair, Beany sat down, falling so heavily into it that the chair would have tipped over had not the monkey cages been there. The chair leaned against the cages and two of the monkeys within them leapt forward, one to each side of Beany, reaching through the wire to take hold of the chair's two sides, stabilizing Beany and slowing everything down.

Beany's breast pocket was over his heart and when Pamela got to him she slipped her hand into that pocket as if she might be able to pull the bullets out. Until that moment there hadn't been much blood, but Pamela's fingers seemed to unplug things, and when she took her hand away, bringing it quickly to her face, there was a torrent, as if Beany were draining onto them, spreading out and covering the land.

Parker and Jerry and the young sergeant all went for the machine gun at the same time, but it seemed to lean away from the other two and into Jerry's hands.

"Don' kill me," the young sergeant said.

Pamela's Peugeot was parked, this time, just on the other side of the monkeys, on the nearest real road where that hammerhead shark had once been, and when she gave the keys to Louis, finding them somewhere with her blood-soaked hand, Louis brought the car around, pushing the cages over with its bumpers and then reaching to open the right rear door from the inside.

Jerry ordered the soldier to help Parker lift Beany into the back of the car, but his voice seemed detached and neither man moved. Rather, both of them stared down at the ground at the unending flow of blood and up at the diminishing figure of Beany as the blood poured out.

Beany Abubakar was dead, probably instantly so, but for all of them time somehow still seemed of the essence, as if getting him into the car and taking him somewhere would allow them to continue, for a while, in believing all those things Beany had said.

While the car door was opened Jerry managed to give Parker the gun, and when he lifted Beany from the chair,

Pamela stood with him, slipping into the car first so that she could receive Beany's body, taking care with the way they put him down. That was all. Beany was incredibly light by then and easy to move. When Jerry ordered the soldier into the front seat of the car, this time the soldier complied, and when Parker got in the back he let the barrel of the gun rest up against the nape of the soldier's neck, keeping it there even when all the car doors were closed.

There were no words then, only the quick departure of Pamela's Peugeot, only Jerry Neal, standing in the heart of Jankara market, at the center of an expanding circle of wet ground. It had not occurred to Jerry to ask Pamela where she thought she could take the man, who she thought she could find to do him any good. It had not occurred to Jerry to ask such things because he knew the answers, finally, as well as any of the others did. Though it was late on New Year's Eve day and though news of the success of the military coup would soon be spreading around the country and around the world, in Jerry Neal's mind's eye he could see Pamela's Peugeot safely traversing the country once again, the soldier providing safe passage, heading toward Onitsha where it would deliver Beany Abubakar's bloodless body to his mother and to his two growing sons.

When Jerry got back to the International School, it was early in the morning on New Year's Day, 1984. He had left Smart's place quickly, going back inside only for his bundle, and he had walked across Lagos during the night, letting no man see him in the shadow of a bush or a tree, existing with quietude, like only the night itself went by.

No one was at the school. The teachers were still on holiday, the maintenance crew still at home. Jerry walked past his office and when he got to the parking lot he retrieved a second key to his flat that he kept taped beneath the bumper of his car. When he let himself into his flat the first thing he noticed was that Jules had cleaned everything well, that there wasn't even any dust, though the place had an unlived-in feel.

Jerry walked into the bedroom, letting his filthy clothing fall to the floor as he walked. Before heading in to take his bath he stopped to look at the series of photographs of Charlotte that lined his wall. Here was Charlotte as a girl, there Charlotte as a grown-up woman, over there Charlotte standing with her sister and Charlotte alone. He tried to remember what had happened to the photograph that he'd taken with him to jail, but he had no idea at all.

In the bathroom Jerry was pleased to find that the water was hot. He filled the tub to the top and then climbed into it, sitting down in one motion, only watching his legs beneath the water and feeling his pores opening, the particles of dirt floating away. Jerry looked over the edge of the tub at his bundle sitting there. He was still wearing his cap, of course, but he let one hand rise from the water and take it from his head. He then reached down with the other hand and, pulling the bottle of Power 99 from the bundle's top, drenched his putrid hair and scalp, rubbing hard with his fingers and closing his eyes. The smell in the room was unmistakable but it wasn't that which had sickened everybody in the back of the truck, that which he had smelled under the mango tree. Rather the Power 99 mixed with the water well, lathered thickly, and turned the tub black when he lowered himself down into it to rinse his hair clean.

When Jerry Neal came back into his bedroom he was normal again, his old self, though slightly thinner than he cared to be. His hair was combed and he had shaved and when he put on a clean shirt he regained, somewhat, the bearing of a principal.

Jerry was in his bedroom a good long time and he heard it first just as he pulled on his trousers, a second and third time when he walked into the hallway to find a clean pair of socks. It was his telephone, ringing loudly in the other room. The sound of it seemed foreign and harsh and insistent, but with each ring his resolve to ignore it slipped away.

When he got to the telephone he was fully dressed, clean, and angry enough at the sound that when he picked the receiver up he held it away from him, ready to fling it down. "What do you want?" he said.

Though he had not spoken loudly, a voice responded, talking fast, and when he finally brought the receiver closer, he heard only the last part of what it said.

". . . been calling for days," said Charlotte's voice.

"Charlotte?" he said. "Hello, Charlotte?"

Now there was silence on the line, as though he had breached some surreal sense of etiquette by calling her name. "Charlotte," he said again, "answer me now, I'm ready for anything, believe me."

"Jerry Neal, I just don't think that's very funny at all," said Marge.

Jerry felt himself grow cold and slumped into the chair next to the phone.

"No, Marge," he said, "you're right, it isn't."

"Where have you been? I've been calling for days. Why didn't you come home for Christmas?"

Marge's voice was Charlotte's again, the same tenor, the same sensibility. Jerry had loved Charlotte so, still did, of course, but she belonged to another time and shouldn't be calling now.

"I've been gone," he said. "I decided to see something of Nigeria this time out. I won't be coming home for a while."

Marge started to say something else but then thought better of it, and though it was a terrifically expensive call, they were both quiet for a long time, their thoughts, their lives, even their senses of what it meant to be alive, meeting somewhere above the Atlantic Ocean, far out in space.

"Marge," said Jerry.

"Jerry," said Marge.

But that was all, for then, mercifully, the Nigerian telephone system remembered itself and the line went dead.

PANEL NUMBER THREE

February 25, 1984, p.m.

The school courtyard was packed an hour before the auction began, with parents and visitors bunched around their tables, voices filled with laughter, glasses filled with wine. To some it might seem strange, but this was the social event of the year, a chance for the entire school community to come to-gether in a philanthropic mood, to bid large sums of money for insignificant goods.

Joseph and his crew had finished their work and were out of the way now, standing behind pillars or sitting down on stools in the carpenter's shop.

In his office Jerry Neal changed quickly into a tuxedo, then reached into his bottom drawer to find a pair of well-shined shoes. The tuxedo was his own, but it fit him poorly now. Though it was nearly March and nearly two months had passed since his normal life had resumed, he had main-tained the thinness he'd acquired in the outside world, and he had to press the tux to him a few times with his hands.

When he left his office and stepped into the courtyard, the first person Jerry saw was LeRoY BaLoGuN, who had ar-ranged his work area and was already tapping away at the third panel, slowly letting the end of the story unfold. It had been the school board president's idea to have LeRoY finish

255

the final panel while the auction was under way, but LeRoY
had readily agreed. He had made his sketches in the village
but would pound the panel while people ate and drank
around him, while other items were auctioned away. And the
last item sold would be the panel itself, bringing extra money
to the school and fame to an artist to whom fame was long
overdue.

LeRoY's work station was to the left of the auction block
and near a table which was reserved for his own friends and
colleagues, for other artists and people that he knew. At a
quarter to eight the auction guests were mostly settled and
the dinner had been served. At LeRoY's table Jerry sat next
to Pamela, but among the artists from the Onitsha house
only Sondra had accepted the invitation, and though she
had come early, she had now gone off somewhere, so Jerry
and Pamela were alone.

"I went to the Ministry of Internal Affairs today," Jerry
said, "did I tell you that?"

"You did," said Pamela, "you got your visas. I am sure
there was no trouble."

It was true. Jerry and Sunday had gone to see the new
minister, who had personally stamped the passports of the
teachers who'd arrived that previous fall. It had been easy,
the minister had been kind, it had taken no time at all.

Jerry sat up straight and looked around. There were many
tables, well-dressed people everywhere. He could see Lee
Logar sitting across the courtyard with Lawrence Biko, the
school's attorney. It was odd to realize how distant he'd become from those two men. Both had meant a lot to him at
various times, yet it seemed to him now that he had left
them behind, abandoning what he knew for a strange world
that seemed ordinary to him now, even as the world of those
two men had become strange.

"I don't see her," he told Pamela. "I expect she won't
come."

"She will come," Pamela said. "She'll bring Bramwell too,
I am quite sure of it."

Jerry didn't believe that Beany's mother would come to the auction, though Pamela had been saying she would for days. Since Beany's death his mother had become a kind of outlaw. The new government was afraid of her and had even sent representatives to the school once or twice to see if Jerry knew where she was. They had not bothered Nurudeen, who was studying again and living with his mother in Jerry's flat, but they had been anxious about Beany's mom.

When Smart and Louis and Parker arrived they went straight to LeRoY's bench, so Pamela and Jerry got up to join them there. Sondra had returned and stood just to Jerry's left, so he was once again sandwiched between the two beauties, Sondra's indigo a pleasant darkness against Pamela's white gown.

The school board president would be the auctioneer but he wanted to start late, after plenty of wine had been served. In this man Jerry saw what he himself had been. The man was forthright, decidedly vigorous in his relationship with each task and each new day. There was nothing wrong with the man, perhaps, but lately he had been making Jerry feel tired, and as Jerry watched him testing the microphone, tapping it and then leaning back to speak to the A.V. man, he saw himself as he had been in Oregon and in Abidjan and during his first three years in Lagos. He had been sure of things then and he had been smart, but wasn't he still that way now? He had run the school, since his return, precisely as he'd always run it, calmly and with no mistakes. What was the difference, then, between a man at one moment and a man the next? Between not knowing something, and then knowing it well?

They were back at the table again when Pamela put her hand on Jerry's arm.

"Look who's here," she said.

The school gate had been empty for a while, everyone eating and laughing with the unending wine, but when he looked Jerry saw that the gate was now full. Beany's mother was there, regal in white robes, a headwrap down low on her

forehead, coming just to the edges of her eyes. She carried
Beany's walking staff with her, the cane Beany had had at
the Ikoyi Hotel, and she seemed to tap it on the ground in
time with LeRoY's hammer.

Pamela stood so that she could better see who else was
there. Behind Beany's mother was her grandson, Bramwell,
but that was all. Pamela waved and said, "Over here," but
though their entrance seemed monumental to Pamela and
Jerry, the other auction guests, the parents and the wine
drinkers, seemed not to be aware of it at all. In fact, while
Beany's mother made her way to the table, they clamored for
the arriving dessert.

There were chairs enough for everyone, and one more for
LeRoY, should he ever decide to sit down. There had been
music playing but when it stopped it took Jerry a minute to
remember that that was his cue, that it was time for him to
introduce the auctioneer.

"Good evening," he said. He had walked to the standing
microphone beside the podium, but when he spoke his voice
was thin and distant and his eyes on the table he'd just left,
on Beany's mother and his first-born son.

Jerry moved closer to the microphone and spoke again. He
welcomed everyone and then pointed at LeRoY, telling them
what he was doing and even pushing the microphone in
LeRoY's direction, so that they might hear the amplified
sound.

Jerry could feel his facial muscles working, he could hear
the now solid booming nature of his voice, he could even see
himself as others saw him, trim and tuxedoed, smiling and
tan, the same man he'd been before, the one who'd run their
school for them these last three years. When he turned the
podium over to Leonard Holtz everyone cheered, standing
with prolonged applause, smiling hard at Jerry as he sat back
down. He had been through so much, their expressions
seemed to say.

"My, my," said Pamela.

At the center of each table were bidding cards, large squares of colored cardboard with numbers on them. When Louis picked one up, Pamela took Jerry's hand. She then told Louis to put the card back down.

The first item to be auctioned was a carton of imported potato chips, the kind that come in cylindrical cans. Such potato chips were unavailable in Nigeria and Leonard Holtz was asking for an opening bid of fifty naira.

"Seventy-five," said someone from the back.

This was a friendly auction and part of its etiquette was that as each bid was made, others from the audience craned their necks around and smiled.

"Eighty," said someone else, making the audience sway.

The potato chips sold for one hundred and ten naira, about one hundred and twenty-five bucks, and the auctioneer moved on to the second item, dinner for six at the Chinese restaurant at the top of the Eko Hotel.

"Let's start this one at eighty-five," said Leonard Holtz.

Bramwell was sitting on his grandmother's far side. Nurudeen was back in the flat watching a video. Jerry knew that Bramwell had been living with his grandmother and it struck him how different the boys' lives would likely turn out to be, Nurudeen falling under a Western sphere while Bramwell followed his father's path, learning his grandmother's ways of the world. "Brammy, go and bring us another bottle of wine," Jerry said. He gave Bramwell some money and watched while the boy made his way across the courtyard to the makeshift bar.

It was just then, just after Bramwell left, that the auction audience noticed the soldiers standing at the door. There were three of them, and then three more. Leonard Holtz could see them better than anyone else, and though he was holding up a handmade doll and about to start the bidding again, he said, "May I help you?" The quality of his voice in the microphone made everyone feel startled, but some of the audience nevertheless craned their necks and smiled, nodding as if the soldiers had come to bid.

It wasn't clear who, among the soldiers, was in charge, but

the way they stood there reminded Jerry of the three men he and Parker and Louis had faced on the morning of the coup, of the unlucky young sergeant who had followed them into Jankara, and he felt a certain vertigo settle in. When the voice came, however, it did not belong to anyone at the door. Rather, someone at one of the auction tables had stood up, a Nigerian who was not in uniform but in formal tribal clothes. This was the man who had purchased the potato chips, though Jerry hadn't gotten a clear look at him before.

"If we could speak for a moment outside we could let these good people continue with their evening," said the man. He was clearly addressing Beany's mom, and when she stood away from the table it seemed to Jerry as if Beany stood up too. Her white gown seemed now to be a business suit, her headwrap a tribal cap identical to the one that Jerry had worn. "Who is speaking?" Beany's mother asked, and when she continued, saying, "Move into the light, let me get a bet-ter look at you," it was Beany's voice that she used. Jerry and Pamela both looked at her but they could no longer find the woman in the spot where she stood.

The table where the man sat was at the center of things, a fourteen-seater, but the man himself was not connected with the school. This was Tunde Phelps-Neuman, whom Jerry had last seen in court. Then he had seemed short but now he was tall. He was a reddish-looking man, a thin man with a mild and freckled face.

"I am sorry to say that you are under arrest, madam," Tunde Phelps-Neuman sadly said, but though he spoke to the image of the woman before him, for everyone at Jerry's table Beany was suddenly full-blooded again, coming from his mother one last time, standing above them and leaning against his cane.

It was clear from his demeanor that Beany expected some kind of exchange, that he wanted something public to hap-pen to make the miracle of his return worthwhile, but Tunde Phelps-Neuman's embarrassment was too strong and too ordi-nary for that. He was a let's-get-through-this-quietly man, and he only said, "I am sorry about this interruption." He was looking at Beany but speaking to everyone else.

"When will we ever be ruled by men who can keep their promises?" Beany asked, but by this time Phelps-Neuman had moved away from his table. He took a few steps forward, but as the first three soldiers moved in from the door, Jerry, who had been catatonic in his chair, suddenly found his voice.

"Mr. Phelps-Neuman, this is U.S. Embassy land," he said. "It is part of the United States. You have no power to arrest anyone here."

Phelps-Neuman very much wanted to finish the job he'd been given to do, but Jerry's comment stopped him. He didn't know anything about embassy land.

Jerry nodded, allowing a slight smile. He could feel the man's indecision, believed he could see a willingness to relent on his face. When he heard the auction gavel pounding behind him he even briefly thought that Leonard Holtz would come to his aid by trying to resume the bidding. Leonard, however, was mad.

"What are you saying, Jerry?" he asked. "This isn't embassy land. This is Nigeria. This is Nigerian land and he can arrest this woman if he has the power to do so."

It was true, of course, the ground was as much Nigeria as Onitsha had been, as much Nigeria as Jerry's prison cell.

Jerry did not know what more to say. He had stood up next to Beany and spoken on Beany's behalf but when he looked again it was, of course, Beany's mother standing there, looking a little unsteady after the tremendous effort she had made.

Jerry tried to speak again, but he had waited too long, and Phelps-Neuman had found his voice. "Please," he said. He then ordered the three soldiers to Jerry's table where they surrounded Beany's mother and escorted her away.

For the longest time there was silence in the schoolyard. Still angry, Leonard Holtz had his gavel raised, but everyone watched the doorway that the soldiers and the old woman and then Phelps-Neuman had gone through. In a moment, though, Tunde Phelps-Neuman came back, walking over to the table where he had previously sat. He picked up his carton of potato chips and carried it back to the auctioneer. He had bought the potato chips but he said that he wanted the money he had spent on them to be considered a donation to the school. He said he hoped the potato chips could be sold again.

That was all. When he left, this time, a little applause began. Certain parents, first Phelps-Neuman's table mates, but finally others too, applauded him as he walked back out the gate. His generosity with the potato chips had disarmed them, mitigating the irritation of the arrest, and though Jerry and his own table mates sat stunned and silent, alone with what they had seen, Leonard Holtz put his anger behind him and held the potato-chip carton up so that everyone could see it when the applause died down. "What we have here," he said, "is an example of generosity in the extreme."

The bidding began on the potato chips again, and near Jerry's table, where he and Pamela and Sondra and Smart and Parker and Louis all still sat, LeRoY resumed tapping with his hammer, imitating the auctioneer but getting the whole thing down, turning the possibility of miraculous life into the most incredible kind of abstract art.

LeRoY did it right before their eyes. And at the end of the evening Leonard Holtz was triumphant too, selling first the potato chips and then the whole of panel number three for unheard-of sums.